TREASON

Contents

Stories

Swings

One afternoon in June, Mrs. Whiteside invited Martha Stites and her two little girls to go to the circus. Martha needed a change; her husband had left her just before Easter, and ever since then her girls had been cranky. Mrs. Whiteside often heard them squabbling when she was weeding along the fence that separated the two yards.

She arranged for her nephew Roy to run them out to the fairgrounds. He was a chinless wonder—his own mother, Mrs. Whiteside's little sister, called him that—but he could be useful at times. However, he said they'd have to fend for themselves after the show because he was taking his steady girlfriend to the movies. Mrs. Whiteside was possessed of great ingenuity and she knew they would manage.

The circus had already begun when they arrived; Mrs. Whiteside realized at once they had missed nothing of importance. As they walked in, a band of worn-out ponies was being ridden around the one ring by a band of worn-out people. Next, a shabby tumbling bear rolled in, followed by two cross tigers and a couple of depressing clowns. It was definitely a third-rate affair, and Mrs. Whiteside, who had read the advertisement carefully, felt cheated.

The tickets had cost a great deal and she had felt obliged to pay for all four.

Right away the girls began to nag for popcorn. Their mother, who looked winded, said she'd already spent too much money on junk; on the way in, she'd bought them two overpriced plastic flashlights for waving in the darkness between acts. Mrs. Whiteside could have told her the flashlights wouldn't last, but she bit her tongue. Already one of them only lit when it was shaken hard.

Before any more complaining could start, there was a drumroll from the band on its perch over the stadium and the hot lights went out. When they came back on, a man was standing in the middle of the ring. He stood with his feet far apart in high white clogs, such as Mrs. Whiteside had herself worn long ago to the beach. He had on a floor-length white satin cape; the edge rippled as though something alive was running through the hem.

Mrs. Whiteside searched her program. The man's name was listed as Evan Dale, and he was an aerialist.

"He's going to have to take off that cape before he can do a thing," Mrs. Whiteside said.

Judy, Martha's youngest girl, chimed in, "I bet he could climb the ladder with it on." She was a square-shaped eight-year-old; her feet were shoved into black lace-up leather shoes because she was pigeon-toed, and her fat knees made hills in her plaid cotton skirt.

"Maybe he'll wear it all the way up and use it to fly down," Cissie, who was eleven and fanciful, suggested. She had the possibility of good looks hanging around her already, Mrs. Whiteside thought, like a cockeyed blessing, one not to be hoped for. Her mother had started to curl her straight blond hair, and it stood up on either side of her face like a pair of fans.

2

Cissie was next to Mrs. Whiteside, and Martha sat between the two girls, to prevent disputes. She had a look on her face that made Mrs. Whiteside ask, "One of your headaches?"

"No," Martha said, not even bothering to turn her head.

Then the band thundered, and Evan Dale looked straight at them. Mrs. Whiteside saw Martha put her hands up to her face.

"What's wrong, Mom?" Cissie asked.

Martha didn't answer. Mrs. Whiteside saw she was still wearing her wedding ring, gold, with a grimy-looking diamond; she wondered why Martha hadn't disposed of it when Ronny took off.

Judy was twirling her flashlight on its string.

"Stop that, you'll put somebody's eye out," Mrs. Whiteside said, but Judy kept on twirling.

Then Evan Dale's fingers felt for the hook on his high rhinestone collar. He unfastened the cape and it fell off him like the spiraling skin when you peel an apple. He stepped forward, showing off his white tights and wide glittering belt. He wasn't wearing a shirt of any description, and his chest was as bald as a potato.

"I always like hair on a man, myself," Mrs. Whiteside whispered to Martha. Cissie heard and gave her an evil grin.

"How come he doesn't have any hair on his chest?" Judy asked, waving her flashlight.

"I guess he's got it some place else," Cissie said, and giggled. Mrs. Whiteside gave her a terrible frown, but Martha acted like she hadn't heard. Evan Dale was lifting his arms in a gesture of triumph, and the audience was clapping.

"Shaves under his arms, too," Mrs. Whiteside remarked. Cissie bit her own right hand to stop laughing.

Then Evan Dale put off his high white clogs. "I wore shoes like that to Nags Head once," Mrs. Whiteside said. His assistant ran for the clogs and carried them to the side of the ring, where he arranged them on a special stool.

Finally, the aerialist set his toes on the bottom rung of a rope ladder that led far up to the top of the stadium.

Mrs. Whiteside saw Martha take a clean handkerchief out of her pocketbook and wipe her face. The sun was shining hard through the little high-up windows, bringing the smell of cement and animal manure up to the stands.

"This was nothing but a cornfield when I was coming up," Mrs. Whiteside observed. She felt she needed to get Martha's attention.

Martha was watching Evan Dale climb the ladder toward a sort of crow's nest of ropes near the roof. When he reached them, he stood up straight and hooked one arm over the trapeze that was hanging there and pointed his left foot in the air and waved at the crowd.

"I believe he's got a wire fastened to his belt," Mrs. Whiteside said.

"He never uses a wire, or a net—it says so right here in the program." Cissie's voice had a switch to it, and Mrs. Whiteside stared. She was not used to being corrected. One reason she lived alone was that she liked her own way, as she was willing to tell anybody. But Cissie was too young to appreciate such statements. Just you wait a few years, she thought at Cissie, darkly. The way you're going, some boy is going to take advantage of you in the back seat of his daddy's Chevrolet, and then where will you be?

Now Evan Dale sat on the high trapeze bar and clamped a thick white rope between his thighs. The rope ran down to his attendant standing on the ground. At a signal, the attendant grabbed the rope with both hands and jerked. The trapeze began to move back, then forward, and Evan Dale, sitting on the bar, leaned with it, far forward on the upswing, far back on the down. His long yellow hair rippled out behind him, and his feet in some sort of satin slippers pointed at the top of the stadium.

The drumroll began again as the lights went out and Mrs. Whiteside reached across to grab Judy's hand in case she was frightened. "Ouch, you're hurting me," Judy said and snatched her hand away. A spotlight played on Evan Dale, swinging miles above them.

Martha was gaping up at him. "All right, now," Mrs. Whiteside said, and she reached across Cissie and touched Martha's shoulder.

Martha shrugged her hand off as though it was a fly. Mrs. Whiteside began to feel unappreciated.

Suddenly, Evan Dale let go of the trapeze and threw himself out into the air. The spotlight bounced, then followed him, and most of the women in the audience screamed. Evan Dale was falling through the air like a released comet, blond hair streaming, and then he hooked onto another trapeze hanging a long distance from the first one. "How he got across that open space is more than I know," Mrs. Whiteside said in a hurt voice, remembering how much she had paid for the four tickets, but Martha and the girls didn't hear her. They were glued on Evan Dale.

Now he was swinging from the second trapeze by one leg, upside down. The crowd beneath him whooped and clapped. The glass beads in his belt gleamed like a hundred pairs of eyes, and Mrs. Whiteside wondered what they saw. She hoped they didn't see Martha sitting there gaping.

Out of the blue, Judy said, "I'm going to get some popcorn," and she pushed over their legs and was gone. Mrs. Whiteside tried to snatch her as she passed.

"Judy is gone after popcorn," she warned Martha, "and as far as I know, she hasn't got a penny on her," but Martha just shrugged one shoulder all the way up to her ear and went on staring at the aerialist.

"I had a swing once," she said.

Cissie asked, as politely as a grownup, "You did?" which astonished Mrs. Whiteside. The girls might have energy—in fact, she knew they did—but their manners had been completely neglected.

She glanced at Evan Dale, who was flexing his legs on the trapeze, pressing the rope between his knees.

"Grandpa put it up for me in the old maple tree," Martha said. Mrs. Whiteside had never before heard her speak a word about her early life.

"What maple tree?" Cissie asked, keeping the conversation going.

"The one in the side yard at home."

"Where was home?" Mrs. Whiteside asked, to show her interest.

"The house is gone, and the swing, too," Martha said.

"In Glasgow," Cissie told Mrs. Whiteside, as though she ought to have known, and Mrs. Whiteside was left to wonder helplessly if they meant Glasgow, Kentucky, or Glasgow in a foreign country.

At that moment, Evan Dale slid off the trapeze again and spun into the air, landing on the top rung of the ladder. He had completed the move before everyone started gasping. "Quick as a wink," Mrs. Whiteside said. She thought his act must be about over.

He teetered as he stood on the top rung of the ladder and reached out with both arms to steady himself, and the audience, which had just started to relax, began to gasp and clap again. He wobbled on one foot until everybody understood it was just a joke but they went on clapping and laughing. "He's a clown, as well," Mrs. Whiteside said; she had never been in favor of humor, which seemed to be mainly a way to catch decent people off guard.

Then there was a terrible moment when Evan Dale seemed to be falling off the ladder upside down, only to right himself slowly, like a bottle coming up in a stream. He bowed low once he was righted and back on the ladder, and everyone in the audience clapped. Martha stood up to applaud and Mrs. Whiteside had to rake at her skirt to get her to sit down.

The band began to play as the aerialist worked his way jauntily down the ladder. He reached the ground quickly and turned his back to his assistant so his cape could be placed on his shoulders. "I bet that one leads a dog's life," Mrs. Whiteside said.

As Evan Dale fastened the cloak under his chin, the band groaned its way into "Old Folks at Home," and people stood up to leave.

"Where's Judy?" Mrs. Whiteside asked. She had her hand on Martha's arm to get her going.

Cissie said, "She's probably down at the popcorn machine."

Martha never said a word.

"She'll be trampled underfoot," Mrs. Whiteside said, shoving Martha along. She stumbled out of the row as though she was tipsy, and Mrs. Whiteside had to grab her and turn her toward the stairs.

The crowd was already thinning by the popcorn machine and there was no sign of Judy. Martha had come to enough to check in her purse for something, but it was not her wallet or her house keys. Mrs. Whiteside took charge, saying, "We're going to make a complete tour of this place."

Martha took Cissie by the hand and started off in one direction while Mrs. Whiteside went in the other. After a few minutes, they met on the far side of the ring.

"I haven't seen a sign of her," Mrs. Whiteside announced. "We'd better find the manager." Martha nodded, looking as though they had misplaced a pillow, and Cissie was so excited she forgot her age and ran ahead of them like a child.

A man who was milking money out of the pop machines told them to try the exit to the left.

Mrs. Whiteside led the way. She was truly frightened now and wondered if she was somehow to blame; the whole afternoon had been her idea, without her suggesting the circus they would all have been sitting safely at home.

She hurried through the exit and onto a bare piece of ground where trailers and trucks were parked in a pack. One trailer looked like an office, and Mrs. Whiteside marched up the three outside steps, Martha and Cissie crowding behind her.

She hammered on the thin metal door. A fat man in a greasy shirt came out.

"A little girl has been lost," Mrs. Whiteside told him.

"Started for the popcorn machine and hasn't been seen since!" Cissie exclaimed.

The fat man looked at Mrs. Whiteside and then he craned around her to see Cissie and her mother. He studied Martha for a long time while Mrs. Whiteside held her gaze sternly on his wet-looking face.

"Well, I haven't seen her," the fat man said, after a while.

"Are you the manager?" Mrs. Whiteside asked in disbelief.

"Sure am. Maybe she went over to the cages."

Mrs. Whiteside wanted to remind him of his responsibilities, but the fat man retreated inside the trailer and closed the door in her face.

This time, Martha led the way toward a bunch of rolling cages, parked near the circus trucks.

In the first one, two tigers were lying down, filling the cage from end to end, tufts of their hair sticking out through the bars. In the next cage, the bear sat propped in a corner. The stink around the bear was strong. By the door to the tigers, a fair-haired man was shoveling chucks of raw meat onto a tray.

"Have you seen a little blond girl back here?" Mrs. Whiteside asked, and suddenly she was glad it was Judy and not Cissie that had disappeared.

The man looked up at her. "No, I have not," he said in a voice Mrs. Whiteside would later swear was born this side of the Ohio River.

"We saw you up there on the swing," Cissie said.

"Yeah?" He opened the tigers' door and flung in the trayful of raw meat; the tigers considered it attentively.

"You were so good!" Cissie cried, sounding, Mrs. Whiteside thought, just like her mother.

She glanced at Martha. She was standing rooted to the ground.

"The little girl is wearing a plaid skirt, dark-colored," Mrs. Whiteside said.

"I haven't seen her," Evan Dale repeated, slamming the door to the tigers' cage.

Then, out of the middle of nowhere, Martha began to talk. "I had a swing at home," she said. "The ropes were fifteen feet long. When I pumped hard, I could swing all the way across the creek and touch the blackberry bushes on the far side with my toes."

Evan Dale looked at her. "You still got it?" he asked.

"Grandpa cut the ropes down when I was thirteen. Said he didn't want every Tom, Dick, and Harry looking at my underpants."

"Isn't that just the way?" Evan Dale asked.

"The child we're looking for is wearing black lace-up shoes," Mrs. Whiteside said.

Martha was talking fast and feeling in her pocketbook for something. "We live real close, off Brownsboro Road, it's called Manorside. We've got the only frame house on the block. It used to be a farm." Before Mrs. Whiteside could say a thing, Martha had a piece of paper and a pencil out and was writing something down. She handed it to Evan Dale and he looked at it and folded it and pushed it down into the bib pocket of his overalls.

"We have six rooms and two baths and a front porch that's screened and a fireplace with a creek-stone chimney," Martha rattled off.

"I live right in back of her," Mrs. Whiteside said. "If that child doesn't show up in about a minute, I'm going to call the police."

"Is that her?" Evan Dale asked, and they turned around and saw Judy poking a stick through the bars at the bear.

Mrs. Whiteside ran to her. "Oh, honey! You had us almost scared to death."

"What'd you do with the popcorn?" Cissie asked.

"Ate it," Judy said, still poking.

Evan Dale strolled over and took the stick out of her hand.

"That bear has a bad temper," he said.

Martha was looking over his shoulder.

"Don't you ever wander off like that again!" Mrs. Whiteside scolded. She took hold of both the girls' hands and said, "We're going home right this minute." Then she remembered they didn't have a ride.

Evan Dale took in the situation at a glance and offered to drive them anywhere they wanted to go.

"It's only about twenty minutes from here, we'll call a taxi," Mrs. Whiteside said, but he wouldn't hear of it, and Martha was aiding and abetting him.

"It would be so nice of you," she said.

While they waited outside the stadium for Evan to fetch his car, Mrs. Whiteside found herself at a loss for words. She had the uncomfortable feeling that she was permitting something wrong to happen, although on the face of it Evan Dale was probably no worse than the men who drove taxis. She wondered if she should offer to pay him, and decided it would be only right.

Then Evan Dale came steering around the corner in a perfectly presentable ten-year-old Dodge. Mrs. Whiteside had halfway expected a pickup. The girls crowded into the back seat and Mrs. Whiteside had no choice but to sit beside them. That left Martha to inch her way into the front seat, alongside Evan Dale.

Afterward, Mrs. Whiteside would always say the ride passed in complete silence, other than when Martha had to give directions. There *was* a conversation she couldn't hear.

When they got to Martha's house, Mrs. Whiteside reached over the seat with a bunch of dollar bills, but Evan Dale brushed them aside. He jumped out and came around and opened Martha's door, and she stepped down like a queen. Mrs. Whiteside scrambled out after the girls. As soon as they were in the front door, Evan Dale drove off, honking his horn lightly and looking back.

In the hall, Mrs. Whiteside folded her arms on her stomach and gave Martha a piece of her mind. "You better start looking for a decent man," she said. "Ronny's been gone three months and it looks like he's not coming back."

"I'm not looking for anybody," Martha told her. "If they want me, they can come find me."

About eight o'clock that same evening, Evan Dale's Dodge pulled up to Martha's front door. Mrs. Whiteside was on her patio picking dead leaves off her geraniums when the aerialist stepped out of the car. He was wearing ordinary-looking khaki pants and a white shirt, and he looked like an insurance salesman except for his hair, which was too blond and too long. He was carrying a large paper bag.

After a few minutes, Mrs. Whiteside saw Evan Dale and Martha come out the back door. They were carrying Ronny's red toolbox, and Cissie was tagging along behind. Martha and the aerialist consulted together—Mrs. Whiteside was not close enough to hear what they said—and then Evan Dale went in the garage and came out with Ronny's extension ladder. He set it up against the beech tree at the corner of the yard.

He climbed that ladder as quick, Mrs. Whiteside would always say, as any monkey, which is just what you would expect, although he was longer and less bent-up, she saw now, in his ordinary clothes, than a monkey, and somehow more human-looking than he'd been in his tights.

He climbed to the highest big branch on the beech, and Martha climbed up after him. They were so high Mrs. Whiteside felt dizzy looking at them, and Cissie, on the ground, started calling to her mother to come down.

Evan Dale balanced himself on the branch and opened his bag, and Mrs. Whiteside saw it contained a long, curled-up rope.

He squatted down and dropped one end over the limb and tied it with a quick knot, and then Martha handed him the other end and he hitched it in the same way. He tested both knots to see if they would hold, and then he said something to Martha and she started down the ladder.

Martha brought a board out from the garage—Mrs. Whiteside thought it might be the one she used to put under her houseplants—and Evan Dale fixed it in the loop of the rope. He pressed down with both hands to see if the seat was secure, and then he stood back and looked at Martha.

She backed herself up to the board and sat down.

By now the light was fading, and all Mrs. Whiteside could plainly see was Martha's long white feet pointing toward the top of the tree. She had shuffled off her shoes.

Evan Dale gave her one hard push, and then watched her swing. Cissie stood and stared.

After a while, he folded the bag and put it under his arm and started out of the yard, leaving the ladder and Ronny's toolbox where they lay. Mrs. Whiteside didn't see him leave, but she heard the car start. Martha went on swinging.

After a while, Cissie went into the house and lights sprang on in the windows; later Judy came out and called her mother, but Martha went on swinging.

Mrs. Whiteside stood watching so long she could feel the stone floor of her patio coming up through the soles of her shoes. She strained to see through the darkness until finally it was no use and she had to go inside.

She expected to see Martha out there swinging barefooted every evening that summer, but she never went near the swing again. She stayed indoors, as usual, shut up with the hum of the air conditioners except when she took the girls somewhere in her car.

The girls argued over the swing at first—Mrs. Whiteside heard them, over the fence—but before long they too lost interest. The grass grew back under the swing, and the tall weeds Martha had brushed with her bare feet stood up straight again.

Just after Labor Day, Martha married a man named McHenry and got ready to move to Cincinnati.

When she heard the news, Mrs. Whiteside took over a pan of her brownies as a goodbye present. The living room was full of boxes, and the curtains had been taken down from the windows. Martha was on her knees, wrapping china in newspaper, and she thanked Mrs. Whiteside and told her to put the brownies in the kitchen. The girls were still at school.

"I wish you the best of luck," Mrs. Whiteside said, and then she asked what was going to happen to the swing.

Martha looked up from the plates. "Why, I guess it'll stay right here," she said.

The people who bought Martha's house took the swing down first thing. Mrs. Whiteside thought they must have distrusted those knots. They looked like the knots magicians put in handkerchiefs, big and showy and liable to come undone.

A New Life

On the third day after the baby was born, the air conditioner in Mina's hospital room began to sing. "Over the seas," it crooned in a rich female voice. "Over the seas, over the seas to Ireland." Frightened, Mina stared at the thing, clamped between the jaws of the plate-glass windows. Then she got up to look at herself in the mirror and was shocked to see how ugly she had become; her face peered out like a starved tiger's from the tangles of her reddish hair. Do something about yourself, the fierce lecture began. Don't just stand there! Have them come and cut your hair or brush it yourself, at least. The voice was her mother's, but her mother had never spoken to her so savagely. Gentle, a little timid, she had seldom done more than glance, weightily, over the barrier between the front and back seats when they were being driven interminably somewhere.

"Over the seas," the air conditioner droned like a bee engrossed in a flower. Mina doubted that the song existed, but she knew she was responsible for it because it had aroused the other voice, the voice of the lecturer, and that had always been hers.

She had waked early that morning, before the streetlamps were turned off outside her windows. Raising the shade, she'd looked out at the green shoulders of the park trees, which she had passed so often, blindly. A million small new leaves were fluttering in the morning breeze, and she'd felt surrounded by lightly clapping hands. A little later, she heard her baby cry as he was wheeled to her down the hall, and the new milk had tingled in her breasts, spilling out in two small cloudy drops. For the first time, there were no choices: the baby was hungry, and she was there to feed him. She'd spent most of her life picking and sorting, trying in anguish to decide what was important, what was at least worthwhile. She had always been told that the serious things, the work, must be put first, yet she felt that she was losing everything in the process. With the baby, work was play, the searching, deadly play of his mouth on her nipple. There had been no need to sort and pick, and she dozed while he fed. The air conditioner's song died down and she heard the voice strike through. Sleeping night and day, it said. You've done nothing but sleep.

That's not true, she answered. I didn't sleep at all. I wouldn't even let them give me Pentothal.

Arguing with the voice never got any further than that: a statement and an answer. Her conviction wilted in the silence that followed. She was not sorry to find herself fading into agreement. After all, she'd grown up with the voice; they had lived together in more or less perfect harmony while the slow scenery of her childhood passed. On the silence of the country house, on the silence that lay between her parents, the voice had struck blow after blow, forging maxims that had seemed both discreet and comforting: work, learn, be honorable, watch your weight, avoid the fond whims of the flesh; scorn the vicious purple lipstick and the low ideals of the people you find around you. When she went away to college, she'd heard, for the first time, the strange clang of it; people there spoke to each other while she spoke in asides, against the clatter in her head. Fortunately, she had met Stephen that first fall, and they had spent most of their evenings and all of their weekends together. She didn't need to tell him about the voice because he too had the shining look of someone who is directed from within. Looking back, Mina saw them straight as a pair of candles in the midst of the jangling confusion, the dirt and disorder of their friends. A week after graduation, they married.

For a while then, Mina lived in a peaceful gabble of lists and compliments. Eventually that chorus too died down and she heard her old voice again, ranting on a sharper note. When Stephen came home at night, he found her standing with something in her hand, a potholder or a book, as though he had interrupted her; she had not dared to tell him that sometimes she'd been standing like that for half an hour, listening to the lecturer. She was afraid that he would be disappointed with her, for, like her parents, he loved her liveliness and efficiency.

When she became pregnant—passing on, by plan, to the next important task—the voice took on a new tone, conspiratorial and wary, as though to guide her through a perilous swamp. She felt the danger too; she'd been nearly overwhelmed by appetite and energy. Once she sat down in front of a loaf of bread and ate it, slice by slice, from one end to the other, and all the time, the baby had lunged in her stomach as though it rejoiced. Afterward she rushed to the scale, but it failed to register the pound of pleasure. At that moment it seemed unlikely that she would ever be thin or well-disciplined again.

As the baby was born, she'd seen the top of his head, dark and wet, in the mirror over the delivery table. "I'm glad!" she said, or nearly shouted. Her words splashed on the white masks around her. Shameless, she turned back the sheet to admire her body. Stark again, it retained the look of the labor it had accomplished, like a tractor parked beside a plowed field. She had been so proud that she had not even noticed the sullen silence inside her head. "Seas, seas," the air conditioner crooned, and she leaned forward to listen and heard instead the other: Everyone feels this way, everyone. It's called postpartum . . . The tune rose, sliding over the rest.

Determined to avoid another harangue, she got out of bed and went to the door of her room. She'd never opened it before, and she was surprised to find that it was very heavy. She crept out and looked up and down. There was no one in sight, and so she began to walk, following the arrows to the nursery and keeping close to the rank of closed doors.

The broad glass windows of the nursery flashed with light and she hesitated, wondering who might look out at her from behind the babies. At last she crept forward and peered in. Their boxes stood in a row against the window, each topped with a card of typed facts; she read those before looking at the babies. Two had been born on the same day as her own child and she was amazed by that, as though she might share something with those women—a lifelong link, buried in the flesh.

Her own baby lay propped on his side, one mittened fist beating the air. She hated those mittens; when he was first brought to nurse, she toyed with them tentatively, tracing his fingers inside. Her own mittens had been canvas, tied on at night with stout pink laces. Years after she had stopped sucking her thumb, she'd seen them hanging from a hook in her closet, like a pair of small chained hands. The baby's mittens were made of flannel, close and soft.

As she watched, he began to cry, his mouth shaping sounds she could not hear. She pressed closer to the glass. A nurse sat on the other side, marking sheets of paper, and for a wild moment, Mina imagined rapping on the glass. Then she noticed that most of the babies were crying while the others lay asleep among them, undisturbed. It seemed the order of things that some should sleep, and some should cry while the nurse sat marking her papers. Mina's concern withered, and she went back to her room. Closing the door, she was startled by the silence. The air conditioner had halted its song.

She sat on the edge of her bed, waiting for the voice to start up again; she expected it to take advantage of the silence. After a while, she began to wonder if the voice and the song had fused so that one could not break out without the other. Leaning back, she heard, for the first time, the dim scurry of traffic outside her window, and then the lunch cart rattling down the hall. All around her, women were sitting up in bed, smiling, pushing back their hair.

When the nurse brought her tray, Mina thanked her profusely and saw a glint of recognition, a submerged smile, in the woman's eyes. Immediately, Mina was ashamed of her misplaced emotion. She ate a leaf of lettuce and two slices of tomato, cold and grainy with salt. After a while, the quiet dark-eyed nurse, her favorite, came to take the tray away, and Mina closed her eyes so that she would not have to talk.

As soon as the nurse had gone, the air conditioner picked up its song, quickly, in the middle of a line: "To Ireland." Under it, the other voice marched; hysterical, hysterical, it said. Mina put her fingers in her ears and heard the voice, without the song, stamping in her brain.

She snatched her fingers out. The tune ran over the voice, melting its ferocity. She fixed her attention on the tune; it was essential to find or forge a permanent connection. Ireland. She had been there once on a summer jaunt with her parents; the memory was vague. It had been only one of many carefully planned trips. She did remember that the hotel in Dublin was something of a fraud, for in spite of its grandeur, it was built over the railroad station. No one had remarked on the constant noise of trains, and Mina had not opened her bedroom curtains to see what lay outside. Finally, one night, feeling stifled, she had snatched the curtains back. An iron network of tracks spread below her, leading away as though she were the lode —a long arrangement, precise yet ecstatic where the double lines dissected, curved, and shot off. A small engine was marching there. She dropped the curtain quickly, feeling the coal soot fret her hand.

The next afternoon, in a tearoom, she disagreed with her parents over whether they should order scones or save the calories for dinner and suddenly, passionately, declared that she wanted to go home. Her father had already ordered the scones and pushed them gently toward her. Her mother reached across the table to pat her fiery hand. They seemed to understand why she was so angry, but she herself hadn't understood at all. Afterward, she hadn't been able to mention the scene in order to apologize because the anger stuck in her throat like a splinter of glass.

The air conditioner dozed off into silence and she was left alone for the rest of the afternoon. At five, a nurse brought in a large bunch of pink roses, and tears came suddenly into Mina's eyes. She hadn't been expecting flowers, and she begged the nurse to take them away: "They'll just make a mess for you, shedding their petals in here." But the nurse told her that good money had been spent on the roses. "And what if your friends visit and don't see them!" Mina could not remember the faces of the couple who'd sent the roses and was ashamed of her vagueness and ingratitude. She got up to wash her face and comb her hair before the baby was brought. She did not want him to find her slovenly.

He took the breast eagerly, without opening his eyes. Mina lay waiting for him to finish. Her nipples were sore, and his strong tug hurt her; she looked down at his avid face and he did not relent, a whole and complete male who would use her for one thing or another the rest of her life. He was wearing his mittens, and the sight of his blind fist flapping against her arm made her weep. When the nurse came to take him away, Mina asked for a sedative and saw for the second time a gleam of recognition, a shaming in the woman's eyes.

The pill came in a little plastic cup; she licked it up surreptitiously. Then it was time to prepare herself for Stephen. She dreaded visiting hours; all the doors were open, and voices disrupted the silence of the hall. The men sounded fierce and excitable as they wove their ways between their wives' rooms and the nursery. They came bearing books, flowers, fresh nightgowns, all inessential, yet after they had left, Mina could feel the depression, thick as wax, sealing the women in their separate rooms.

Stephen burst in exactly at seven, tired, smiling, trailing the hot smells of the city day. He whirled toward her with kisses, the newspaper—white hopes extended. She was ready for him. "Don't you think it's warm in here?"

"A little. I'll turn this thing up." He moved toward the air conditioner.

"Yes, please." She waited while he turned the knob; the rush of air increased but the song did not begin. "It's been singing at me all day," she told him gaily.

"What does it sing?" He was used to her whimsy.

"Oh, some foolishness." She was suddenly uneasy about telling him. "Over the seas to Ireland, something like that."

"Did you ask the nurse to give you something?"

"Yes, and she gave me a pill as though she expected it." She was overcome by disparagement and began to cry.

He walked over and held her solemnly, aware, she thought, of the increased weight of his responsibilities. She wondered if he had felt chained and weighted when he stood beside her in the labor room. "Did you want all this to happen?" she asked.

"Of course!"

"But doesn't it occur to you, even if we didn't want it, even if we changed our minds . . . I can't remember when I wanted it!"

"Don't you remember, in Vermont?"

"I remember we walked to the top of a hill, through an old orchard. That time in Dublin I wanted to jump out my window and get on a train and go anywhere."

"Alone?"

"I guess that was the point."

"This room is too cut off."

"But it's worse," she said, "when someone is here."

At that the song began, with a shout. She looked at Stephen sharply.

"I brought you the mail—a magazine, and three bills." He turned away, opening his briefcase. "Also, your beer." When he brought out the bottles, she touched his hand.

"You can't hear anything, can you? I know you can't."

"I'm going to turn that damned thing off."

She snatched his arm. "No, don't. It's not the song I mind, it's the voice underneath and that's stopped now."

He smiled at her. "I always thought one voice was enough."

"Oh no! You've got to have a tune, as well. The voice keeps saying I'm no good." She made a face like a sad clown and they both laughed.

At nine o'clock, the speaker over Mina's bed announced that visiting hours were over, and Stephen stood up and uncapped a bottle of beer. "For night sadness," he said, patted and kissed her and left Mina to drink all the beer as quickly as she could. Then she lay back in the nest of her pillows. After a while, she began to feel flushed and easy, and she feasted on something Stephen had said: "You make such a pretty mother." He'd said it quickly, embarrassed by such obviousness. She wished she had forced him back to repeat and elaborate, to examine her face, her breasts, her thin slack body and tell her that she was all pretty, and well equipped for the task. How surprised he would have been, surprised and, she imagined, a little disappointed that she needed so much reassurance. He would have stared at her, seeing the mauve ribbons in her bed jacket and the mauve ribbon in her hair.

The baby was carried in at ten o'clock and fastened to her breast by a brisk nurse with red iron hands. Mina's nipples stung, and the baby drew and drew in a frenzy; he did not seem to get a drop. Mina knew that if she asked, they would give him a bottle, and felt beforehand her guilt at her choice. Failure lay on all sides and her successes were as thin as ribbons. The baby would be brought again at two and there was nothing she could do to prevent it except give up, abandon the whole nursing thing. The tight silence in the room molded itself to her body, and she longed for the song of the air conditioner. It purred instead, mechanically tranquil. At last the baby was taken away and she turned out the light and lay waiting for the two o'clock feeding. It seemed to her that she was being eaten alive.

At two, the night nurse snapped on the lamp and dropped the baby like a small bomb on Mina's bed. "Just ten minutes, each side," she warned. "I'll be back for him." This time, the baby's eyes were open, and he was not crying. He looked up at Mina calmly, his hands in the flannel mittens, folded on his chest. She looked at him for a while, aware of the way they were enclosed in the yellow bell of light from the lamp. She began to feel, against all reason, the baby knew her; he looked up at her so confidently, waiting to begin. Cautiously, she took his left hand and peeled back the mitten.

She had not seen his hands since the night he was born and for a moment, she was afraid. Then she peeled back the other mitten and held his hands closely, as though to prevent him from doing some harm. Finally, she let them go. His left arm lifted, and the hand unfurled slowly. His fingers were thicker than she had expected, with a flake of skin at the corner of each nail to remind her of the way he had grown, week by week, inside her.

Then the air conditioner began to sing. She groaned and caught his hands again, waiting for the voice to start. After a while, she heard it far off, chanting venomously. Anybody can. Anybody can. Anybody can have a baby. Then the air conditioner's song rose, drowning the voice, which finally went down with a shriek. "Over the seas!" the air conditioner shouted.

Mina put the baby to her breast and lay back in the pillows. He sucked and sucked and then, for the first time, he began earnestly to swallow. She listened to his long hard gulps and saw a bubble of milk forming at the corner of his mouth. His bare hand waved as though to set the beat for his delight, and his face, suffused, flushed pink. She looked at him with amazement. At the same time, she noticed something new, a creamy warmth at the front of her body. Something feels good, she told herself cautiously. She did not want to examine the feeling too closely, and for a while, she just savored the baby's warm head, pressing against her arm. The air conditioner's hum rose a little, and she fell asleep before the baby had finished.

She woke when he was lifted out of her arms. Opening her eyes, she saw the nurse pulling the mitten back over his hand.

In irritation, she sat up. "I'd like those mittens left off, please."

The nurse glanced at her and smiled. She started to pull on the second mitten, propping the sleeping baby against her hip.

"I want those things left off," Mina said, this time raising her voice.

The nurse looked at her again.

"He should be able to suck his thumb if he wants to." She was beginning to tremble.

"Don't you know he can't get his hand to his mouth?" the nurse asked kindly. "You want something to help you get back to sleep?"

"No!" Mina shouted. "I want those things off!" A great blush of satisfaction spread over her face.

Sighing, the nurse uncovered the baby's right hand. Mina watched while she freed the other. The baby's hands curved inward like little cups. "Now he'll scratch his pretty face for sure," the nurse said.

Mina was so surprised she laughed. It had never occurred to her that there was a reasonable explanation for the mittens. "Never mind," she said, catching her breath as the nurse looked at her uneasily. She watched the baby go and remembered that in two more days, she would take him home.

After that she lay awake for a long time, listening to the air conditioner croon. She knew that sooner or later the old voice would break through, but she was not afraid: the song and the voice were finally braided together. Among the strands, she thought she would be able to find her own voice, magnified, intense and brilliant as a streak of blood.

Grand Canal

You thought you knew the painting so well you'd never see it fresh
again, no matter how many more nights you spent sleeping in the
bed right beneath it: a big painting, the one collectors were said to
hanker for, would pay any price for a decade after it was exhibited.
It was the ethereal blue of the canal they wanted, the tilted head of
the woman wearing a white hat in the gondola, the golden glow of
the distant bank of houses—realism, but realism with a varnish of
magic. Now, that painting is "whereabouts unknown."

There have been times when you should have sold it but the
thought never crossed your mind.

Not that you valued it.

How can you value something you can no longer take in or
appreciate?

This is what you value: outside your window, your garden,
this August, the shrill blue of the sky, the mountain range now
hidden by pines planted years ago, nourished by everything that
passed through your irrigation pipes. They grew and grew and
you lived from then on in the core of your creation, the place you,
Matilda, made with your own heart, brains, money, and blood (or
at least sweat),

. . . the beautiful little house, all air and light, built on the plateau you discovered on a downward drive into the arroyo, a plateau to which your house was so perfectly fitted by your friend the furniture maker who cut down only two trees for the foundation, and those trees, stripped and varnished, became posts for your portale;

. . . outside, sunflowers, yes, but also hollyhocks and lavender and even roses where before there was only gravel, sand, and the stone points chipped by the tribe stopping there, to watch for game passing through the bottom of the arroyo; and you gathered those points and put them in a pueblo pot, honoring the past you recognized but knew nothing about;

. . . and the coyotes still yelled at dawn and dusk, and in spite of the neighbor's cruel leg-shattering traps, managed to survive and even flourish, now and then crossing the road with a swagger as though they owned it.

You made your creation and lived in it, reverently, among things you carefully assembled, or grew.

So why did you keep your father's painting, Matilda? Why does it still hang, disregarded, over your bed?

"The past," you often say to whoever will listen, "is not worth remembering," sententious and probably not even true.

Years ago, you examined the painting every night in the semi-darkness, how it poured its azure and golden colors down into your dreams, as well as its waters and rigid rooftops. But now the time has come to deal with that, something about the end of summer, cold weather: the reckoning.

So, take the unscented beeswax candle, Matilda, since you woke up long before light, kneel on your bed and by that breeze-blown flame, study the painting.

Blue water, yes, obviously blue, although you remember it as
a little murky (didn't all the sewers and drains of Venice empty
into it?), lined on both sides with the peach, melon, lemon, and
linen gray of the old three-story houses, their balconies hung with
unnamable flowers (not your hollyhocks, Matilda, not your lavender, sunflowers, roses), their peaked tile roofs crowding the sky,
for in his wisdom, the painter had only allowed room for a slice of
sky since it was, to tell the truth, uninteresting, interrupted here
and there by those cocky, crooked chimney pots;

. . . and now you can't avoid it, Matilda, you must lower the
flickering flame and study those shapes he painted on the water,
seven of them, gondolas, yes, you must name them, there's no
avoiding it now.

With the gondolas comes the stink of sentimentality, striped
shirts across brawny shoulders, leghorn hats with fluttering ribbons, some sort of song tossed onto the water, and whether you
want it or not, Matilda, you are fifteen again, standing on that
bridge, the old bridge, the Ponte Vechio, with your little camera
slung from your neck and held, proudly, in both hands, and he is
beside you.

You never thought of his age, then, but now, calculating, you
think he must have been fifty, you his last child, the others cast to
the four winds along with their mothers, none of whom, mothers
or grown children, you would ever know; they were always far
away, in Israel, Egypt, Australia,

. . . and your mother, Matilda, for whom you were named,
where is she? Not a question to ask, or to ask yourself, as you stand
on the old bridge in Venice with your little camera in your hands,
beside your father, who is setting up his tripod.

Do you remember, Matilda, how you felt about that tripod,

long-legged, awkward as a crane, difficult companion on all your journeys, too large, too fragile, too important to be easily accommodated?

You used to watch him extricate the thing from its specially made satchel, which he had designed himself to protect it during all those trips. And did he protect you as assiduously, Matilda? Should the question have been asked then, on the old bridge, the Ponte Vechio , arching over the Grand Canal in Venice?

Not then. Not now. Some other time. Or, probably, never.

Once planted, the tripod claimed its space in the hurrying or loitering crowd.

Then, squatting, he raised the cumbersome camera from its leather case (you carried it sometimes, when he trusted you), clamped it on the tripod, and started the process that took him far away, farther and farther each month, each year.

Because no one ever saw his photographs and yet they were essential.

Adjusting, flicking, his gestures small and specific as when he worked a comb through your snarled hair, made sections, braided; you watched once in the mirror and wondered who had taught him to do that and did not want to know;

. . . and would not allow you to wear bows. Too silly. Too *jeune fille*. Rather, rubber bands, dun-colored, like your hair;

. . . and, at night, always made you take it down—"So the hair can breathe"—and spread it, in kinks, over the shoulders of your cotton nightgown.

Enough of that now, Matilda. Raise your wavering flame, again, study those seven boats (unfortunately, gondolas), the girl with her leghorn hat, the man twisting to point at something, the child, girl or boy, trailing her or his hand in the too-blue water.

What you would give, now, to see a torn leaf of newspaper, a bottle, floating there, but "No garbage," he said, about the canal, and other things: your longing for ice cream, not gelato, your fatigue at the end of the day, head down on the café table, whining about the August heat.

"No garbage."

You knew what he meant. You were floating too, Matilda, out of a house, a yard, a school and all that went with it, floating out from under your needy mother's hands. "She'll be my apprentice," he'd told your mother. "August in Italy, an education."

Was she, finally, Matilda, ashamed of holding you back from this "great opportunity"? (And he was paying for it, as well.)

Perhaps someday you'll know.

So, she packed your suitcase, slipping in everything she deemed your favorites, the sandals with beads, the little pink camisoles, the flowered shorts—but when he saw those things he called them "inappropriate, suburban," and bought you jeans and shirts and hiking boots like his,

. . . the boots awfully hot in the Venice summer but he said you were both adventurers and laced his up high over wool socks no matter what the temperature. And so you did, as well, and every night hung your sweaty socks off the headboard of the bed in the small hot room you shared in the pensione, until your socks were stiff and crusty and you had to wash them in the sink and wear them next morning damp: one of the small pieces of garbage you chose not to complain about but he never would have noticed.

Then Matilda, the camera he bought for you—you hadn't asked—unwrapping and assembling it with a patter the whole time to instruct you (he wouldn't let you read the manual) of which you remembered almost nothing, yet you set the aperture, adjusted the focus (never on automatic, he wouldn't permit it), lined up your shot the obvious way and then when he showed you all the other options—crouching, leaning, stepping back—you learned gradually to shift the lens a fraction to the left or right, to lengthen or shorten it, to catch a tile, the turn of a wall, the stone wet from last night's rain (but never a spire, never a vista), and from that to insinuate the whole of it, canal, boats (gondolas), balconies, old houses, without "the obvious," as he called it, until one day two and a half weeks out he said, "You'll do. You have talent. And you listen."

Then you knew you were no longer what people in the cafés and on the streets observed, a daughter, but instead, one of two artists, working together.

After that you never called him Daddy.

Now the glass candleholder is hot in your hand, Matilda, the wick is burning down into a pool of wax; you could turn on the light, you know, it's almost morning.

Instead you come back to the painting with a jerk and go over its elements again: water, sky, pastel houses, gondolas, and their shadows and reflections. "Too sweet," he once said, "should be the garbage scow," and you understood that kind of garbage was distinct from the one he railed against, and had more to do with attitude.

Now you see what you've never seen before, Matilda, up there near the top of the canvas, and you hold the candle high and strain to see better: a bit of gray, not sky, not cloud, and how is it that in all these years you've never noticed it?

Could the paint, aging—it's been five decades—have started to peel?

He wouldn't approve of that, would he, Matilda, if he was still

alive and standing beside you now (and you in your nightgown),
holding his cane. The photographs on which you have built your
reputation do not flake, do not peel or fade.

The old camera on its tripod only a humble way to record the
scene so that he could transform it, later, in his studio, the coffee
cans of brushes, some only one hair, the squashed and squirming
tubes of oils with their delicious names: Carmine. Ochre. Sienna.

No.

Paint can never betray, flake, age, to reduce that sky to a scrap
of tattered gray.

Yet there it is, and he no longer beside you or anywhere else,
to explain.

Are you vindicated at last, Matilda? Will you admit to yourself
if to no one else that the failure, in this instance, of his medium has
restored you to primacy? Your photographs do not flake or peel.

But how unworthy: to mount your primacy on the happen-
stance appearance, fifty years later, of a patch of tattered gray in
what he had intended to be blue sky.

No.

It won't do.

Leaning closer, you see the gray is only a wisp of cobweb
the cleaner missed. So blow out your wavering candle and go to
fix your breakfast. It's almost eight, high time. The others will
be stirring.

Instead, you take another five minutes, hesitating, before you
fire up the percolator and pour your cereal and do all those other
things that are part of your invincible routine, five minutes you
would prefer to forgo, for they bring back, not the feel of your
little camera between your hands on the Ponte Vechio but the day
some time afterward when you came to his studio unannounced

because of some emotional knee scrape for which you wanted comfort (even knowing, as you did, that he never gave comfort of that kind).

And stumbled in, blurry with tears (was it your first boy-friend?) and found him painting, as you expected but had never witnessed—he was secretive as an owl—and discovered the transparency illumined on his canvas. Yes, there it was, the Grand Canal in all its candy perfection, blue, peach, melon, lemon, linen gray, the girl in her leghorn, and the gondolier in his striped shirt. And your father, filling in the colors, directly on the big canvas.

Did you say anything, Matilda? You may regret it now, you may have regretted it for fifty years, but you did.

You stood there and stared until he felt the weight of your eyes and said, without turning, "What is it? What do you want?"

And you said to the back of his head, "I never knew that was how you did it."

He went on filling in peach on the old house third from the left and at first you thought he hadn't heard you and so you repeated, shamelessly, "I never knew that was how you did it."

And without turning, he snarled, "I can't draw." He made it sound low, filthy. "I won't draw. All I care about is the color."

And he had taught you, without words, that art was the highest calling, worth all sacrifice, yours, as well, and you had believed him. And so, for all these years you have slept under the painting and yet refused to acknowledge it, hanging on to it after his death although collectors still call for it.

Remember, Matilda, how in his last year he came to your annual show in the big city gallery, how you avoided him cringing in a corner; he was crippled by then, wasn't he, slope-shouldered like an old raven in his wheelchair, and she, the latest nurse or wife, parked him in front of the long wall holding your black-and-white photographs, each one larger than his largest canvas,

. . . wrinkled heap of Sierras, vast Salt Sea, stone idol face of the Hoover Dam, and he looked briefly then gestured for her, compliant nurse, last wife, to roll him to the next wall. There it was, implacable, black, white, and all grays in between, the cold clear Colorado slamming across the photograph, scouring, tearing, so huge it took the entire wall;

. . . then another gesture and she rolled him to the third wall where the boulder studies hung, each darker and more menacing than the last.

He sat for twenty minutes before saying to the air or to anyone nearby, "She'll do. She has talent. And she listens."

Upstate

A Novella

1

I am standing on Shultz Hill at six o'clock in the morning: Labor Day. To the west, the Hudson River Valley is streaked about equally with industrial smoke and fog. The river itself is hidden by a fold of hills. Beyond it lie the Catskills, those humpbacked purple mountains, which we never climbed in our eight years here. To the east, the Berkshires back up against a cloudbank , reddened by the hidden sun. At my feet, the little hills and valleys of my country are lined with banners and processions of mist. It is an old, failed landscape, the farms gone—my place was one of them—and the fields grown back with sumac, heaven trees, and scrub pine. Even on my hilltop, I can hear the buzz of early-morning traffic to Poughkeepsie.

Eight years ago, I bought the white house, which I can see in the valley: a small frame house, with eight rooms divided four downstairs and four up. It was the cheapest advertised that Sunday in the Farms and Country Homes section of the *New York Times*. Waiting for the real estate agent to unlock the door, I heard the traffic on the highway beyond the yard and a row of old maples. I was carrying Jeff, and Molly and Keith were picking along behind me. "You do hear the road," my husband observed.

"That's just 11H," the real estate lady said, "an old two-laner they'll never get around to widening. You can't actually see it from the house."

A few hours later, I had decided to buy the house, with money my grandfather had made off railroads in Florida.

"Do you want it?"

"Yes, do you want it?"

"Yes. But you do hear the highway . . ."

I was a righteous person, nursing my third baby, protecting my two older children from most of the rigors of the world and satisfying my husband to the best of my distracted ability; fortunately, his demands were minimal. I had packed my life so tight there was no room for one alien impression, one mistaken impulse to intrude. So, buying a house on a whim was like buying a mad hat or a chocolate ice cream cone: it just didn't fit. My husband was too kind to point that out.

The sun moves up out of the cloudbank, blinding me and casting my stork-tall shadow across the grass. A blue jay screams in the woods behind me. The grass as it warms smells sweet. Across the river, the trees shimmer and turn green and the traffic on the highway picks up. It is morning, time to go home.

I turn down the path. The first climb, and the last. At eight o'clock, the auctioneer and his men are coming to set up their tent in my yard. We are selling eight years of accumulation—"household effects," the advertisement called it—because the house has been sold and we are moving on.

We?

I think of the children sleeping, each in her or his cell. Their light breath fills the house, lifting it slightly, ballooning out the thin frame walls.

My husband is here too, for the auction, installed in the downstairs guest room. We have been married for fifteen years and separated for the last five months. His hairbrush and shaving gear are laid out on the toilet tank in the bathroom, as neatly aligned as they were on the shaky nightstand in Florence, in the room where we spent our first careful, sticky night. He had a zip-up bag which contained all the necessities, even a pack of rubbers which he slipped under the pillow, not quite escaping my eye. Those were the old days, and my diaphragm had stayed in my pensione with my guidebooks and camera and list of letters to write home. He was kind then, too, and I was delighted to have his full attention, if only for the few minutes when we made love.

I stop at the edge of the highway, feeling self-conscious in my rubber boots and old Mexican serape. Pale faces peer from the interiors of speeding cars. At last I cross, at a dead run. I hurry up the gravel road, wondering what David will think if he wakes up and finds me gone.

I cross the patch of parched grass between the concrete slaughterhouse and the side porch. My begonias are blooming in cracks on either side of the door. I slide it back and step into the smoke from the burning pancakes. David is standing at the stove in his white pajamas, pouring batter onto the griddle. He glances at me, smiles, and pours another dab. "Good morning, Ann. Enjoy your walk?"

I grunt. His civil behavior is a cross I will not bear.

"The children are still asleep," he says, to reassure me.

"They wouldn't be frightened if they woke up and found I wasn't in bed. They know I take walks in the early morning."

"Would you like some pancakes?"

"No, thank you."

"I put blueberries in them, Ann, the way you like them." He

41

is proud of his newly acquired cooking skills. I am thinking of the price of the blueberries, charged to my account at Mrs. Hunter's fancy fruit market. "Yes, but I paid for them."

"You sound like a teenager," he adds agreeably. I notice his slight hunch, his sideways glance.

"You put me in my place." I push my boot heel into the crude wooden bootjack which Edwin and his eldest son made for me last Christmas. Stepping on the back of the jack with my other foot, I imagine that I am stepping on David's neck.

"I see you still have that thing," he says, sitting down to his pancakes. His pajama fly gapes, and I catch sight of a mass of dark curled hair. He closes his fly with one hand, then pours maple syrup liberally on his pancakes. "I thought you said you were going to get rid of it."

"It has been in and out of the garbage several times," I admit, embarrassed. Watching him eat, I am annoyed by his silent assumption: he has always said that Edwin caused it all. "I am going to keep everything he gave me," I add defiantly. We both know he gave me nothing else.

I hang the bootjack on its nail and stop its swinging, gently, with my hand. Edwin's handiwork. Why is it that making love once with Edwin under a full moon in a wet field mattered more to me than fifteen years of discussion, dinner, parties, agreement, affection, shared meals, plans, children? Edwin, the maker, with his small strong hands, the opposition between thumb and forefinger maddeningly delicate, precise. Edwin, the wizard, the healer, the one who splits the soul.

David eats, his fork traveling to his mouth at regular intervals. Now and then he wipes his lips with a folded paper napkin. He has set the sugar bowl where he can reach it for his coffee, next to the vitamin pills and lined up silverware on either side of his mat. Next to his right hand, he has laid a yellow legal pad and a sharpened pencil. I see the date written across the top.

"What are you going to write on your pad?" I ask, smiling. I am being reasonable, to match him.

"Just a few thoughts. When are they coming to set up the tent?" Consciously, he tips only half a teaspoon of sugar into his coffee.

"In half an hour, at eight. Tom wants to have everything set up and ready to start the auction at ten."

We both glance into the living room where the furniture is huddled in a corner. "I notice you've decided to sell your aunt's sewing table," David remarks. "It's very fine. Don't you think you ought to keep it for the children?"

"I've told you several times. I'm keeping almost nothing."

"It seems to me you ought to keep something from your family for the children." He catches a runnel of maple syrup on the side of his fork and carries it to his mouth.

"What are you keeping from *your* family?" I ask.

"Nothing really. I don't like that heavy Victorian stuff. My mother asked for the pair of Ming lamps—I told her I'd see to it that she gets them."

"Be sure to put a label on them."

"I will, as soon as I'm finished here. Surely you're going to keep the grandfather clock?"

"I don't think the children are going to want a grandfather clock."

"Why should you decide for them?"

"They can have my diaries," I say, "when they want them. That's the whole story: money and desolation. The furniture, the silver, the china—the trimmings."

"I don't like yard sales."

"This isn't a yard sale. It's a cut higher—an auction. The last yard sale was a disaster." I like to make concessions when I can. "People parked all over the grass, and they wanted to see what else we had in the house."

"That woman from Red Hook came into the parlor and actually asked me the price of the chair I was sitting on."

"You were very polite. You even offered her a cup of coffee."

We laugh and the weight lifts. I go on eagerly, "It was a real disaster, a mistake in judgment. Do you remember, it began to rain after lunch, and we had to haul everything inside? We only made something like nine dollars, and that had to be divided among the three children." I do not remind him that I was helpless with giggles of relief all day, rattling my change box like a leper's bell. It seemed we might be getting rid of the past.

Since then, I have wanted to throw out the rest of my possessions. When David moved out, my wish began to grow vigorously, sprouting roots and leaves. I am bound to my mistakes by these chairs and tables, these nesting ashtrays and mismatched lamps, all remnants of other pasts, some mine and now partially detached, some connected to other people's lives. It seems to me that change will come more quickly without the framework of my mother's good taste, my own extravagance, David's mother's vulgarity, and his own cleverness at spotting a good buy.

I imagine the way the living room will look cleared out, full of sun, as it was when I first saw it. I am making space here again, clearing the way. I am also hoping to make a little money. With it, I will be able to buy the essentials for the apartment in the city where I will be living alone with my two younger children.

I look into the living room again. My family's things—the

sideboard from the Georgia house, the Shaker rocking chair, the cradle we never used—are pushed together with the carved wooden knickknack shelf, the icon with its staring eyes, and the curly-legged rosewood chairs which David's mother contributed. Around and beneath these objects lie the things we bought ourselves—the little round mirror from the antique store in Claverack, the tool chest the children used for blocks. Everything has fused into a molten lump.

I remember unlocking the front door on winter Fridays, my arms full of groceries, the children scrapping at my heels. The furniture loomed in the dark like the real inhabitants of the place. The overstuffed chairs by the fireplace were as gross and misshapen as the farm wives whose yearly labors took place in the downstairs guestroom. The china cabinet loomed like a maiden aunt. I only loved the house in the beginning when it was nearly empty. Then there was the sweet smell of baby powder, the pine fragrance I used in the vaporizers, the fine stink of diapers. As the children began to grow up, the house began to feel stifling, and then the parties started.

Last New Year's Eve, I sat on the basement steps with Edwin, his cool hand down the back of my jeans. Looking down, I noticed a cow snake lying on the warm cement next to the furnace. "Look," I said. Edwin got up, went down the steps, took up the broom and, with a whack, broke the snake's back. Then he opened the basement door and scraped the snake out, where it lay in a loop on top of the frozen snow. "You could have kept it to eat the mice," he said, coming back, the cold air fresh in his dark hair. Sitting down again beside me on the stairs, he put his hand again down the back of my jeans. His fingers were chilly.

Now Edwin and I do not see each other anymore, and I do not know what to do with what I have become. In a year of living alone, I've seen enough to know that my carefully selected opposites at dinner parties will never warm my hunger. Even Edwin had his doubts, calling me names when I was too greedy. He did not believe me when I told him that he wasn't enough. He wanted to be accepted for his sex—but also to be honored as a friend, revered as a doctor, appealed to as an authority on the problems of childhood, respected in general for his commitment, his moral stance. The many splits in this man were so wide and so various that my ceaseless attempts to bridge them were as futile as a spider flinging a thread from one fence post to the next.

Yet Edwin is the only man in the world who seems worth reassembling, to me, or loving in pieces (he would say, to pieces), the only man in the world whose honest pain cannot be comforted, whose rage cannot be placated, who exists independently of my love and attention (although not his wife's), like a meteor on a dark country night.

David has taken his plate to the sink. "I think you're making a mistake with this auction," he calls over the running water.

I walk over to him, realizing as I do that there is a space of inert air, as resistant as plastic, between us. "We talked about this months ago, David. I told you I wanted to get rid of practically everything."

"I don't believe you can do it."

"I know. Also, I need the money."

David adds wearily, "Everything I make goes back to the farm."

This is something he will not discuss. He squeezes soap onto the dishes. We've been going over this ground too many times and now it is parched.

"When are you going to decide how much you can afford to give me for the children?"

"My lawyer is talking to your lawyer next week. I doubt if you're going to clear very much on this auction by the time we've split the proceeds and paid the expenses. Labor Day—whose idea was that?" For the first time, he is crisp.

"Tom thought it was a good idea—the end of the summer, people feeling restless, ready to buy. He should know, I thought."

"Tom? Well, he's in the business. I never heard anything good about him, though. He has those auctions in that rundown inn in Hillsdale, doesn't he?"

"Yes, those and that one which was really quite good—the Hull place on the river."

"Still, I would have thought Labor Day was a bad time to choose, especially with the weather. People are going to the lake."

"We'll just have to see, won't we?" My tone has turned to the nasty, harsh, self-justifying voice I used with my children when they were too young to argue back.

Attracted by my sharpness, he asks, "How are you managing living alone? Are you all right?" He is coming with the bandages.

"I like it a great deal. I've always liked living alone. The year before we were married, when I was working in New York, was one of the happiest times of my life." That of course is not entirely untrue. I add, "Being up here alone for eight summers with the children was what convinced me I wanted to live by myself."

"I don't know how you can say that."

"Well, it's so, in a way. The more conspicuous reason may turn out in the end to have been less important."

His eyes slide around the curve of my cheek before catching on my ear; they hang there briefly while he speculates. "Don't you think it might have been worth something—another year of trying or so?"

"I don't know. Nothing would have changed."

He gets up to let in the cat who is scratching at the kitchen door. He waits until she has finished rubbing against his legs and then sits down so that she can jump onto his lap. "It might have changed," he says.

"Why? You weren't hurting, and I was half-asleep."

"I was starting to notice a little something."

I laugh, hear the teetering sound and stop. "A little something. Such as that we never wanted to fuck anymore. When I used to talk about it, you'd say I was being pessimistic."

"You were always so black. You never wanted to talk about the good things."

"What were they?"

He fingers the gilt edge of his mother's antique coffee cup, carefully drying it. "It's late to talk about that now. First you made up your mind you wanted a separation, and now you want a financial settlement as well."

"I thought you wanted it too—to straighten things out, so we didn't have to go to court."

"I told you, if you want it, I'll agree. If you want a divorce, I won't fight it."

"Anything I say. Why is it I'm not worth a fight?"

"Because you've already made up your mind," he says.

And yet I want him to fight for me, to struggle against the current that is sweeping us apart. I sit down at the table and put my hands carefully on my knees.

After a pause, David asks, "Where are the children?"

"They'll be up soon." I now see he has reached the limit of his endurance; the children will provide a little padding. How easy it still is for me to read his signs. David's mother, the dragon lady, used to ask me why I couldn't understand her son. She had taught him a set of signals which worked quite well in the rest of the world, worked superbly well, in fact, in his investment firm and at dinner parties. I tried to explain that I could read him well enough but that his vocabulary was too limited. My own is simplified enough, but it is entirely different. It is only in the last year that I have been forced to add a few qualifiers to what is after all only the old sordid, all-engulfing search for love. Now I know that I must also learn to survive, and that is another language.

"There they are," David says. I think he means the children, then see that he is looking out the window. Tom's green pickup has turned onto the gravel road. It stops at the slaughterhouse, and two men climb out. "I wonder if we ought to offer them coffee," David says.

"I don't think they expect it."

David goes to the window to watch them. The two men let down the truck's tailgate and begin to haul out a mound of canvas.

"What percentage are they getting?" David asks.

"The usual."

"What," he asks quietly, "is the usual?"

"I've forgotten. You can ask Tom when you take him out the coffee."

"I'm not going to take them out coffee. This is another example of the way you get your finances into such a mess: you simply don't remember detail."

"I thought they were your finances too."

"You were handling the money, paying the bills," he says wearily, having been over this ground too many times.

"But you still haven't told me what happened to your salary all those years, or why you kept it in a separate account." I lean across the table to snap a dead bloom off the purple petunias I picked and arranged the day before.

"I've explained as well as I can. You are determined as far as I can see not to understand. I told you about the expenses for the house, the mortgage . . ." Catching my eye, he turns abruptly away. "I'm going upstairs to dress." I glance at the fingers holding the dead petunia. My nails are cracking, the cuticles rising. And my hand is brown, worn from the summer working in the garden.

He walks off rapidly, unbuttoning his pajama jacket. Before I have to remind him, he remembers that he is no longer sleeping upstairs and turns into the guest room.

How well-mannered he is, how discreet still, even in the midst of what I must assume is outrage and resentment. He will never look at me with fury or abuse me; he will maintain our calm, and I will always feel something of a fool as I flounder and toss in it. Of course, he has explained everything—but when?—and of course, I have failed in the whirlwind of my resentment to listen, to understand. I have always been distracted by my worry over what he leaves out.

Yes, I know about his miserable childhood, only son of a mother addicted to drink and antiques. I know about her struggle to pay for college, graduate school—and the even harsher struggle to make the contacts he needed to be invited to join Smith and Harper, one of the most respected midrange investment houses. I know he used to view our marriage as his reward, and again I look down at my worn-out hand.

His explanations remind me of my mother's lectures on sex, illustrated with a photograph of the naked Perseus in my book of Greek myths. I paid more attention to the snakes around Medusa's face.

2

It was a party that started it. Almost two years ago, Mary Cassaday, a neighbor I'd seen in town doing errands, invited us to a dinner party. The week before, Molly came down with impetigo, Jeff was at home with the flu, and my husband cancelled a business trip I'd been counting on him to take. Mary Cassaday's invitation, a sky-blue note with her handwriting streaming across it, consoled me completely—dear Mary, the true mother of invention, who would spend two days cooking in order to provide me with an excuse to see Edwin. In the city, he had been very busy. He did not return my calls. I knew better than to complain. So, Mary's pale-blue note was as large a factor in my life as the presence of the children—perhaps larger. I knew Edwin and Flora were going because she asked me to buy her a new dress.

Flora was teaching and had no time for inessentials. She had always hated shopping, anyway. Although she was a size larger than me—occasionally in my dreams she loomed like a mountain—I was able to choose clothes for her unerringly. So on the day of the party, I brought over a substantial brown-and-white box lined with tissue paper and tied with a white ribbon, the dress inside.

She looked at the box disapprovingly when I laid it on her kitchen table. "I hate to think how much it must have cost."

The children had gone fishing with their father, and the house was quiet.

"Wait till you see it. It's worth every penny—you told me you wanted something well-made." I took off the box top, folded back the tissue paper, and revealed a handsome clinging black woolen dress with a jacket to conceal the décolletage. Flora looked at the dress as though it might strike her. "Try it on," I urged. Her unwillingness charmed me. She was neither a liar nor a hypocrite, would not spare her own feelings or anyone else's, and her honesty, once accepted, proved instructive. She began slowly to unbutton her denim shirt.

Her big breasts flashed as she pulled off her shirt. I looked away. Flora's fleshiness was an aspect of our situation, which I was trying to ignore. She was, too clearly, my opposite. Where I was flat or even concave, she was full and round. Her belly would have filled my indentation, her popped navel, relic of three pregnancies, would have stuffed my sunken one. I did not help her lift the evening dress out of the box.

She dropped the dress over her head and turned so I could zip up the back. Feeling at the neckline, she said discontentedly, "It's much too low-cut. Edwin won't like it."

"I know. That's why there's a jacket." I held up the little garment for her to slip in her arms. She pinched the front closed tightly with one hand, then turned to survey herself in the glass door. It was difficult to see anything except dark shifting planes. "Don't you have a mirror?" I asked.

"Just Edwin's shaving mirror in the bathroom, and that won't do much good."

Watching her turn uneasily, fingering the dress, I wondered

whether Edwin's dictum grew out of her unease or whether he had imposed on her the image she now held as though with the tips of her fingers: a large woman, very competent, and by her virtues entirely unsuited to a black evening dress.

"It's tight over the hips," she complained.

"No, it isn't. It fits perfectly."

"Edwin doesn't like me to wear anything tight."

"I know that, silly."

"I'll try it on again later," she said, turning her back for me to unzip her. "Maybe I'll like it better. You wouldn't mind frightfully returning it, would you?"

I slid down the zipper and studied her broad white back. That was a safe zone. "Of course I'll take it back. That's our deal." Suddenly I was annoyed, and I wondered why I was always trying to please Flora. She paid me, of course.

"How much did it cost?" she asked suspiciously, turning away to put on her clothes.

"One hundred and fifteen." Without thinking, I had cut thirty-five dollars off the price.

"That's terrible!"

"Not really," I began to show her the seams. "You'll be able to wear it for years."

"I have the money, of course, but I do resent spending it on clothes."

"I know, but this is an investment." I heard the servile saleswoman's whine in my voice. "Look, Flora, if you don't like it . . ."

"Oh, I like it, it's very smart. It's just so different from what I ordinarily wear."

"It's time for you to get rid of that old corduroy skirt," I said, brusque as my mother.

"Edwin likes it."

"I don't care whether he likes it or not. It's not flattering."

Instead of contradicting me she began to complain about Saul, who was doing badly in school. A line of vexation settled between her eyes. Generally her children were a credit to here, quiet, well-mannered (except when they were with Edwin, and Flora took no responsibility for that). Saul had recently broken out of the model. Someone had reported seeing him sneaking on the back door of the Broadway bus. "Edwin won't take him seriously," Flora complained. "You know how he is."

"He doesn't like to scold."

"Except when it's Frank. He's after him all the time. He won't leave him alone. Frank cries easily."

I thought of Frank's anxious face. He always caught his first cold in September and kept it until spring, and Edwin could make him cry at any hour of the night or day by reminding him that he was "sickly." The other children drifted off one by one when Edwin began to point out their faults—he was always fair about it and even asked them afterward what they had felt when he lectured. Still, they drifted off to watch TV or do their homework until only Frank was left, a thin figure of misery, staring at his father through streaming tears. He was a courageous child, the only one of the three who always looked Edwin in the face.

"Sometimes Edwin frightens me," Flora confided. "Last night he hit Frank and knocked him down."

I gasped. Edwin's violence had never broken out in front of me, although I had felt it, root and stem, in all his lovemaking. "What did you do?"

"Nothing. What could I do? Trying to stop Edwin only makes him worse. I've learned that at least in fifteen years."

"Poor Frank," I muttered, stunned by her complicity.

"He has to learn to be tough. He'll never get by sniveling and crying."

"He's only eleven."

"That has nothing to do with it. He simply won't make any effort. He's not doing at all well in school this semester."

I turned toward the door.

"Don't leave."

"I have to go home and fix lunch."

"Let David fix lunch for once."

"I have to go."

She sighed. "I wish you wouldn't. Edwin will be coming soon with the boys. He'll be so disappointed if you aren't here."

"Don't you ever want to do what he does, Flora?"

She considered it from afar. "Well, of course sometimes I'm curious. Edwin's the only man I've ever had. I'd like to see what it's like with somebody else before I'm too old. But Edwin feels I'd probably get involved emotionally if I tried it."

"So he doesn't permit it."

"It's not like that. It's never like that with us. Our marriage comes first. Neither of us would think of doing anything to threaten it. Edwin feels I'm more emotional . . ."

"Well, perhaps he's right."

"And then, it's good for us in bed," she went on demurely. "I really don't have much appetite for anyone else."

"I really must be going," I said.

Jeff complained all the way home. "We didn't stay any time at all! You made us leave too soon! Saul and I were going to look for mushrooms when he came back from fishing."

"I'm sorry," I said unfeelingly and turned up the radio to block further complaints. The children's voices continued to nag for my attention, but I was able to maintain my separateness by thinking of Mary Cassaday's party, imagining what Edwin would do there, what he would say, how he would look, and planning to snatch a few minutes alone with him.

Driving up to our house, I saw David raking the leaves near the porch. He waved. "Did you have a good time?" he called pleasantly as I stepped out of the car. I was annoyed by his useful compliance. My friends had automatically become his friends, my family had replaced his family, and now it seemed that my love affair too was becoming his—a source of vitality and vicarious excitement.

"Why should I have had a good time?" I asked, passing him rapidly. "I only went there to pick up the children."

"Was everybody there?"

"No, only Flora." Grudgingly I added, "The rest had gone off fishing."

"If I had known it was only going to be Flora . . ." I went into the house before he could complete his customary compliment. He liked Flora and would have been pleased if we had all thought that they were having "a thing."

The afternoon passed with the usual procession of obligations. I tracked down the bottled-gas man, who hummed away around the house hauling out the old canister and putting in another. Then he waited silently just inside the kitchen door while I wrote out his tiny check. Handing it to him, I watched him fold it carefully and store it in his shirt pocket.

At six, Mrs. T. the babysitter arrived, looming large in the doorway in her scarf and coat. She took off all her layers, then sat at the kitchen table to give me the week's gossip. The light bulb burned above our heads, and the children argued on the stairs while she told me about her brother's disloyalty, the pecuniary malpractices of the telephone company, and the probable fate of the proposed Grand Union. Meanwhile, Jeff and Keith began to fence in the living room with a pair of plastic swords. Molly settled herself on the couch, the cat in her arms, and started to croon and smooth it. Used to her sudden changes, the cat arched against her arms. "I must go up and dress," I told Mrs. T.

"Why, yes, go right away," she said, chagrined because she had not unloaded all her wares. She followed me into the living room and hissed, "Scat!" at the cat. Melvin leaped out of Molly's arms. "Dirty thing!" Mrs. T.'s voice sawed across my daughter's complaint.

Upstairs, I plunged into my ritual. Drawing a bath, I poured in capfuls of sweet oil; the dinner party gave me an excuse to pamper myself. I knew that in the other house three miles away, Flora would be getting ready, and I imagined Edwin in the bathroom with her, and perhaps even sharing her tub. I lay alone in my tub with my jealousy, my rubber duck.

David was already dressed and shaved, having used the downstairs bathroom. We avoided seeing each other naked. Six months of abstinence had made us both unusually polite. David arranged himself to suit my unspoken demands, dressed and undressed apart from me, and slid into bed beside me as apologetically as a stranger. I knew he hoped I would continue to put up with him as long as he continued to put up with me.

We went downstairs. The children were eating their supper in the kitchen in brutalized silence. They had offended Mrs. T., who was clashing pots in the sink. She made a face at me and shrugged at Jeff, who was crying into his soup. I could not afford to inquire into the trouble, which might cloud or even forestall my pleasure in the evening. I hacked off a slice of bread, buttered it lumpily, and offered it to Jeff. He pushed it away. "I hate dark bread." I kissed each one of their resisting faces. David kissed them too, and we walked out of the house together.

A starry night: I took his arm, reminded of the nights of our first autumn in the country. After a day spent taking care of children, we would walk a little way down the dark road, afraid to be gone for more than a few minutes, holding each other's hands. Pleased by my touch, David announced, "I thought it was a very nice day."

"Yes."

"A little hectic, as always, but the children had a good time."

"Yes."

"Molly seems to be coming down with a cold."

"So it seems."

We got into the car. David started the motor and negotiated the front gate. Snapping on the radio, I flooded the car with the ridiculous songs which had become my panacea and my revenge. David turned the volume very slightly down. "Do you mind?"

"Not at all."

There is a point in a marriage beyond which the only hope lies in silence—total, smooth, and entirely accepted silence, a wax over the unknown.

We were both fixed in our separate worlds by the time we reached the bright glass house ten miles up the river in the little town of Ransom. Light streamed out of the walls and roof of the house, which was a frame for panels of glass. Hurrying across the bridge to the front door, we were both animated for the first time in days. "That dress is very becoming," David announced.

"You don't think it's too tight?"

"Not since you lost weight."

Mary Cassaday welcomed us with open arms. Her beautiful delicate face was decorated with threadlike lines. It seemed that they would drift off any minute and leave her face smooth again. In a husky whisper, she directed me mysteriously to lay my shawl upstairs. Mary was full of secrets and suppositions, turning the dreariest country evening into a field for intrigue. I loved her imagination and often asked her to repeat stories about the people we knew, stories which were always more thrilling than anything reality offered, or to describe the days when her children were small, and she turned them out into the snow, in desperation, to work on a poem.

Upstairs, I laid down my shawl and wondered what Flora would think when she saw it. She disliked the brightness of my clothes and might well cover my red shawl with her beige one. I stood for a minute by the window, listening to the stream that curled around the foundations of the house. The country sound swelled and filled my attention, and I was for a while relieved. I smiled, looking at the double bed, and entertained the vision of the four of us—David and me, Flora and Edwin—sitting up as straight as dolls against the plump pillows. Perhaps after all that was what we wanted: a family erotically entwined. The relief of laughing made me generous, and I understood for the first time how Edwin could lose himself talking to his patients or chopping wood, lose himself more effectively than he even lost himself with me, for with me, guilt admitted a pinpoint of light.

I arrived on the stairs as Flora was coming up. Edwin, below in the hall, was wearing the wrinkled prep-school blazer and shrunken white pants that made him look like the ill-fated captain of a mutinous ship. He snatched Mary Cassaday into his arms, kissed her ear, and hugged her firmly, rocking her back and forth; she fell in with the motion. I went down the stairs. When I held out my hand, Edwin took it, startled.

Without a word, he turned toward the living room, and I followed, mastering my panic, chattering to Flora. "I'm sorry you didn't wear your new dress."

I left her to make the round of the little circle of friends standing near the fire. Helena greeted me with an exclamation of pleasure, holding me off to admire my green-and-blue striped dress. "I've been calling you all week!" she said. "We really must talk," and she looked at me with a surmise that frightened me. "Why did you call . . . ?" I began, but Charles came over and slipped his arm around my waist. "The prettiest girl at the party." We were all in line again.

Winty Cassaday made my drink and brought it without a word. Hooded in his reserve, he took up his post beside the fire. He was the only person I did not dare to kiss. Frugal, hardworking, he was not a weekend visitor but a full-time country schoolteacher. He had served the local high school for thirty years, which everyone said was a waste and an example of his lack of self-confidence. He had a degree in philosophy from Harvard. Winty had no illusions about education; he simply liked to live in the country. At parties, Winty was never talkative or drunk or flirtatious, but simply totally removed. Mary was his only vice, apparently. The summer before, I had walked with him in Mrs. Lyton's rose garden, crying because Edwin had not been to see me for a month. "You should leave him," Winty had remarked at the end of our promenade, and I realized he had mistaken me for Flora.

Parker Harris drew me to his side. "You are looking simply

marvelous, as always. What a smashing dress." The compliment was not undone by his irony. Parker was a slight, dapper man with a blond moustache; his eyes were very bright. We began to talk and laugh together—Parker with his sense of style would never let me complain. He lent tone to my life, to all our lives, which he seemed to see objectively, in a glassy blue glare, as though lit from above by a fluorescent tube. Eddy Lang, Parker's friend, who rumor claimed had supplied all the money for the big house they had bought at Long Wharf, came up and kissed my hand. I was delighted by the attention. His lips on the back of my hand seemed real compared to the feel of my own lips on everyone else's cheeks. He began to tease me about my long hair, which I had been threatening to cut. "I see you are still hoping to draw up a prince." Parker and Eddy both disliked Edwin, whom they accused of being irresponsible. Parker and Eddy were both very careful, even cautious in their dealings, sensitive to the slightest swing in mood or opinion in the people around them. The local gentry, the river folk, scorned them for basing their lives on sexual preference. In spite of their charm, they fell into the same category as the millionaire who had installed his mistress in one of the river places. Parker and Eddy did not ignore the slights, the turned backs at the supermarket, the invitations ostentatiously ignored, the fawning friendliness when a new piece of upholstery or an extra man was needed. They were not bitter. They often seemed quite gleeful at the sight of the discomfort they caused. They were an idea whose time had not yet come, and they had been unfailingly kind to me.

Looking at their trim small bodies, I wondered if they took pleasure in each other, in spite of Parker's waspishness and Eddy's bad back, or whether they had settled, like the rest of us, for the voyeurism of middle age.

Mary Cassaday was lighting candles in the dining room and calling us in a whispery yet penetrating voice. As we went in, I saw our reflections, as white as ghosts, in the dark windows behind the dinner table. Mary seated us according to a written plan. I was on Edwin's left. Too lucky: I knew it at once. Edwin did not look at me or pull out my chair. We were made for difficulties, after all, not for the obscenely smooth working of a benign fate.

Edwin sat down and turned immediately to Ellen Cassaday, Mary's eldest daughter, who was seated on his right. I was frightened. What had I done? Then I remembered the moment on the stairs. I turned hastily to Eddy on my right and launched into conversation. His brown eyes were dead, and I wondered what kind of hell Parker had made of his day. I asked him about his sister. Eddy was the pillar of a large, tottering family. He gave them money, which they accepted, and advice, which they invariably ignored. He sent them to colleges and other institutions, shaken by their failures but never in despair. "Lou-lou has gone out West to take the cure," he told me. "This time she seems really to want to change." He went on to say that he was running out of money. His small advertising firm had been hit hard by the recession, and he did not know anymore whether or not he would be able to send his youngest niece to college.

I listened to Eddy with difficulty through a numbing clang. Edwin had turned sideways in his chair to enchant Ellen. His back, broad as a wall, was set in my face. I reminded myself that he did not go after young women; their expectations were too high. As I heard pretty Ellen Cassaday laughing, I remembered Edwin's fascination with mothers and daughters. Certainly at some point in the last five years, he had fucked Mary, behind a sofa, at a party, behind a tree. To get into her daughter would cap the memory and prove, as well, that he was appreciated—his medicine effective on both generations. I was beginning to feel sick. I could not eat. Where was the gentleness, which I mistook for love, when he first touched me in the wet field a year ago? I thought then we were alone together. Now we seemed only to exist in terms of our effect on others. I had become Edwin's tool, his weapon in the long-drawn silent battle with his wife. "You don't know what he's like," Flora had called after me a year ago, a lifetime ago, when I started out with Edwin to pick wild grapes for jelly. Our first public escapade—and we made plans then for more.

Eddy was talking steadily, softly, trying to find my attention. Knowing that something was wrong, he was offering me a picnic, a night at the races, a chance to taste a new white wine. I accepted all his invitations, ducking my head, afraid to trust my voice. "Nobody believes in goodness anymore," Flora declared across the table. She was trying to work up an argument with Winty, who was known to go to church on Sundays. I heard everything she said at my outer edges, preoccupied with my contract with Edwin, that sun-signed, sun-sealed promise we made in the grape arbor: no marriages and no divorces. I had laughed then, seeming to agree, tossing my head, unable to predict that the delightful flirtation would harden into genuine slavery.

Suddenly Edwin turned to me. He did not look at me as he began to talk. "Mary shouldn't have put us together. It was a mistake. You see, it isn't fun anymore."

I was silenced, pain undoing rage.

He went on, "There are three types of schizophrenics. One shatters like a glass. One dents like celluloid and fills out again. The third doesn't break or dent. It gives off a tin clang. Do you know which kind you are?"

I did not answer.

"You are the third kind."

I turned my head on its hinge and asked Eddy about his niece, Lulu . He told me she had slashed her wrists on Labor Day weekend when her parents were away and she was in the house alone. He was horrified by their negligence. The girl had nearly died. Tears were filling my eyes. They crawled slowly down my cheeks, which were so hot the tears dried at once. Eddy glanced at me and took a sip of wine. "Excuse yourself," he said.

I left the table with a clatter, knocking off my knife. Edwin had turned his back and was laughing with Ellen. I saw David across the table staring at me. With my napkin balled in my fist, I went upstairs.

Mary's bathroom was cold: a window was open. I sat on the toilet lid in the dark, slit by a triangle of light from the open door. Their voices came up the stairwell. I stuffed part of the napkin in my mouth. We fell into bed together the last time—a sunny Wednesday. I licked Edwin down his chest and up again. It was too much. It was always too much, after the first time. I had never seen the smile I had seen on his face after he had fucked somebody's wife during the second half of a country concert. He came out of the men's room in time to drive Flora home, and he was beaming.

I knew all that about him. I was not deceived. For a year Flora had been providing me with the details. She was proud of him and exasperated by him about equally. His absence, his torture, felt like love to me, the real thing, pain and pleasure unequally mixed. The absence of decency meant honesty, the absence of warmth meant truth, the perpetual threat of rejection meant that we were working on each other like yeast, rising to new heights of perception and pain. I wanted to suck his little nipples and claim him for my own because he was unclaimable, a scourge of God, a gift of love.

Finally I turned on the bathroom light and brushed my hair with Mary's silver-backed brush and washed the tear-scales off my cheeks. Then I started down the stairs in my beautiful dress, which was too well fitted, too flattering. Eddy was waiting for me at the bottom.

"All right?"

"Yes."

We went into the living room.

3

September, just a year ago: a fusty Saturday full of wood smoke and the threatening claustrophobia of early fall. During the morning, the sun burned through layer after layer of mist. By the time David and I had been to town to buy the groceries, the *New York Times*, and pots of chrysanthemums, the day had turned hot, and the children were complaining because the swimming pool had already been covered.

We unloaded the station wagon, each child agreeing to carry something, which turned out to be a jacket. There were, as always, six brown bags of groceries to take into the house. David and I hauled them in and began putting everything away, opening cabinet doors into each other's faces. We were both perfectionists and would have preferred to do the job our own way. I stacked a can of chicken soup on top of one of David's pyramids, and the whole thing collapsed, cans rolling off the shelf, one of them bouncing on David's toe. "Ow, ow, ow!" he shouted, hopping on one foot, but he smiled his enigmatic smile and picked up the cans and began to rebuild his pyramid on a wider base.

Molly and Jeff careened through the kitchen, firing the cap guns David had bought them in lieu of allowance.

I shouted, "Get out of here!" David tried to soothe me.

"Why do you buy them cap guns?" I asked. "You know I can't stand the noise."

"They wanted them."

"What if they had wanted dynamite?" I began to lecture and tone down my irritation. "Shooting cap guns is one thing they don't need to be taught. Everything else—books, models, all the worthwhile things—mean one or the other of us has got to help. We never help them anymore, have you noticed? Neither of us seems to have the patience." I was growing calm, having shouldered half the blame.

"I help Keith with his homework."

"I mean, working with their hands. They don't know how to put anything together or even take it apart; Keith asked me the other day to screw a lightbulb into his desk lamp. They don't seem to understand how anything fits together, and now they've given up even asking for help, so we won't be irritated. They just do what they can do alone. They seem to accept the fact that we're both permanently distracted."

"They do well in school."

"Maybe because it's all abstract, or because they can ask for help there." Suddenly I tasted my fatigue, the sourness of the last late night in the back of the throat. "All we do here is go to parties."

"Helena was expecting us last night. She would have been upset—"

"I know. There are always reasons, good reasons. But we came here in the beginning to be quiet, to be with the children, and now we're never with them. Mrs. T. has to come on Friday and spend practically the whole rest of the weekend here." I was bargaining on the fact that David would not mention that it was me who accepted all the invitations.

"If you don't want to go to Saul's birthday party—"

"That's different," I interrupted hastily.

David did not ask me why.

I went on in the humming voice of perpetual strain. "Sometimes I wonder if they are going to grow up just heathen— the children—or simply unskilled, manual illiterates."

"I don't see what that has to do with our going to parties."

The children streamed through again.

"Get out of here with those guns!"

Giggling, they fled outside, slamming the door.

David suggested, "Let's get those chrysanthemums out."

We went back to the car; I waited while David brought the old red wheelbarrow. Together we loaded the six pots of chrysanthemums. David took up the handles and began to trundle the wheelbarrow down the hill to the flower garden. We'd arranged it badly, the weight all to the front, and the wheelbarrow began to lumber rapidly, jerking David along. "Watch out!" I shouted. The wheelbarrow toppled over on the hill, one clumsy leg sticking up into the air. The chrysanthemums bowled out. David began to pick them up, breaking off the bent branches and laying them in a little pile. He apologized for loading the wheelbarrow badly—anything to avoid a fit of rage, which would have left me sweating and trembling in the void of David's calm.

We carried the plants to the edge of the flower bed. David took up the shovel. With its edge, he began to feel for a giving place in the gravel. We had ordered the garden to be made in the foundations of the fallen-down barn, and the gardener, taking advantage of our ignorance, had added a bare two inches of topsoil to make the beds. There were rocks everywhere under the briefly flourishing plants; they dried up and died in just one hot summer. Each spring we replanted, at great expense, since the frost heaved up most of the perennials. The garden was our most important creation, radiant with tulips and daffodils in May, a scorched desert of drooping petunias in July. Now it had entered its empty period, which the chrysanthemums would disguise. Behind the singed petunias, in front of the iris, David found a spot that gave and began to dig a small hole.

I returned to gnawing at my subject. "You know, David, sometimes I think we only come to the country to see the Fields."

"It's lucky for us they are here. Our kids get along so well."

"They're not really friends, though, have you noticed? Except for Jeff and Saul. The others just hang around together. It's the grownups, really, who enjoy each other."

"Yes. It works very well." He took one of the chrysanthemums and edged it into the hole, which was too shallow.

"You'll have to dig more," I said.

He lifted the plant out and began to pry at the hole with the shovel. "I'm afraid I've hit rock," he said after a while.

Crouching down, I felt the dry earth at the edge of the rock. I clawed away at it, my nails clogging as the dirt piled up. As a child, I had clawed the dirt at home to get rid of the stripped feeling after my grandmother cut my nails. "Here, use the trowel," David said, dismayed, but I continued to rake with my nails at the dirt. At last I uncovered the rock and lifted it out, straining. It was flat and wide, an old-time occupant nearly a foot across. I hoisted it up, longing to hurl it, but it was too heavy. I staggered to the edge of the flower bed and dropped it with a thump in the long grass.

"Good for you," David said. He sunk the plant into the deepened hole and began to stamp the dirt around it.

"Do you think we've learned anything about plants in eight years?" I asked when I had my breath back.

David paused to consider the situation. "Yes, I believe we have. The catalogs are very helpful."

"We haven't learned much about anything else."

"I don't know what you mean."

I did not have the courage to go on. Digging in the earth had reminded me of sex. Sweating and straining generally did, as though physical effort was the most important component of fucking: simply the effort required to lift the arms and legs, tilt the pelvis and rotate the hips, combined with the more obscure but equally arduous effort required to raise a flagging penis. David and I had begun several years before to ration this effort. We now did not sweat together in bed, unless we had the electric blanket turned too high, yet it was exhaustion which provided us finally with the excuse to stop fucking altogether. For six months, we had rested, hoarding our energy for a later date. All in all, it was a relief. Looking back, it seemed that the exercise wasn't worth the effort, raising hopes for intimacy which were certain to be dashed. I had never come with David, and he had stopped coming with me; this underground blight had finally undermined our affection. David was parching me, leaching me dry as I was parching him. He did not give me money, and he did not give me his prick. The connection was as odious as it was vital. That he was a good father, in his absent way, and a decent man no longer mattered to me at all.

"I'm not going to be able to stand it much longer," I said ruefully, stunned by regret.

He unpotted the next plant with a tap. "What?"

Choking back tears, I did not answer and he did not ask again. We had both learned to avoid questions which had no ready answer. Instead, I turned away. "It's nearly noon. I'm going to get the children ready for the party."

"All right. I'll come up to the house in five minutes."

Walking up the hill, I began to imagine Saul's birthday party, and my anger evaporated. I knew I would see Edwin there, possibly touch him, possibly steal a word or two alone. We would be able to plan our next meeting.

I lifted my head and really looked around for the first time that day. The willow behind the house was yellow, its streamers separated by sharp lines of shadow. It grew over the cesspool, which it clutched with its roots. It sprang a few feet higher every year, clearing the peak of the house, planted by a second wife two generations ago.

Behind the willow, my land fell away into a shaggy, overgrown field full of straggling hay, which was bleached now and bowed to the ground. Tom Goldsmith had refused to cut it this year, saying it wasn't worth his time. It worried me to see the land lying idle, covered over with milkweed and cockleburs, but I didn't have the money to pay Goldsmith—he had taken the hay before as a fair exchange—and I knew the time had come for me to accept, as my neighbors had, that the land had lost its primary use. Next summer there would be sumac in the field, the year after, scrub pines. The pasture would cease to have any justification except as a backdrop for our lives.

Beyond the field, a low limestone ridge marked the boundary of my land. Keith had found an old dump back there. He came running into the house to tell us that he had uncovered all sorts of treasures, including a doll buried to her waist in the dirt. We all rushed back to see, but when we pulled the doll out of the dirt, we saw that her legs were eaten through. Her obliterated face maintained a lipstick smile—a dead toy, abandoned years ago with the mottled tin coffeepot and the busted buckets.

I saw the children running from underneath the willow, running in all directions as though they had exploded. "Time to go to the party!" I shouted. Suddenly, I was pleased with it all—the close, smoky days, the house, the life I had laboriously made around children and dinner parties and the conversation of friends, all illuminated now by my secret life with Edwin.

Jeff came barreling toward me, and Molly and Keith followed behind. I had the uncomfortable feeling that the older two had been talking. They did not play anymore, turning that activity entirely over to Jeff. Instead, they talked and refused to share their long, half-whispered conversations. I suspected them of analyzing. At least Jeff had not outgrown his games. "They hid from me!" he whined, coming so close to me his face nudged my side. I imagined a calf butting its mother's bag, getting down to the business of nursing. I turned away, ignoring him. "You're not listening," Jeff complained.

"I'll listen when you tell me something I want to hear," I told him, catching his hand and pulling him toward the house.

At the porch door, I looked back and considered them separately. Three children, all inconceivably mine, they clustered close to me to complain. Keith was looking, as always, sour and fat: at thirteen, he had lost his bones, and his shirt buttons strained across his plump chest. Molly was wearing one of his shirts and a pair of his jeans that hung loose from her hips: She was only ten, and she had not yet given up her hope of being transformed into a brother—not a boy plain, but a boy caught and held in the mystical union of brotherhood. She refused to put on anything except Keith's clothes, maintaining her faith in flies and leather belts and torn striped jerseys that showed her startling breastbone. A beautiful girl, a little witch, the source of my undoing—as sometimes

I thought when I saw her perched on Edwin's lap. She was the only one of my children he liked, and she liked him too. All the girls' mothers I knew joked about their daughters' seductiveness, yet it still seemed strange to me that Molly was so flirtatious when she genuinely, painfully wanted to be a boy. The two wishes—to be seduced and to be seductive—were after all not contradictory, perhaps not even connected at all. Edwin responded to her, feeling her round bottom gently with his hands, as though she were a glass bauble dangling on a thread. Perhaps, after all, this was what Edwin wanted.

Jeff, whining along behind, looked like a ghost with his cobwebbed blue eyes and his shaggy head. His last hysterical fit at the barber's in New York had convinced me never to have his hair cut again. David was supposed to do it at home, but since he was opposed to anything that smacked of force, he was against it too, and eventually I would have to cut Jeff's hair myself. I would not have minded cutting it if it were not for his screams, my own child staring at me, panic-stricken. He had the same fear of being seen naked. At school, he went through elaborate contortions in the bathroom, hiding his genitals behind a towel, and when it was time to change for gym, he had permission to go and lock himself in the supply cupboard. Otherwise, he would not go to gym. These concessions sealed his disability. I imagined him as an old man shielding himself in men's rooms, trying to explain with a joke that he had never, in seventy-three years, been seen without his pants.

It was easier, although I worked harder, when they were small. Then their needs were clear and mostly connected with feeding and elimination. Still, sometimes I cleaned their nails with my nail or inspected their ears or tried to catch them on my lap, but mostly they grew like cabbages, flourishing in my distraction, in some rich soil of their own invention. Only the recent intimacy between Molly and Keith alarmed me. When I heard them whispering together, I longed for the evil days when Keith hated his new baby sister and had walked the house at night, howling, clutching his ears, wetting his bed when I forced him back into it, and then screaming at the sight of the dark patch on the sheet. With Molly goggle-headed in the shoulder sling, I'd held Keith in my arms, trying to quiet him until my own arms were stiff as pistons with resentment, when he must have felt in my soothing hands the clutch that would have torn his hair out if I'd lost control. David was away that summer, working on the provisions and charters for a Saudi bank, and I was more proud than angry to be left with it all. David's contribution had always been minimal. I had wanted it that way. The babies had needed me, separately, completely, devouring whole areas of my attention and patience until there was not an inch left for my discontent to sprout. All I had wanted in those first years was to get from one day to the next, or possibly, to sleep through the night. As soon as Molly was out of diapers, Jeff had come along. Devoured, devouring, I was satisfied for a long time with the pride I felt as a single-handed homemade mother of three small children.

"I wish you'd get some help," my mother had observed on one of her whirlwind visits from Florida. She'd brought me a bright pink dress which I was too thin and too pale to wear. I did not try to explain to her that I would never give over to some stranger even a tiny piece of my children. After all, they were all I had. On evenings in the city when David and I went out, I was pleased if the telephone-ordered sitter proved to be ugly or old: the children would not like her. Now, of course, if Edwin had been free in the evening, I would have quickly arranged the sitter, not caring whether or not the children fell in love while I was away.

We crowded onto the porch. "I wish you children would wash your faces and brush your hair before we go," I said, realizing too late that I had put in exactly the inflection which would allow them to refuse.

"My hands are already clean," Molly said.

Keith, in parody, waved his hands in my face. They were enormous, the half-inch nails lined with dirt.

Jeff grumbled, "Last year you made us put on all clean clothes for Saul's party, and we were the only clean ones there."

I laughed. Then I did not much care how I looked myself. Now the time I would have spent on getting the children ready could be spent on my own appearance. "I'm going to change, and I don't want to be bothered," I announced, marching off toward the stairs.

The children went into the kitchen and began to open and close the cabinets. "No eating!" I shouted down the stairs, knowing how wounded Flora would be if they turned down her spaghetti.

Upstairs in the bathroom, I spread the bathmat on the muddy floor (there was never time to clean the house, and we existed quite happily in dirt), stripped off my denim shirt, and washed myself, shivering, from the waist up. The house did not warm up or dry out from October until May. Even with the windows open all weekend, there wasn't time to get rid of the sour damp smell that had accumulated during the week. For generations, the house had been crammed with people—relatives, farmhands, an occasional boarder; the big locks on all the inside doors recalled their need for privacy. The men had worked on the farm, the women had cooked and cleaned and raised children, and the house had never been empty or quiet or properly outfitted or decorated. It had been a funnel, a chute to the outdoors, or protection from it.

How they would have stared at my pink towels, my crocks of dried weeds: so much for effect. Of course what would have astonished them most of all would have been my need for a city freezer and a country one, two enormous refrigerators, and enough food to feed a small army.

It was one of the things our little band never discussed: our twinned lives. We all kept egg cartons and mashed milk containers to start our fires; we all reprimanded our children for eating junk and kept odd dried bits of leftovers in our refrigerators. I remembered how angry Flora had been with me once when I had poured the bacon grease down the drain: we could have used it!

I put on a tight pink shirt—I enjoyed showing my nipples— and a clean pair of blue jeans. Anything else would have looked planned, which in our circle would have signified frivolity. We were all serious people after all, the women perhaps more so than the men, and spending time getting "dressed up" would have branded us as "silly."

Downstairs, there was a crash, and Jeff came screaming up. I pushed him away when he burrowed into my thigh. Threatening him with being left behind, I started for the stairs. That threat frightened me a good deal more than it frightened him: I was terrified of delay as though the party were dissolving before I could get there. At my heels, Jeff launched into an endless litany: teasing at school, boredom at home. Injustices, injustices—I have never been able to explain them to my children, and their number was always legion. It did not matter now. I was armed with expectation—eventually his tears would stop and anyway, with the children for an excuse, I was going to spend the rest of the day with grownups. There would be plenty to eat and drink, a bonfire lighted later, and the promise, the miraculous promise of Edwin.

We were cheery in the car. David did not even make the children fasten their seatbelts. He drove a mile or two above the speed limit, which surprised me. Usually he drove with dazzling caution, noticing wetness or ice on the road which I could never see. Now he was at his ease, the fingers of one hand resting idly on the wheel. It was unlike him, but I did not mind. Sinking into my delicious euphoria, into the cottony layers of expectation, I looked out the window. The landscape seemed formed for my delight. Old fields sloped up from the road to barns and white frame houses. There were sheep in one pasture and a special set of trapezoid barns, which we'd always admired.

We turned onto the lumpy tree-hung side road. The children cheered. They shouted at their father to speed up over the big bump in the road, but David slowed down and began to explain to them about the car springs. We passed quietly over the bump without losing our stomachs. I remembered sailing over it with Edwin years before, his children shrieking on the roof of their car. They were quite small then, and I was startled by Edwin's nonchalance. My own three were safely strapped into the back seat with David. "Do you think they will hold on to the luggage rack?" I asked Edwin politely, and he laughed, showing me his eyeteeth. "Perhaps we'll be lucky and lose one or two." He was able to say that sort of thing because he never appeared to be burdened by his children; he simply included them in his life. They went with him everywhere. I had often seen them monkeying around in the supermarket, shattering crackers in the diner, or creating some mild disturbance in the movies, with Edwin in the lead, beaming with charm to cover their dishevelment.

We turned into the little gravel drive, passing the trashcan on wheels which Frank, their eldest, was responsible for wheeling out every Sunday morning. In spite of their exuberance in public, the Field children were well-trained. Edwin and Flora did not seem troubled by the uncertainty that dissolved my rules as soon as I made them. I was still torn between the wish to do everything for my children and the conviction that they should at last begin to grow up. Edwin and Flora, I thought, had produced a set of small grownups with glee and a good sense of responsibility. It seemed as fine a recipe for raising children as any I could imagine.

The Fields' little white house looked neat and bright inside its border of geraniums. Edwin had laid the brick terrace himself three summers before. That was the first time I saw him without his shirt, and I remembered being surprised that a man with so little hair on his chest could look so male, his muscles long and smooth under his glittering wet skin. I had lived my life with an eye to appearances, clothes jerked around on hangers, men who seemed costumed, and so Edwin's bare chest had seemed a statement of intent, a signal of intimacy. Of course, nothing had happened then. Jeff was a hectic five-year-old, and I was drained and preoccupied. Two years later, when Jeff was in school all day, I stored the image of Edwin's bare chest carefully among my fantasies—there were very few—waiting for the ripe time.

There was no one in sight as we drove up to the house, except for the dog, a dismal yellow mongrel that everyone hated except for Frank, who slept with Porky on his chest. Edwin, who walked Porky every morning in the city, had once referred to the dog as the ultimate pleasure. This raised my hopes that he and Flora had stopped sleeping together. Although we'd visited the house at least three hundred times, Porky began to snarl at us, and when Jeff reached out to pat him, the dog snapped. David avoided the source of conflict and led us all safely into the house.

A great pot of spaghetti sauce was popping away on the stove. Dishes and clothes lay everywhere. As always, the hosts had vanished. I called, and they appeared, emerging from the cellar, the bathroom, pounding down the stairs. Frank stepped out of the coat closet and smiled with his father's mystery when I asked him why he had been hiding. Flora, her hair flying, dabbed my cheek with a kiss, brushed my forearm with her muscular breast and turned away to stir the spaghetti sauce.

I looked for Edwin, sorting through the milling bodies. He was there, but he passed me quickly without a look or a smile, heading for the telephone. Sometimes when we met, he lifted me up in his arms; other times he did not seem to see me. I was never sure of the difference, although I was sure of the hurt. Now I quickly reassembled myself—it was important not to show Edwin any sign of pique or pain—while he began to dial.

The children stormed outside, and Flora and David sat down to their ritual cups of coffee. They had an odd friendship, foreclosed, narrow, and lasting. They began their standard dialogue, touching humorously on their difficulties as the responsible adults in their families. Flora's condescension, as always, annoyed me. Meanwhile, Edwin was talking on the telephone, his back turned to me as he leaned against the wall. The call was long, detailed, and yet perfunctory—I was grateful for that—dealing, I finally realized, with a repair he was having made to his car.

Watching me watch him, Flora asked me if I would like a cup of coffee too and smiled tenderly at my guilty start and refusal. Standing in the middle of the kitchen, I knew that I was upholding all their expectations: I was the child who had drawn the short straw, who had to be "it." "Aren't you at all attracted to Edwin?" Flora had asked me curiously over the years. She had watched us together, before we were lovers, with her faint antici-patory smile. Her obvious certainty, which I was just beginning to recognize, took the edge off mine. It was beginning to be clear to me that I was the last of Flora's country friends to draw the short straw.

Flora had remarked several times that fall that she knew I had "a thing" for Edwin. She seemed to find it amusing, as though I had finally revealed myself to be as foolish as she had always surmised. My authority and independence regarding "the thing" were gone and she had even begun to advise me about my children, remind-ing me to take them to have their shots, handing out aspirin as though I would not have any at home. David seemed to enjoy the situation too. "I have a tiger by the tail," he observed once when I had spent the evening dancing with Edwin. At times, I grew tired of pleasing them and remembered my role in school. Bright, stiff-necked, spoiled, I had been the clown who could be counted on to say anything, do anything, and of course, to scream and cry when I was punished.

Finally Edwin hung up the receiver and said, "How are you?" without looking at me so that I was not quite sure who he meant. Then in one stride he came and took me in his arms—those long arms, the wrists as narrow as mine. He pressed me confidently, knowing that I would never lean back or wriggle away; I leaned against him for a moment. "A real kiss," he said, and I tipped my head back. His lips brushed mine. He smelled as neutral as water, having a great love of baths. After sex, he would plunge into a hot bath and scrub every inch. He liked me to sit in the water with him. When he had finished washing, he would lie back and talk, the faucet dripping on his shoulder, and I listened with the great-est care, as close to his hidden spontaneity, his secret wishes, as

I would ever be. I hoped for illumination, for the final breaking of his code. Out of the water, Edwin talked in short bursts and enigmatic phrases, which, between ignorance and wishfulness, I could not quite decipher, yet it was our secret language shared with no one else. Like a primitive, Edwin used a code so precise it fascinated me, and explained exactly what he wanted.

He lifted me off my feet and swung me around, our poor substitute for the orgasms we wouldn't have. "If only we had more time!" I used to plead, as though it would all work if we had hours to play. Of course, Edwin did not have time to give; I had to be sandwiched between appointments. Now, for an instant, he swung me off the ground, and I felt as light and helpless, as exuberant, as a child. Then he set me on my feet and disappeared down the steps to the cellar.

Indian giver, I thought.

"Now have a cup of coffee," Flora advised. I wondered how much I was like her: We were sisters under the yoke. Sometimes at night, I ground my teeth until my jaws ached at that thought. At other times, our union called up terrifying fantasies: Flora's nipple stoppering my mouth while Edwin fucked me. Flora's mouth on my neglected clitoris. That image was more than I could bear, even in the far reaches of sleep, and I would wake up sweating. Now I sat down and accepted her cup of coffee.

Flora pushed the gritty sugar bowl in my direction. It was crusted because her children, starved, sometimes ate out of it with their hands. She looked at me with kindness. "Tell me, before Helena and Charles return . . ." (The two of them were mutual friends I hadn't known were coming.) " . . . how do you think they're getting along?" If I had been a little younger, she would have distracted me instead with a good smack.

"I think they've gotten everything straightened out. Apparently Charles has started seeing an analyst, and it's really working."

"Edwin told me you said analysis is just another form of exploitation."

I was careful not to let her see the hurt. Edwin was not supposed to repeat our conversations. "I was only arguing that ideally treatment should be free."

"Then the patient wouldn't respect it. You know what you get for free is useless, without any value—a handout."

"Paying doesn't mean that much to me."

"You can afford that attitude."

Swiftly, I shifted: money was a dangerous subject. "Generally, I guess I don't have much faith in doctors."

"Since when have you been so disillusioned?" There was a smile like a point of ice in her eyes.

"Since Jeff was born," I answered rapidly. "The obstetrician— you know I switched on purpose—insisted on forceps—"

Edwin emerged suddenly from the cellar, and I lost the last half of what I had meant to say.

"I've never claimed to do anything more than replace neurotic misery with ordinary unhappiness," he said.

"That's saying a lot, even if it's misquoted," I grumbled, annoyed because his mere reappearance had robbed me of what I had intended to say. The births of my children had been turning points for me, all lost in the good-humored glance he gave me.

David, making his way into the conversation, asked, "Who else do we have, after all, for help?" I could hear my own opinions caught like flies in his waxy voice: he was never quite up-to-date. "We can't turn to priests anymore, or parents. Who do we have for trouble except doctors?"

"We might do better with nothing," I said, refusing him the right to compliment my lover who was not, after all, my cure.

"There are a lot of other things to turn to," Edwin said. "Liquor, drugs, sex." He grinned. "Charles told me last July they were thinking of a separation," Flora said, turning us off the track. "I told him I thought it might be a good idea. They ought to think things over."

"We had them here afterward to talk," Edwin observed. "They were hardly speaking to each other at that point, but I think we got them started again."

"Perhaps they are saved, then," I said.

Edwin went on. "I used to think those two held each other up. Now I think they've made it easy to fall apart." Before I could answer, he went to the telephone and began to dial. Watching his finger feeling for each hole, I remembered how he felt for me like a blind man, his fingers hardly discriminating between nipples and buttonholes. I loved his blind fingers. It was only afterward, when the talk began, that he discredited what he did so well by instinct, because it was by instinct and not by love or will.

I strained again to hear his cautious conversation cupped into the telephone. Flora and David had begun to talk about schools— this was Flora's area of expertise. She knew each week which of the city private schools had reached its apex and was beginning to slide down the other side. She spoke intensely about one such school, which had begun to deteriorate, and as she leaned toward David, convincing him, I imagined how the other mothers might listen, overawed as she introduced them to the system.

"I think five o'clock should suit," Edwin said into the telephone, and I lost track of the rest of Flora's monologue. His neat life was full of holes gnawed by my suspicion. He had been faithful to me for the first six months of our affair (a word which neither of us used, out of moral conviction or a fear of the end)—except, of course, for Flora, our companion in all our dreams. Later, at a party, he had begun to work on my cousin, flattering her, smiling at her, asking her directly what she liked in bed, until she melted into his hands. I don't think he ever saw her again—that would have been intentional—but it did not much matter. He was demonstrating to me that he wanted his effects back. I knew that he had reached the limit of his commitment and would begin, out of guilt and despair, methodically to destroy it. I knew for a whole day and then forgot. It was too painful. I needed my little bite of pleasure. I needed perhaps even more the flimsy, ever-failing conviction that I was special to him, that my mouth, my words, or my tenderness, had turned him into a lover. Now I succeeded in distracting myself from Edwin's telephone conversation by getting myself a slice of bread from Flora's loaded refrigerator. The sight of all that food reminded me of the children, the meals, the planning, the solidity of their life, backed up protectively behind our partial life together. I buttered the bread and slowly consumed it.

Flora was telling David about her concern for Helena's children if the marriage should fail. "Sheila is impossible as it is. So rude. Helena simply ignores it. She lets the child get away with anything. I told her the last time she came here she couldn't eat with her hands at my table, not at her age. She's practically nine years old. Helena of course wouldn't say a word, though she thanked me afterward for pointing this out."

"Maybe that's why Charles is bored," I said.

"What?" They both turned to look at me.

"Maybe, like a five-year-old, he keeps hoping she'll set him some limits. When he was off with that girl—what was her name?—at Mary's last party, he came in looking like a child who wanted to be whipped."

"Helena just turned her head away," Flora said. "I thought at the time it was a mistake."

"Resignation is boring, though, at least when you're looking for something else."

"Reaction?" She eyed me. "I think you have told me something quite perceptive."

"Use it, next time you get them talking."

David intervened smoothly. "I don't believe they speak with anyone outside anymore. Flora and I just wanted to get them started."

Flora nodded. I looked at the two of them, fellow conspirators over the coffee cups. "Let's hope they're not two hours late this time," Flora said, glancing at the clock. "I'd like to get lunch over with."

Edwin changed positions and leaned against the wall, listening intently to whoever was talking to him on the telephone. Pricked, I asked Flora, "Do his patients often call him on the weekend?"

She smiled. "That's one of the questions I never ask, Ann."

David observed, apropos of nothing, "This fall, it seems as if everyone is breaking up."

4

Tom is knocking at the kitchen door. I can see him through the window, his head turned away to preserve my privacy. I slide my feet into my shoes and go to let him in. He glances at me before asking, "What about setting the tent up in front of the house? People would see it from the road."

"All right."

He turns away, beckoning to his partner, Fred Shingle, a small surly-looking man who hangs around the drugstore in the village. "You know Fred," Tom tells me.

"Yes. Good morning."

Fred ducks his head.

"We'll set it up in front of the house, then," Tom says, turning away. He is a short man with a large belly swinging out over his belt. His monkey face is sad and mean. This house belonged to his family for three generations; I have a snapshot of Tom and his brother as children eating watermelon on the side porch. Tom was not particularly happy to let the place go and he is not particularly disappointed that we are leaving. We are a strange breed to him, living according to rules which have nothing to do, as far as he can see, with seasonal changes or economic survival.

"We'll get the tent set up, and then we'll start moving things out," he says to me over his shoulder. "Good warm day, they'll be coming in crowds." An authentic country man, he gauges the sky. Yet I've heard he was a failure as a farmer, sitting drunk in the kitchen all day.

Jeff is standing behind me, so close I nearly fall over him as I turn around. "Are you going to sell my bed?" he asks for the tenth time. He looks sleepy and cross, having just arisen from the bed I'm selling out from under him. His pajama bottoms hang on his hips below the navel. He has my body, lean and tense, and I wonder if he will ever be strong or if he will have to settle, as I have, for a certain degree of flexibility.

"We've been over this, Jeff," I tell him patiently. "You know the rule. You can each keep one piece of furniture from your room, in addition to your toys. You didn't choose your bed."

"I'm too big for that damn rocking horse!"

"Do you want to change your mind?"

Without answering, he edges toward the kitchen table and begins to shuffle through the cereal boxes.

"You'll have to decide in the next few minutes," I tell him. "Tom and Fred are putting up the tent, and then they're going to begin to empty the house."

Jeff leaves the cereal and runs to the living room window. Over his shoulder, I see Tom squatting by an enormous bundle of canvas. "Is that the tent?" Jeff asks, and his voice and his face change, becoming animated, hopeful.

"Yes, that's the tent." I am as proud as if I stitched it up myself.

"It's going to be a really big one," he says. I kiss the back of his neck where his thin blond hair lies like tiny feelers on his pale skin. He still smells babyish there, powdery. He is going to allow himself to be drawn into the spirit of the occasion.

It is this optimism, I think, that David finds so hard to accept. If the auction were held in a spirit of defeat, of humble acceptance of life's blows, he might be able to tolerate it. But the springing of hope out of destruction is what he finds obscene. Last night, when the children and I were running around the house slapping red tags on the objects we wanted to keep, it felt like a game (until we came to their rooms, at least). David, standing in the middle of the hall, watched our foolish careening as if he couldn't believe his eyes. He told me I could do as I pleased, but had not planned on seeing me enjoy myself.

He has reserved a few items for himself—his clothes, of course, and a collection of books and prints. He was supposed to take more to furnish his own apartment, and I was sorry when he did not arrange for a moving truck to arrive because whenever David fails to make an arrangement, he is making a point instead. Perhaps David will interpret this auction, or my enjoyment of it, as evidence of my instability. To fight me, David would have to place himself in a posture of defiance; he would have to agree with himself to use the past as ammunition; he would have to think of himself as a man capable of rage.

Outside the window, Tom and Fred are crouching and darting, dealing with a maze of ropes. Jeff, fascinated by their expertise, watches with his nose against the glass. I go back to the kitchen and pour myself another cup of coffee.

When I turn away from the stove, Keith is standing by the table, eyeing the boxes of cereal. "Cereal again," he complains, not looking at me. "At least I hope you remembered to get some bananas."

"There's one on the bottom shelf of the refrigerator, but it's brown."

Keith sighs, abandoning breakfast, and drops into a kitchen chair: thirteen years old, already in despair. His pajamas gape at the waist, showing his fat white middle. "You always used to cook real breakfasts, eggs and all, before."

"That's because Daddy was cooking real breakfasts every other morning. I had to keep up. He would cook sausages, I would cook bacon, or vice versa. We argued once about which took the most time."

"Where is Daddy?"

"In the guest room getting dressed." I do not allow myself to remind Keith that this process always takes a while.

He looks toward the door to the porch, then shifts his eyes regularly around the room to avoid looking at me. "Daddy asked me to go down to the Caribbean with him at Christmas. He's going sailing on Uncle Sheldon's yacht."

I will not show my surprise. Calmly I remark, "Sheldon always did prefer your father to me. I suppose it's natural. You can't very well have sibling rivalry with your brother-in-law, and Sheldon really did hate me when we were little."

"It's either that or sitting around in New York for three weeks."

"If you're going to eat, eat. I want to clear the table."

"I'm not going to eat. You're in a foul mood, aren't you?" When I do not answer, he goes on. "New York at Christmas really stinks. It rains, and you're always in a bad mood, and there's nothing to do."

"I can't afford to take you to the Caribbean. Grandpa's money that we lived on all these years is nearly gone. Two houses, three children, and a husband used it up."

It is not the first time he has heard this, and it is not the first time he has refused to believe me. "I guess I'll go with Dad and Uncle Sheldon."

"Have a good trip," I say.

For the first time, he looks straight at me, and I see the wretched torn boy beneath his arrogance. "It's all right, Keith. I expect you'll enjoy yourself. I *want* you to enjoy yourself. I'm just angry because the money's gone, and it wasn't only me who spent it. You don't want to hear that, and I won't say any more for a while. Talk to your father. You'll have plenty of chances, once you're living with him."

"He told me he'll have his place fixed up in another couple of weeks. Can I take my stereo?"

"Of course. It's yours."

The collaboration between my husband and my eldest son sticks like a splinter of bone in my throat. I carry my rattling coffee cup and saucer into the parlor. It is important not to burden Keith with any more guilt. Yet when I think of him sitting in the evenings with his father sharing confidences, I am ready to die. This is the child I bore and nursed and raised when David was so busy he never even met the pediatrician, so fastidious he could not bring himself to change a pair of diapers, so clumsy that when he tried once to feed Keith his strained apricots, he upset the little jar into the lap of his pin-striped suit. And now they are united and solid against me: two males. It is the tie that binds.

Until the separation, they were united by distrust. Keith, after all, had edged David out of my attention. A baby is so much more satisfying than a dry man. Keith was hungry, angry, and kept me up night and day with his shrieks, his kicking, his active, changing pace. He was a racer from the start, and he kept me to the mark— with him I reached, for the first time, the limit of my endurance.

David watched this from the sidelines, intrigued perhaps—it was another tiger of a sort to be held rather gingerly by the tail.

Now they are united against a common foe. I remember their voices late at night after I have gone to bed. They sit by the fire with their glasses of crème de menthe and their well-documented injuries. David told Keith about Edwin, and my son was devastated. "Frank and I used to be friends," he told me with tears in his eyes. After that, he began to avoid me. His moon-look of devotion and patience, which I had depended on without even knowing it, has almost entirely disappeared.

"I don't want to live with you without Daddy," he told me dryly, finally, when I was discussing our separation. "I don't want to live with you without a man." He imagined, I suppose, an adolescence devoted to making drinks for my friends and taking me to movies. He is going to live with his father instead, where he hopes to be free of demands and disillusionment. For a moment, standing in the sunny parlor, I am frightened by my willingness to let him go. I am letting everything go. Where will I draw the line? Then I remind myself that it is because my other two, my babies, will still be with me: I can afford to lose one limb.

Molly comes running into the parlor, her face flushed and strained. "The Fields are here! I saw their car!"

David is behind her. "It can't be," he says, and goes to the porch to have a look. I stand rooted in the middle of the floor. My heart is pounding. I thought they might see the announcement of the auction in the local paper, but it never occurred to me that they would come.

David returns. "It's true," he says. He has turned pale, and for the first time I am sorry for him. He fears the embarrassment of confronting Edwin. What will he say?

For his sake, I call back my sangfroid like a genie escaped from a bottle. David is watching me closely. "They're welcome," I say. "After all, it's a public event." I have not realized until I say those words how much I want to see Edwin.

"I wonder what they want."

I do not answer, unwilling to be drawn in, although my curiosity hurts like heartache. We have spent a great deal of time analyzing Edwin's and Flora's motives—assuming that their motives are separate—and that effort took the place of analyzing our own. Those lines of comparison might have been worth drawing. Instead, we attempted to make of the Fields a common enemy, to unite briefly against them, but that was not possible for me. I genuinely cared for Edwin and that disrupted the common cause.

"What are we going to do?" David asks.

"We are going to behave as though everything is normal. Don't frighten the children. There is nothing else we can do." For the last time I am asking him to be a fellow conspirator, and he seems to agree. When Molly comes rushing back with the latest bulletin, we both greet her with an appearance of disinterest. I repeat to her that the auction is, after all, a public event.

Deflated, she sits down at the desk and begins to draw a series of large faces on a pad. "I wanted to help with the auction," she complains, swiftly shifting ground. "You promised to wake me up early so I could help, and then you forgot."

"There really isn't much more for anyone to do, Molly. You helped me tag the things we want to keep. Tom and Fred are going to take the furniture out. Maybe you can help with that."

She looks around the parlor. "In this whole room, we're only keeping that ugly lamp."

It is made from deer's hoof, brittle with age. "That was in your grandfather's lodge in the Adirondacks. I was always fond of it."

"It's ugly," she says. "Why aren't you going to keep this desk?"

David sits down and opens his newspaper; behind it, he will listen to our conversation.

"That desk is too small to be practical," I repeat wearily. "I need a big desk for paying bills."

"But it's so pretty!" She lifts one of the little brass pulls and lets it fall with a jingle.

"I know, and I remember how you used to enjoy sitting on my lap and opening and shutting all those little drawers. But there won't be room for two desks in our new apartment."

"It sounds like a stinky little place."

"It's all we can afford. I'll take you next week to see it. It's bright. It's full of sun. Your room has a bookshelf."

Keith has come in, chewing on a piece of raisin toast. "I thought that desk belonged to your grandmother."

"It did. It came up with all the other things from Washington when she died. This desk was always in the corner of her bedroom. She kept flowers on it and a photograph of her first husband—not your grandfather. He came around too late to be admired. The desk was a kind of shrine. She never actually used it. She sat up in bed with a tray on her lap to write her letters."

"Why isn't Daddy taking more stuff?"

"Ask him."

We all look at the newspaper. Slowly it shifts, and David's calm face appears. "What is it?"

I motion to Keith to repeat his question, but his mouth is conveniently full of raisin toast, and he simply stares. "I told your father weeks ago he could take anything he wanted, but he never could get a moving truck here," I say.

"Why can't he just keep the things he wants here?"

"Because the new people are going to move in." My voice is crusty, dry. I am so tired of explaining, tired of my own righteousness. Where is the soft woman Edwin used to take in his arms?

"Well, nobody is going to sell my things," Keith announces.

"You've told me that many times, and I've told you it simply can't be. Now we haven't been through your room together, and nothing is sorted, but you're simply going to have to make your mind up to let the furniture go. The house has to be cleared out. Your father and I agreed on that. We can't take all your junk to the city; there wouldn't be room for it there." As I pile argument on argument, I begin to lose my patience. Turning away, I knock my shin on the rocker. I lean down to rub the bump. "Now get dressed, both of you. It's nearly time for the auction to begin. You may want to go outside when the people have all come."

"I'm not going out there," Keith says.

"Why not?"

He does not answer, and I know he means to guard the door to his room.

"He says it's too embarrassing," Molly explains.

"It is," Keith says. "We're getting rid of everything we own."

"I've told you over and over, I'm sick of telling you—we have to have the cash to live on."

"I can't bear the idea of everybody picking over—" Suddenly he is crying, furiously beating me off with his hands when I try to comfort him.

"Keith," David says, lowering the paper. "It will be all right, son." He adds to me, "This is all very upsetting."

"Of course it's very upsetting. And it's going to get worse. We are going to have to clear out Keith's room." At that, the boy breaks away from me and dashes up the stairs. I hear his door slam behind him. "There isn't going to be any way around this one," I tell David.

Looking at his calm face, his benevolent soft brown eyes that match his corduroy country suit, I am frightened by the extent of my own power. Pushing against David has always been like pushing against cream, or foam; I am left with the desolating awareness of my own strength. Normal assertiveness begins to seem in his presence like the high-pitched barking of a hysterical dog, leg-chained to a lamppost. I begin to falter. "I need you to persuade him, David. We really have to get his room cleared out."

He lays the newspaper aside. On his lap I see the yellow pad. "There's your theory as well. I don't believe that people can start over, fresh, forget the past."

Molly glances up from her drawing, scenting a confrontation. We both look at her, wish her away, and then settle for her presence as a potentially useful ally.

"Of course there's my theory," I admit, cornered. I listen to David's silence for a while. In the next room, Jeff, oblivious, is pushing a metal toy tank around the floor. Upstairs, Keith is guarding his room. It seems to me that they are all waiting, listening for my explanation, and I realize that I have counted on their grudging consent. "You'd better tell me what you're getting at," I tell David.

He doesn't answer. I didn't expect him to. I slip into silence along with him. I'll never be able to shed my past, even if I wanted to. I'm keeping that loveseat because I used to sit there while my grandmother told me her stories about all the terrible things that can happen to women in this world, but even if I didn't keep the loveseat, I'd hear her voice. The most I can do is just to change my way of life, and that's hard enough—change what I eat, what I wear, how I spend my time, the rooms I live in. Maybe eventually rearrange things so I can go outside in good weather and stay inside in bad, be with people I like or be alone. But that's ambitious. "All I'm trying to do now is just revise the look of the rooms where I'm going to live." David glances at Molly. "Is that ridiculous?" I ask.

David looks at his yellow pad, touches a line with his finger. "That's not ridiculous. But I'm not sure that's all you're trying to do."

"Anyway, it's too much!" Keith shouts from the top of the stairs. "It's too much, and it's not fair!" Then he stumps off to his room again and ostentatiously slams the door.

"Keith gets to keep everything. It's not fair," Molly whimpers.

I look at my husband. "David, you are going to have to deal with him. You can't expect the other children to give up their furniture when Keith is keeping everything he has."

"I'm sorry," David says. "I don't remember agreeing to help you with this. It was all your idea. I told you to go ahead and try. But I warned you it wouldn't work. The children wouldn't stand it. You were determined. There was nothing I could say. But I'm not going to bail you out at the last minute when it all starts to go wrong."

"It's not all starting to go wrong. You are not going to sabotage it." My power, or the illusion of my power, has drained away, leaving me watery. I go into the living room to escape their complicity—Keith and David, Molly and David, each couple united against me. I look down at Jeff, still busily running his tank across the floor. Thank God there is one extra for my side. As I watch him, the sun is abruptly cut off, and I turn to the window to see a straining patch of canvas slowly moving across the panes. While we were arguing, Fred and Tom have been putting up the tent. My helplessness vanishes: the tent is going up.

Molly has followed me into the living room. "Look, the tent is going up!" I exclaim. She glances at it perfunctorily. Jeff raises his head and stares, then darts to the window.

"It's going to be really big!" he says.

Molly begins again at my elbow. "I want to keep my cradle. It's not fair. Keith gets to keep everything in his room."

"Keith is not going to keep everything in his room. Now go up and get dressed."

"Daddy says I should get to keep my cradle. He says it's an antique."

"Daddy and I agreed on a set of rules," I tell her. "We agreed two months ago, but now he wants to forget that." Before she can begin again, I lean down and put my arms around her. "I'm sorry, Molly."

She stands distrustfully within the circle of my arms, her body thin as a stalk of celery. After a while, she begins to mutter, "We used to have a good time, and now we don't ever have a good time anymore."

"We do have a good time still." I sift my memory for examples. "We went to the Bronx Zoo that day—"

"It's not the same," she interrupts, and I do not contradict her. Of course it's not the same. I hold her for as long as she will allow it, and then I let her go. The suffering of children arouses such terrible guilt in adults who are responsible for them. I must cling with all my strength to my faith that my happiness is worth as much as theirs.

David comes into the living room behind me. I catch a whiff of his shaving lotion, which makes me gag.

"The tent's up," Jeff announces at the window.

"You are going to help me with Keith," I tell David.

David looks down at his pad and corrects a word.

"What are you writing there?" I shriek.

"Mommy, don't scream like that!" Jeff is suddenly beside me, pulling at my arm. David tucks the pad quickly away.

"Just some notes."

"My God, I can't stand it." I grip my hair with my hands.

"I'll get you a glass of water," David says. We look at each other. Hatred, so much more nourishing than love, is briefly illuminating his face. I know that I am looking flushed and vital too, rage speeding fresh blood through my veins. The energy with which we are trying to hurt each other was never available for loving.

"It's all right," I say, patting Jeff's shoulder and at the same time trying to put him a slight distance off. "Don't worry." He goes back to his window.

I walk to the desk and pick up his yellow pad. At the top of the first page, David has written in crisp black script: *Examples of hysteria.* There are fifteen numbered examples. The first one reads, *Shouting at Keith, completely out of control.*

So he is planning a custody battle. Suddenly I'm calm. I remember the years when David and I were gentle and kind to each other, offering tidbits of comfort and understanding, adjusting a pillow, pouring a drink, united by our distrust of common reality. That was when the sex began to stop. Two invalids must spare each other. Instead, we lay side by side in bed, chastely, companionably, like two children sharing a fear of the dark.

It was better that way. The disappointment otherwise was

too much for either of us to bear. David had stopped coming with me—he blamed his allergy medicine—and I had never come with him, even in the beginning when everything seemed possible.

For years I prevented myself from seeing the situation. I cooked and bought and made babies instead, filling up the gaps, and of course, I read. Eventually I stumbled on an article in a woman's magazine, which convinced me that there was one cause for the despair which gnawed me after David was gone. I admitted in a French restaurant that I had never had an orgasm, either with him or with anybody else. It was wine-choosing time (or whine-choosing time, as Edwin, my pun-maker, would say), and David looked up from the list. "I'm sorry to hear that," he said, with mild surprise. He comforted me then as he had for other disappointments, with a soft pat on my shoulder. The magazine, I told him, advised women to try a vibrator. That made sense to David, and he bought me one the following week, shielding me from the embarrassment of having to buy one for myself. It sat on the bedside table in its cheap box, a plastic wand I filled with two D-cell batteries; when I turned it on, it buzzed away like Jeff's tin tank. I was half-afraid of it. Finally one night, when David was in the city, I tried it out. It gave me an intense spasm, a revelation, which should never have come to me so cheaply and so fast. Fascinated, I tried the device again and again, hurrying the children into bed in the evening so that I could experiment. There was relief hidden in that device, but after a while, it seemed to lose its magic, and the spasm did not come without ditch-digging work and fantasies, which embarrassed me. And I no longer had the warmth of David's body pumping away vaguely above me for comfort. When I came, it was purely mechanical.

That was when the hope began. With Edwin.

It was the day after Thanksgiving, and all our children were playing Monopoly in the parlor; we had locked the door and fallen on the sofa. He took me rapidly, pulling off my pants, pressing his penis into me. It was over so quickly. As he washed himself in the bathroom next door, I pressed my hands between my legs. "It's no good for me this way. Get a sitter for the boys tonight so we can have some time together."

He looked at me, alarmed. "But I don't want to get a sitter. The children depend on me to be with them, especially when Flora is away."

"Flora asked me to take care of you when she went back to town."

"You are taking care of me." He smiled, came to the bed, reached down, and touched my hair. It was so rare for him to show this kind of affection my eyes filled with tears.

"Edwin, I need you—I need more of you than this. I need you to stay inside me."

"I'm sorry," he said quietly, "but this is all there is."

"I just want more of what you have, more time with you," I pleaded.

He turned toward the door, buckling his belt. I went around the other way, through the kitchen to come into the living room separately. By then, I had adjusted my expression. It seemed to me that I would not be able to outlive my despair, and yet of course I went on, fixing the children's snack, pouring their milk.

In the afternoon, we all went for a walk in the woods, the older children running ahead along the trail, the younger ones tagging behind, complaining about the cold. Edwin shouted and ran and leaped for the low branches. I ran beside him as though running and playing with him was familiar. To run, to eat, to talk—surely that would take the place of the deep touching he would not give me. "An affectionate relationship is the only thing that keeps two people together," he said later when we were walking back. "That's what you're trying to build with me."

"But I don't want an affectionate relationship if it means just being friends."

He looked at me, taken aback. In the house he went at once to the telephone to call Flora in the city. He discussed this and that with her, his face animated, his eyes fixed on me as I moved around the kitchen, pretending to ignore him. Finally I went upstairs and choked down a Valium, trying to put a cap on my rising anger. He must have hung up at once. He called to me from the bottom of the stairs: "Where are you? Where are you?" mocking his own uneasiness. When I came down, he said, "You see, I won't even allow you to go to the bathroom alone anymore." I wanted that—I wanted his need. It took the place of my own satisfaction. And yet I knew the next time I saw him, he would have forgotten.

Later that evening he took his children home. I woke up in the middle of the night in my small cold room, like the inside of my own head. I lay awake for a long time, my hands clenched by my sides. He had sex with me in the room next to my children. He had exposed them to my desire. He had forced me to do that because he was not willing to find a time when we could be alone—sex snatched like an irresistible bit of filth, a moment's wallowing. I felt constrained, and yet full of flaming energy. I got out of bed. Dressing, jerking on my boots, I went downstairs and sat at the kitchen table until the sky turned gray beyond the pine trees on the rocky ledge. Then I wrote a note for my children and went out to the car. The windshield was frosted over, the steering wheel so cold I held it with the tips of my fingers. I drove down the two-lane highway between fences beginning to appear out of the dark. There was not a single other car. Chasing my own headlights, I drove as fast as the car would go: eighty, then ninety, till the trees leaped, and I was frightened. I slowed down and turned onto the field, stopped the car, and walked to the front door. The dog, as always, began to bark. I tried the door. To my surprise, it was locked. I had never thought of it being locked. I had imagined that I would open it silently and creep up into their bed. I began to bang on the door with my fists. Then I kicked it with the toes of my leather boots. Finally a light went on inside, and I saw Edwin's wan face through the glass panel. He looked scared, and for a minute I thought he would not open the door.

He opened it.

I pushed inside, pushed against him, snatching his forearms, then his shoulders, holding him with all my strength. "I hate you. I hate you. You treat me like dirt. You fuck me with the children all around. You won't find time for me, you don't care." I snatched his limp hand and bit into the fleshy part at the base of his thumb, sinking so deep I could feel the muscle under the skin and tissue. He did not pull his hand back, did not exclaim. His other hand fell on the back of my neck. I unlocked my teeth and looked at his hand: it was set with the prints of my incisors. "Edwin. Edwin." I was sobbing, terrified. He took me in his arms, standing rigid, staring over my head at the meadow appearing out of the shadows of the night. Later, he gave me oatmeal, and we sat in silence in the scruffy little kitchen, waiting for the children to wake up. He was the only man who had ever let me rage, and like a child with a sliver of pride, I inspected from time to time the blue dents I'd left at the base of his thumb.

5

"You're not breaking up," I said to Flora. We were in her kitchen.

She stared at me. Her brown eyes looked small in her large, rosy, always slightly damp face. When she turned her eyes away, the planes of her face continued to confront me with an appeal I did not want to see. "Edwin and I have our ups and downs. But I don't believe anyone could come between us."

"Of course not."

"It breaks up other people's relationships, but we have our arrangement. He can do what he wants on the side." She glanced at Edwin, who was chopping lettuce for lunch.

"I think I'll go see about the children," David said tactfully and made his way out of the kitchen.

"David doesn't like this kind of talk," I said.

"I suppose it embarrasses him."

"Your contract. Its consequences."

She did not respond to my irony. "It works quite well actually. Edwin has his little pleasures, but they don't intrude on our life together. He wouldn't allow them to."

It was on the tip of my tongue to tell her that Edwin and I had our contract too. Edwin had presented me with his terms before our first night in the field. "No marriages and no divorces," he had said, and I, wanting him, had agreed, too naïve to understand exactly what he meant. Later I had begun to wonder about the order of events in his pronouncement. Surely divorces could precede marriages.

Edwin hung up the telephone and passed us, frowning, his mind on something else. I felt the movement of air along my arm as he passed; it was as close as I could come at that moment to touching him. He went down the stairs to the basement.

"Edwin makes a funny little smile when he hears your name," Flora said.

"Does he?"

She fingered her coffee cup. "I know if there was anything between you, you'd think of me. You wouldn't let it get serious."

After a while, she got up to stir the spaghetti sauce. Looking at the way she tied her calico apron, tightly around her small waist, I tried half-heartedly to believe that she loved Edwin and that she would suffer if she lost him. She was entirely lacking in overt affection—never touched him, kissed him, smiled at him, teased him, or asked after his comfort, and might have scorned all such outward shows as either vulgar or hypocritical. It was easy for me to believe that they used each other only as social commodities, escorts at dinner parties, partners in anxiety and planning. I had always discounted the strength of that kind of bond because I disapproved of it.

Our neighbor and friend Helena came suddenly into the kitchen. I had forgotten her and now her presence seemed irrelevant, an intrusion. "Can I put some of these things in your fridge?" she asked, her arms full of groceries, which she dropped on the table before kissing Flora's cheek and then, in the same motion, mine. Without waiting for permission, she began to unpack the bags, slamming meat, milk, and butter into the refrigerator. Dark, small, lively, she reminded me of a skittering field mouse as she darted back and forth. Her five minutes seemed to last the whole day. "It's so much cheaper to do the whole week's shopping at the A&P," she explained as she saw that we were watching. "We came straight from there, and we're going straight from here to the city Sunday night."

She reminded me of our shared satisfaction, our triumph even, when we returned to the city from a weekend in the country; everything that needed fixing in our old houses fixed, and the children packed rosy and exhausted in the back seats of our cars.

Flora got up to help.

"How do you keep the frozen stuff from defrosting in the car?" I asked.

"I never buy frozen things. Not at this time of year when fresh produce on the stands is so cheap."

They talked for a bit about prices, a subject I had always been able to ignore. Flora looked at me and laughed. "Look at her—she's off in her daze again."

I got up and took an egg carton to show that I was involved. There was no room for it in the packed refrigerator. "I was thinking about all the telephone calls I'll have to make when we get back to the city Sunday," I lied. "They pile up over the weekend."

"Well, if you insist on doing all your ordering over the telephone . . . what do you expect? Doesn't money matter to you at all?" Flora teased.

"Oh, I like it," I said to make them laugh.

"Wait till you have to learn fifteen different ways of cooking cabbage," Helena said. "I like figuring it all out, adding and

subtracting, keeping track of what I spend—but when I have to
come down to dealing with what I've bought . . . cabbages . . .
and all the other boring vegetables. I'm the only meat-eater in the
family now."

"You should join my co-op," Flora said. "They give us more
potatoes than cabbages."

Both women lived on the Upper West Side, although they seldom saw each other in the city. Their apartments seemed identi-
cal, long rows of brown rooms high above West End Avenue. My
pale-yellow co-op on East Eighty-Ninth Street was an expensive
luxury, by comparison.

Charles, Helena's husband, a short, stout man in his early
forties, passed rapidly through the kitchen, kissing us all on his
way, even his own wife. Flora and I glanced at each other at that.
Charles went down to the basement where Edwin was powering
up the electric saw. It squealed like a shot rabbit. Flora grimaced,
threw her hands up, and slammed the basement door.

David came in from checking on the children. He kissed
Helena affectionately, held her off to admire her face, and then
began to rearrange the packed refrigerator. He did not need to
be told what Flora wanted because he had a great sensitivity to
domestic arrangement and could always be counted on to help.
After the shelves were ordered, David offered to pick the last of
the tomatoes in the vegetable patch and Helena, very pleased,
followed him.

Flora peered out of the kitchen window, her hand expertly
twitching the curtain aside. "Are those two having a thing?"

"I'm afraid not." It was easy for me to imitate her jaunty tone.

"It would be good for David if they did have a thing," Flora
observed. "Good for his self-confidence generally." She began to

scrape the breakfast plates, now and then snatching a morsel of bacon or solidified egg and cramming it into her mouth. I had never seen her eat, except at dinner parties or off her children's plates. "You wouldn't mind if they were having a thing, would you?"

"I'd be delighted."

"That's the way I feel. It doesn't mean anything after all. It doesn't take anything away from me. Why should I object?"

"No reason at all."

This time she didn't quite believe me. "It's the age, I think," she said quietly. "Forty-five and these men still don't have what they want."

"Do we know what we want?"

Flora shrugged, "Edwin's been trying to finish his book on hyperactive children. He's been trying to finish it for five years. He has the notes and the outline—he finished those last summer when he was alone in the city—but he can't seem to get started on the book."

"He doesn't seem very concerned about it."

"You're right, he's not desperate. He's perfectly comfortable," she said crisply. "It's only boredom that drives him to other women. We call them his fuckees. He never wants to see them again after it's all over. I say to him, 'So-and-so's in town. Shall we invite her to dinner?' But he never wants me to."

I could hardly swallow. "He tells you about them?"

"Of course. That's part of our arrangement. He doesn't tell me at first. He waits until he thinks I'm ready."

"And are you?"

"Oh, yes."

"Don't you ever mind, Flora?"

"No, why should I mind? They don't mean anything to him."

She loaded the last plate into the dishwasher. I did not try to help, knowing from experience that Flora would wave me aside. "It would be different if they communicated—had a relationship."

"Why does he do it," I said, not making it a question because I was terrified by her assurance.

"Oh, he does it for a little adventure, a little excitement." She began to fill the silverware basket. "It makes our life together better actually, especially in bed."

I stood up abruptly. My chair fell over. "I'm going out to see about the children."

"I'll come with you."

"Don't bother." I went out, knowing she would be too wary to follow.

Outside the door, I looked at the flower bed which Edwin had dug last October and filled with chrysanthemums for Flora—Flora, who did not like flowers and was embarrassed by the gesture. I clenched my fists, feeling my own lack of strength in the delicate imprint of my nails in my palms. I would have liked to ram them through. Flora, Edwin's mouthpiece, speaking the truth which I was resisting with every muscle and every fiber, but also with wishfulness, the child's insistence: I will not have it this way because I do not want it this way. I began to summon up arguments for my own case, drawn from thirty-eight years of speculation, denial, of avoiding my own needs and the lengths to which I would go, once aware, to satisfy them. Sweat ran down the insides of my arms, my shirt was sticking to my back. It occurred to me that I was not going to be able to stand this rage. "Get out of this situation," I said aloud. "Get out, just get out." The command seemed simple, and yet it had no force. When I was seven, my uncle threw me up in the air, throwing me again and again and catching me again and again, until I seemed to sail, lost, freed, my body limp as a petal. When Edwin lifted me in his arms, I flew again. Yet what did the connection mean? I wanted to believe it was love, but that meant love has no consequences.

I saw my children up at the swings. They seemed very far away, and I could not interpret their dodging and darting, their particular cries. Pain or joy? Edwin's two oldest boys detached themselves and began to throw a ball back and forth, and I wondered what they, edging into adolescence, thought of this thick hot atmosphere, or were they even aware of it? What did they question, what did they conclude? They looked at me now, sideways, curious and wary, with their father's light gray eyes. Perhaps the most terrible consequence of it all was the danger of losing their trust. They were fed by our lies, which negated their own observations. "I think you like Edwin," Jeff said to me once, long ago, on the way to nursery school. "You kiss him a lot." I told him that he was mistaken, and he looked up at me, his face clouded.

David and Helena were walking toward me from the car; they were in deep conversation. I called, "What are you talking about?"

"You," Helena said soothingly.

"Don't you have anything better?"

"Now, don't get irritated. We've all been concerned about you this fall—that was what David was telling me. We love you, you know, we all love you, and you seem so hectic."

In spite of myself, I was flattered. She had sensed my flourishing disorder, getting rid of my cleaning woman at an hour's notice, with a handful of bills, stripping the bed and remaking it with fresh sheets, and then standing by the front door waiting for Edwin to ring the bell.

"I've been waiting a good time," I said.

Helena looked at me with suspicion. "Well, I hope you know

what you're getting into. I hope you don't wear yourself out. You look very thin."

"Don't worry," I said.

"She can take care of herself," David offered and went into the house.

"I'm afraid I've offended you." Helena began rapidly to apologize, "I've been so busy this fall I haven't had time to think—the legal aid, and then Sheila is a handful right now. She's going through something—I must talk to Edwin about it—she's up at night. I've lost track of my friends. I'm sorry. We must get together in the city and have lunch and a good talk."

Nothing could have been further from what I wanted: no one was going to touch my secret life. "I just saw you last weekend," I reminded her, turning toward the house.

"The weekends . . . somehow they don't seem to count." Still asking for forgiveness, Helena trailed behind me. "David asked me to talk to you. You know that's the only reason I said anything. He thought you'd find it easier to communicate with a woman-friend." She said it ironically, twisting the phrase as we never twisted other hard-used terms—daughter, son, husband, lover. "I promised him I'd try, and now I'm sorry."

"Try what?" Before she could answer, I went on. "How can women be friends or even women-friends as long they are mouthpieces for men?" Seeing her face, I was ashamed. It was too easy to loose my anger on Helena. "Never mind. I'm in a bad mood—I'm starved. I wish Flora would dish out some food."

Let off, Helena began to clown. She pretended to pull out a pad and pen. "Madam, as the married mother of three children, could you give us your opinion of the nude men currently displayed in the centerfold of a certain woman's magazine?"

I looked at her disdainfully, pressing down a laugh.

Humbled, she confided, "I sometimes think I'm the only woman in this country who isn't turned on by the sight of the male sex. I always think of Sylvia Plath: turkey neck and gizzards."

I did not answer.

"Don't avoid the subject," she pleaded. "I was tactless, I guess, but I was just trying to get you and David to talk. Charles and I both feel that once you stop—"

"You all have so much faith in talking."

"Well, words are our only tools."

"If words are our only tools, we're crippled. What about touching? What about tasting or smelling? Don't you draw any conclusions from that? Have you ever smelled a man when he's afraid?"

"I wouldn't want to," she said, wrinkling her nose.

"You're right. It's a terrible smell. Do you need words on top of that to understand?"

"They are our only tools," she repeated.

"If you mean for power . . ."

Edwin burst out of the house with the other two men at his heels. He stared at me, suspicious of my closeness to Helena; I stepped back. He passed, lugging the orange chainsaw. "We're going to cut firewood," David explained.

Edwin glanced back, "Come on!" He looked gleeful, stealing the advantage—taking my husband away up the hill. Charles followed along at the tail like a younger brother.

I watched them go: Edwin strode as though he was wearing a gilt paper crown. "A leader of men," I murmured to Helena, "or at least of women." He had had her too, three years before, in the back of a Volvo station wagon, a fact I usually tried to forget. "That was the act of a desperate man," Flora said when she heard.

Alarmed, Helena went into the house. The screen door closed behind her with a snuffle. I knew she would tell Flora in the kitchen that I was in a bad mood, and they would search out the causes. Later, Flora would reprimand me privately for making Helena feel even more of an outsider, and we would smile at one another covertly, ashamed of the pride we took in our inner circle. Flora and I had been to the same East Coast college, and we could fill out each other's stories with details from debutant parties, heartless families, and the petty desperation of living in a dormitory. Helena had grown up in the South and would never share our polish and dash. She made a specialty of her provincialism, exaggerating her accent and her plainness. Flora knew, however, that Helena often felt excluded, snubbed by Charles's law partners and merely tolerated by their wives for whom she cooked "down-home" meals which would have put her mother to shame: cornbread, black-eyed peas—"Nigger food," Helena herself called it once, sweeping away in one stroke all her attempts to hide her authenticity.

The chainsaw began to shriek at the top of the hill. I looked up in time to see the children running toward their fathers. There would be no pats on the back, no conversation other than jokes. The links between the three men were provided by the women. They had nothing else in common after five years of shared weekends and holidays and were as wary of each other as they had been at the beginning when we had all used the same contractor to refurbish our newly purchased country houses. Then, I had thought the men were suspicious of each other because the contractor favored Edwin, giving him lower prices for the same jobs—Edwin always worked along with him. The suspicions had not faded when the work was done. Even when drunk, the men did not discuss their jobs, their incomes, their wives, or anything else that might pertain. They clung to the fringes—movies, a new book. David and Charles both admired Edwin, who never talked about himself, never complained. Edwin's pride, like Flora's, held the group together.

Watching from a safe distance, I thought there was something ludicrous about the intense way the men were bending over the chainsaw. Even the children noticed it and, impressed, withdrew giggling. Edwin was the only one who was actually handling the machine. Charles and David were both city boys, fast risers from low beginnings, without the country skills that Edwin possessed as though by birthright. They were frightened of the chainsaw. Edwin's ability to tear down, repair, and rebuild had less to do with his strength and dexterity than with the fact that his father had made a good deal of money by patenting the kind of nylon tubing used in lawn furniture. So, he had been able to buy a house outside Toronto when his son was born—a real farm, equipped with machinery and animals and a farmer who knew how to deal with both. The only baby picture of Edwin I had seen showed him at four or five, grinning as he steered a tractor.

Helena came out of the house, her conversation with Flora as fresh as a blush on her face. "Flora is so good," she said with a long, quivering sigh. "She never seems to get tired of hearing me complain, and she always gives me such good advice."

"That's why she herself never has to complain."

"Well, you know, she has her life in shape. She and Edwin know exactly what they want, they know each other's goals, and they accept each other." She spoke with the fervor of a convert. "Now that Flora is teaching full-time, she's become so well organized. She's pleased about her job, and the children are fine. They don't seem to have many problems"— Helena finished quickly and pressed on before I could question— "I mean, problems they can't handle. Flora says they talk everything out in the morning when they take their bath together." She must have seen me wince. "It is amazing, isn't it?"

"I don't want to talk about it," I said. She was silent, and I realized she was about to offer some ill-timed consolation. "Why are those three men not friends after all this time?" I asked, gesturing toward the racket on the hill.

"I suppose they're more cautious than we are. They take longer to get started."

"I don't believe they'll ever get started. They have their chainsaws and their wheelbarrows and their rakes and shovels, though."

"And children," Helena reminded me.

"Yes, the children do seem to be theirs as well."

"Edwin even takes them to the dentist."

There was a shout from the hill: it was Chrissy; the heavy swing seat had crashed into her head. The men were still absorbed in their commotion: not a head turned. And the other children stood staring helplessly. Helena rushed off and snatched up the big long-legged girl and pressed her to her breast, covering her with kisses. As she squatted in the grass holding the child, I decided that the crisis had passed. Even the children were turning away. Yet I could not take my eyes from the tight knot of Helena's arms around Chrissy. There was so little contact between the rest of us that she looked potent, almost erotic.

Helena stood up and came toward me carrying Chrissy, contentedly draped in her mother's arms and sucking her thumb. "Is she all right?" I asked.

"Just a little dazed. I'll sit out here with her for a while."

Helena's dignity embarrassed me. As she sat down on the bench, I went inside.

"Just in time," Flora said when she saw me. "I need you to carry out the food. What were you doing anyway, lurking out there?"

Yes, but—I reminded myself as I was loaded with a tray of hot-dog rolls, mustard and ketchup—yes, but remember the glare of the television set that Saturday night when I lay alone in the huge bed, David out of town, my insomnia growing more ominous as time passed, until it seemed to lie on my chest like an enormous cat, its eyes pressed to mine, its furry weight crushing out my breath. By three a.m., I was convinced that I would never sleep again without David next to me, his placid touch on the back of my neck, his feet meekly gathered together with mine. Dummy love I called it, but it had its place. Then I put my hand between my legs and strummed, forcing the orgasm which only the vibrator brought me, until my clitoris was sore and I was crying, somehow betrayed by my own body, a kind of love that led nowhere, an addiction like a commonplace dependence on candy or cigarettes. I began to count the things I had never done with David: never traveled or cooked a meal or visited a museum. "He's a zero," I said under my breath, snatching up a tower of paper cups. Saying that shielded me, I was at best a very low number, a one or a two—for the list of things I'd never done alone was even longer. David and I together made a paltry figure.

"Chrissy was hit by the swing," I said to Flora to distract myself.

"I knew something like that would happen. The children are overexcited. Let's hope we won't have to make a trip to the hospital today." She opened the refrigerator. "My God! Look what they've done to my cake!"

One side had been clawed off. "How horrible—maybe it was Sheila," I said.

"No chance. It was one of my dirty boys. I don't know how much longer I'm going to be able to stand them—Saul especially. He's impossible this year. His language! I tell you, it's foul." Reaching in, she began to paste bits of cake and icing into the tear. "I fine him a dollar for each one of those words. He's already run up fifteen dollars this weekend." She took the cake out and slammed it on the counter.

"It doesn't look too bad," I said.

"It's ruined, but I couldn't care less. They can eat it or not. It doesn't matter to me." Turning to the freezer, she began to snatch out package after package of hotdogs. "I meant to take these out at breakfast, but we never had breakfast. Edwin was up at five tramping around in his boots. He woke me up—I was furious. I didn't wake up again until eleven, and by then they were all out in the woods, hunting for pinecones for the bonfire. I forgot all about the damn hotdogs."

They were solid as cartridges. "Maybe they'll thaw out over the fire," I suggested.

"All I really wanted to do today was stay in bed."

"You've been very busy," I said, offering a little sympathy. "I don't know how you manage it all. That long day at school, and now you have the teachers' strike to deal with—all those meetings with the union." Flora was mollified. "Have you started to shop for my fall suit?" she asked shrewdly, seizing the opportunity, and I was ashamed to admit that I had not yet begun. She depended on me to choose her clothes, within the limit of her tight budget, claiming she had no time. "Oh well, it doesn't matter," she said, dismissing my effort as well as my failure.

The squeal of the chainsaw died, and I knew Edwin would be coming down the hill. I rushed out the door, hoping to catch him alone, to taste his voice. I stumbled on the step and nearly dropped my tray, awkward and eager as a child. The men were already coming toward me, carrying logs down the hill. Helena was waiting in the kitchen, oddly poised with Chrissy at her side. Edwin crouched down and deposited his armful of logs, the other two men following suit. They seemed to be laying gifts at Helena's feet, and she bowed gracefully accepting. Or perhaps they were preparing to burn her at the stake? I felt as though I was running through water, hurrying clumsily to interrupt the scene. "No bonfire?" I asked. "Later," said Edwin, smiling at Helena. I came up behind them, leaned down, and put my tray on the table, close enough to touch him, but he didn't look at me. Crouching, he delicately aligned the logs, utterly remote from me, engrossed in his task, and would remain remote for as long as he sensed my need. I'd learned never to try to get his attention. Charles asked him, "Do you want the matches?"

"Not yet."

I wished I had something to do.

David began to talk to Helena about the movie we'd all seen in the city the week before. "My wife called it a tour de force," he said, going on to repeat my opinion in full.

"What did you think about it?" I asked with great restraint. I was trying to break David of the habit of quoting me. At dinner parties, I could hear his voice through the jumble of conversation: He would be relating my latest exploit with pride and animation. "She simply told the traffic cop she was not going to pay the speeding ticket . . ." At these times, I felt like a trained poodle walking on its hind legs for its keeper. His impression of me was odd. "You are an eagle," he once blurted out, a few weeks after I had begun my affair with Edwin. No one knew what was going on at this point. Yet the atmosphere we all lived in, the sea of lies, was warmer by several degrees.

That evening, after we all saw the movie, David was already apologizing. "It's just that you express yourself so well. I seem naturally to pick up your opinions."

I said, "What did you really think about the movie? I was so busy lecturing you about it, it's no wonder you don't remember." I added hastily, stricken by his look. Then I explained to Helena, "The movie's about a woman who can only fall in love after she's become a victim, having allowing herself to be abused. The terrible thing about it is that it's partly true."

"You know you don't believe that," Flora said, coming up behind me with the hotdogs in a basket.

"Ah, but I do," I said.

"Thank goodness female masochism has outlived its usefulness," Edwin said.

We all laughed.

I went on, facing him, "Wasn't it ridiculous when she kissed the man's feet?"

"Those Frenchies," Charles added. "They know about darkness."

Flora said, "I hate their movies," separating the frozen hotdogs with Edwin's pocketknife.

Flora settled in with her various evasions. She had her own vocabulary, her own set of perceptions, and it was not necessary for her to enlarge either one or the other to suit the rest of us. She'd found a place and use for each of us in her hierarchy. Even Edwin had his niche, his function as her link to a network of lies and excuses.

Edwin was organizing us into a procession up the hill to the bonfire site, each of us carrying two logs. As we walked, I noticed that David looked crushed.

"I'm sorry I criticized you," I told him.

Despite his intentions, Edwin noticed every change in my voice, more sensitive to my tone than to my expression, which he'd always thought of as veneer, like mascara or my perfume. He was particularly sensitive to the subdued signs of my affection for David, not out of jealousy, which he was not able to feel, but because he wanted to be able to squash my disillusion when I complained about my husband. "But you enjoyed arguing with him about the train schedule last Saturday," he had reminded me a week before, interrupting one of my diatribes. Edwin had a longer view of my life than I could possibly tolerate. He wanted me never to change.

Once in our bath, I had stripped off my wedding ring, and he'd tensed up, and repeated as if instructing me, "Never leave your husband. Never leave your husband. Never leave him. I'll never see you again if . . ."

I didn't believe him.

6

The auction will begin in half an hour. I must do something about Keith. Leaving the others in the living room, I start up the stairs. His door at the end of the hall is closed, and when I try the handle, the bolt rattles in its catch. I knock politely. "Keith, I want to talk to you. Let me in."

He mutters something indistinguishable and does not open the door.

I knock again, too hard, my hand crashing into the wood till it hurts.

"Let me in! We have to talk, Keith. We can't handle it this way."

He does not answer. In the space of seconds, I feel like splitting the door with an ax. I go to sit down on the blanket chest at the other end of the hall, trying to wait, letting my hands rest idly in my lap. I look out over the field where the housing development will be. A year ago, I would have wept at the prospect. I felt like lying on the ground in front of the bulldozer to preserve that colony of pine trees. Now, I'm only concerned with escape.

I get up and go back to Keith's door, which is for a moment transformed into his face set against me. I slap the panel and my palm stings. "Look, I'm not going to try to make you do anything you don't want"—a lie to gain access. He will surely smell that out. "Let's talk about this at least, Keith. Can't you remember the good times? We painted your room together. We went to Hyde Park to get that bookshelf. I know how you feel."

Nothing else for me to do. I remember Keith as a small boy, precariously carrying cups of tea when I was sick in bed, running up the stairs after school with his hands full of crumpled drawings, but sentimentality has no power in this situation.

"I'm going to get your father," I say, calmly facing the closed door.

There is no response, although I sense a stirring, a rustle of curiosity on the other side of the door. He will open for a confrontation. I race down the stairs and into the kitchen where David is waiting for his toast. His Pooh Bear domesticity irritates me as usual. He has spent the whole morning eating and drinking. I stop on my first words—"Will you . . ."—having started on the note he hates most, that of hysterical demand. I begin again more tactfully, "Would you please come upstairs and help me? We have to do something about Keith."

He looks at the toaster. "I'm just waiting for these slices to pop up. Would you like one?"

Once, our life together was made bearable by these gestures, these small courtesies: the delicate porcelain teacups with bluets on them, the well-chosen presents on my birthday and our anniversaries, the cab waiting at the door to bear us to city entertainments. I no longer accept these substitutes because they take the edge off my appetite for the real thing. "There is no time for toast now," I announce. "I need your help with Keith."

"What's happened?" he asks mildly, his eyes on his reflection in the toaster.

"He has barricaded himself in his room, and he won't come out or let me in."

The toast pops up; David takes it gingerly and lays it on the waiting plate. Then he goes to the refrigerator for butter. "Keith and I went over this Friday when we drove up from the city. He wants to take his things with him to my place, and I told him he could."

"You can't do that, David. We agreed to this auction."

"It's your auction," he says, carefully spreading butter in order not to tear the toast. "I told you before, I feel no obligation to help you make it a success. A teenaged boy . . . ," he begins, but I am no longer listening. My eyes are fixed on his short square hand manipulating the knife.

"Everything you do now, even buttering that toast, is to get back at me," I say.

"I've noticed you've begun to interpret everything that way."

"Even my silence about Edwin. Why didn't you ask me to stop seeing him before it was too late?"

"I wanted you to be happy, and you seemed very happy, if a little hectic."

"You profited from it."

"Not really," he says with dignity.

"You accepted it. You wouldn't fight it. You justified my falling in love with another man. It took the pressure off you to perform, to please me, to make some attempt at understanding. Now you've decided to punish me for it anyhow. Now you've decided to take Keith's side."

"We both agreed to that," David reminds me.

"I had no choice when Keith began to make my life unbearable last month, after you told him about Edwin."

"I don't believe there's a connection. Besides, he already knew," he says.

"Knowing and having to confront it are two different things. Edwin is his friend's father. He will never forgive me—he'll need never to forgive me—for spoiling that friendship."

David says resignedly, "I don't see that there's anything I can do about that."

"Back me up, give me your support. Tell him he has to let Tom take the furniture out of his room."

David takes a bite of toast, swallows and glances at me. "I'm not going to do that. I don't think it's fair to Keith. I'll have a truck here sometime next week to take my things and his."

I plant myself at the kitchen table. "David, what are you up to? What are you trying to do?"

"I'm thinking of the children." He wipes his fingers carefully on a bit of paper towel. At the same moment, we both glance at the yellow pad, which is lying on the counter next to the sink.

"This is your evidence, isn't it?" I ask. The first page is thick with his handwriting.

He's quiet for a moment, considering, weighing his chances of making an impression. "I haven't seen you much in the past six months. I'm curious about some things, and so I'm writing them down—observations, thoughts."

"Observations about what?"

He rinses his coffee cup and places it on the top rack of the dishwasher. "I'm trying to be fair about this, believe me. You've changed so much since we separated. The children do need stability."

"No, it won't work, David."

He looks at me with his small smile. "I'm not so sure about that. The law has changed, you know."

"You are not going to be able to take the other two children."

"Only if it seems to be the best thing for them. Of course, you could see them whenever you want."

"Not Molly and Jeff."

"We have to think about their welfare, not just about what we want. It would be a tremendous amount of work for me, taking them on full-time. Of course, I'd hire a housekeeper, a nice, warm, competent woman."

"Warmer and more competent than me."

"I didn't mean that. You've done a fine job with them, especially when they were younger. But when I see the amount of friction with Keith . . . I mean, it's just a matter of time before the other two get to your wrong side."

"My wrong side is the side I teach them from. Of course they complain. You give them everything, seduce them with presents and money and approval they haven't earned. Of course they complain about me. I set their limits."

"That's not what bothers me. You're a little erratic. You must know that. One minute screaming at them and the next smothering them with kisses. It has worried me for a long time, but it's much more pronounced lately with the turmoil you've been going through."

"Is that the kind of thing you've been writing on your yellow pad?"

Before he answers, I reach for it—the counter is just beyond the ends of my fingers—but David is quick on his feet. He snatches the yellow pad and clasps it under his arm. "Just watch yourself," he snaps.

"You're a spy. That's what you've always been."

"Think what you want to think. You kept me away from the children all those years."

"You kept yourself away. You were always busy. Even when you were around, you were preoccupied. Remember when Jeff was a baby? I was going mad, up at night with him for six months. I pleaded with you to take some time off to help me out. You told me to hire a nurse. I didn't want a nurse. I didn't want another woman handling my baby. I wanted you to help me."

"That was in the middle of the Con Ed suit. I couldn't get away."

"Yes, I know, I know. There were always reasons, good reasons. Now suddenly you have plenty of time for them. You have plenty of money, but you never even paid for their school bills!"

"I've always contributed my fair share," David insists.

"I don't believe it. I don't understand your arrangements. The lawyers will have to straighten it all out. All I know is that you never supported us, never had any money, and never even told me how much you earned."

David shakes his head. "I can't believe we're arguing about money."

"Yes, we've fallen that low. I wish to God we'd fallen that low a long time ago. It was my fault. I never would complain. I felt as though I owed you my approval. I never told you how I hated to spend the evening paying bills, with the scraps left from Grandfather's fortune, while you watched television. I felt as though I owed you a living, an atmosphere, a whole life made by hand."

"I did take you out of a pretty desperate situation."

"Yes, you're right. I had to get away from home. And you

seemed so warm, so civilized. That's what I've paid for—your civility. The fact that you never make demands. I could live in my vacuum, in my private dream, with you."

David sighs. "It worked, for a while."

"Yes. But then I began to know what I wanted. You still haven't begun to find out."

"Actually, I have some idea. I do wish you'd go to one of those clinics."

"Where they fix you up with a 'partner'?"

"You can't blame me for all your dysfunction," he says wryly.

Before I can go on, he reminds me, "We were talking about the children."

"Yes." I come back to it from a long way off. "I want you to go upstairs and talk to Keith."

"All right. I'll tell him we've settled it."

"Settled it!" I am, in a breath, beside myself. I begin to beat my fists on his arm. "You settled it! We didn't! You sabotaged me!"

He shoves my hands away, staring at me, appalled. Then he holds my wrists together. "Please, don't let's be violent. You are behaving viciously."

Then, releasing his grip, "I thought we had settled this question about Keith, like two adults."

"We never even discussed it. You sidetracked me. You've blown up my whole plan."

"It was never my plan," he says. Now I can see the gleam of satisfaction in his eyes.

"There's something for you to write on your yellow pad. 'Attacked by wife.'" I rub my wrists.

"I'll get Keith," he says, and leaves the kitchen.

I go to the telephone and dial my lawyer's number in the city.

A syrupy-voiced secretary answers: "No, Mr. Rodman is not in. No, he cannot be reached at the moment. He is in court." She will pass the message on when he returns at some indefinite later hour.

"It's urgent. Tell him to call me in the country. Something has happened here." Used to female hysteria over the telephone, she calms me expertly. "Mr. Rodman will deal with everything as soon as he returns."

I remember his chrome-and-glass office, his practiced smile: a handsome man, a fighter, who betrays his cupidity when he glances at the clock on the building outside his window. He does not have a clock on his desk. He makes it appear that we are friends—he even offers me a cup of coffee—but while I talk, he swivels in his chair and glances out the window. There is another woman sitting among the potted plants in the waiting room.

I am used to these timekeepers. Edwin used to lay his watch on the table beside the bed, where he could see it while we made love.

Keith comes into the kitchen, propelled by his father.

"I'm sorry if I made you mad," he says, having been coached.

I speak to David. "How do you expect the other children to behave now?"

"They don't need to know, do they?"

"They're not fools. This has been hard for them too, but they agreed to give up their possessions. They had to. They didn't have an alternative."

"Daddy has a big apartment," Keith says mildly.

"Yes. He can afford one. He's been saving money for fifteen years."

David says, "This is simply not appropriate, Ann." He puts his arm around Keith, preparing to lead him away. My son shoots a glance back at me, stricken.

"I learned what I wanted finally," I say. "Maybe too late."

"The children have paid quite a price for that." He opens the fridge, pulls out a Coke, offers it to Keith. "It's a small thing, but for some reason you never allowed them to drink soda, even once in a while."

"More to write on the yellow pad," I say.

Keith adds carefully, "Well, it's true. You weren't around much at all, last year. You were never home when I came home from school."

"You're thirteen years old. You don't need me at the door with cookies."

"It was hard on Molly and Jeff too," Keith says.

"Everything is hard on everybody. That's something your father won't understand. You blame everyone else for consequences, but they're not avoidable. From the moment you draw your first breath, you're caught in a maze of consequences. There is no safe place."

"That's a dangerous philosophy with small children," David says, turning toward the living room. Keith turns too, as though attached by an invisible towline.

"It is not a philosophy. It's reality, which is different."

"I intend to protect my children from it," David says. They both go into the living room and sit down side by side on the sofa.

Panic is a small mouthful; I swallow it down. I remember the delights that caused all this to begin: walking in the woods with Edwin, for example. He held me in his arms under the big sycamore at the edge of the pond and asked me to be patient. It was the only grain of hope he ever gave me, the only link to a future.

Tom comes in the door, his hands hanging, looking around for something more to take out.

"There's the sofa," I say.

"I'll have to get Fred for that. What about upstairs?"

"Everything except what's in the room at the end of the hall."

"We have everything else."

"All right, then take the sofa."

He looks at David and Keith. "I was leaving that to the last so you people would have some place to sit."

"This is the last," I say, and he smiles, a little embarrassed, not sure where the joke lies, not sure—any more than I am—whether or not it is a joke at all.

7

Flora began to call in the children for Saul's birthday party. "Saul! Keith! Frank! Chrissy—all of you! Come and open the presents!" She had assembled them in a pile beside the unlit fire.

She'd also baked a cake with green icing—Saul's request—topping it with ten candles.

From the swings, from their clubhouse behind the woodshed, from the porch, the children came, the younger ones running, the older boys strolling as though they hardly cared at all. The three girls came, looking as though they were clutching secrets. They had been plotting something by the vegetable garden. Looking at the children, I tried to imagine their conception, on a night after a party, in the middle of a hot afternoon. It seemed unlikely that any of us could remember exactly when, or why, our children had been conceived. Chance, good temper, a sudden rush of optimism had together or separately produced this little band, tumbling or running or pacing steadily down the hill toward the fire.

As they came closer, I noticed how pleasantly ragged they looked in their bleached hand-me-down clothes—a pied piper's rabble. There were no real friendships between them, other than that between Saul and Jeff. They hung together only as a group,

reflecting the grownups' precarious unity. When we were not getting along, the children fell apart and sulked in corners. When
we were excited, feeding off a new experience or argument, the
children fought and laughed indiscriminately. "The grownups are
the children," I told Edwin once. That was after Chrissy had telephoned the doctor in town because Sheila choked on a chicken
bone. All the adults were off walking in the woods. The doctor
advised bread, and the crisis had passed by the time we returned.
"Thank God, this time we get to play the young ones," Edwin had
said, not to be shamed.

Saul, a knobby nine-year-old, Edwin's youngest, squatted
down by the pile of presents and ripped into the first one. "Read
the card," Flora reminded him crisply; she hated any display of
greed. Saul stopped ripping and began to poke around for the
card. Jeff had drawn it, painstakingly, complaining of the bumps
in the road, while we were driving up from the city. Saul found
the card and showed it around to polite exclamations: a huge
mouth, without teeth, shouting, "Happy Birthday." I was glad
there were no teeth. As Saul handed me the card, I caught his
eye , and he looked hastily away. The children were as unused
to direct looks as cats. Saul had his father's eyes, pale gray, wary
and bright, the eyes of an animal drawn into company against
its instincts.

Monday—five days before—Edwin had rushed in my front
door, late as always, with only half an hour to spare for me between
appointments. He stripped off his watch, then stood with his arms
stretched out so that I could unbutton his blue-and-white striped
shirt. He submitted to my touch with hesitation, fearful that I
would leave a trace or smell, which would be detected by Flora. In
spite of that, I took hold of him with his clothes on. Unbuttoning

his shirt, I put my cold hands on his chest, unbuckled his worn leather belt, unzipped his fly.

Saul was ravaging his presents, throwing paper and ribbons in the air. Flora shouted, "Stop that at once!" Flora insisted that he look at each one again and thank each child. She knew the effort those meaningless toys represented—afternoons in stores while our own children fretted. The cards meant something because they were homemade. Flora gathered them up to keep. We had bullied our children into producing a rudimentary drawing or collage to meet Flora's expectations. She made everything she gave away herself, and my shelves were blessed by her blueberry jam and cucumber pickle, too precious to be eaten.

Edwin went around collecting the wrapping paper and stuffing it under the logs. Crouching, he struck a match. The flame traveled rapidly up through the paper, which glowed blue, yellow, and green; the logs began to pop; soon the fire was burning vigorously, and a thin column of smoke rose through the air. Edwin sharpened sticks with his pocketknife to use for hotdogs.

Flora and Helena settled themselves near the food and dealt out paper plates. Flora's voice, scolding, rose over the crackling fire. "You boys are pigs—don't snatch. Frank, one potato chip at a time. Jeff, you know better than to put your whole hand in the pickle jar. No marshmallow now for you, Chrissy. Those are for later. Don't stuff your mouth! Wait for the rolls! Really," she looked at me, rolling her eyes, "they are disgusting." I smiled back at her. She always scolded more on weekends when Edwin and I had fucked during the previous week.

I sat down by my husband, who speared a hotdog on a stick, then poked it into the fire. He did not need to tell me that he was taking care of me even before he took care of himself. I snatched the stick out of his hand. If I rejected his care, his courtesy, he had nothing else to offer. I poked the stick deep into the fire, pulled it back—too late: the hotdog blazed up, sputtering.

"Give me another," I told Edwin. He got up and went to get one from Flora, happy to oblige.

For a while, we were all as absorbed as the children in roasting and eating our hotdogs. Charles went around with a jug of wine, refilling our paper cups. The children, as a special treat, were given what Flora called "that Nasty Punch—full of chemicals." The grownups, at least, would be half-drunk by the middle of the afternoon.

Frank took my cup without asking permission and gulped a mouthful of wine. Edwin, sitting on the other side of the fire diddling his hotdog over the coals, told Frank without force to behave. "How can I teach them anything when you—" Flora began, then chopped off the rest. Helena rose and moved over to sit by Edwin. The air seemed to stiffen and crack. Charles began at once to lecture. At first I did not understand what he was talking about, although I picked out each word. His monologues led to preordained conclusions—in this case, that we should all petition the village fathers to ban the use of ATVs in the woods. We were walkers except for Charles, who kept a horse and fancied himself in riding boots. One of the ATVs, careening through the woods, had frightened his horse and triggered a nasty fall. He suspected its owner was an overgrown high school student who collected mechanical junk in his front yard and lived in the euphoria of loud noises. I allowed myself to look at Edwin. He had edged closer to Helena, and they were chatting intimately.

I was unprepared for this. It was daytime after all. At evening parties, I adjusted myself, almost numb, to Edwin's flirting. Like

Flora, I tried to look away. Usually, he was too busy to make the effort to disguise what he was doing. Edwin and Helena were old comrades, old friends—as Edwin and I had been. Edwin had helped Helena through Chrissy's bed-wetting crisis, as he had helped me to understand Jeff's stammering. Charles was still lecturing. "I mean, why should we all lose the quiet—the peace," he added abruptly, as though he saw it shining a long way off. David handed me another hotdog, perfectly roasted. Edwin leaned toward Helena, his face a few inches from her face. They had stopped talking. Helena closed her eyes. She tilted her head slightly, bringing her mouth in line with Edwin's lips. His eyes were closed. In the firelight, he looked neutral and tense, a sleep-walker edging toward a precipice.

Flora blurted out, "I'm going to fetch the cake." She lunged up and started for the house as Charles began to instruct David in the usefulness of the local zoning laws.

I slid over to my husband and leaned against him, curled like a snail. I did not look at Edwin. After a long time, I heard Flora returning with her damaged cake. "Birthday cake, any-one?" she asked brusquely, squatting in front of me to cut a slice. "Disgusting," she murmured as she handed me the plate, grimacing toward her husband.

I looked again, under her custody. Their faces seemed to be two halves of the same sphere, moving in unison. Helena's lips were open. They did not quite touch Edwin's mouth.

"Otherwise people who enjoy horses will simply have to live somewhere else," Charles concluded gloomily. David nodded in agreement.

"It's the buildup I hate," Flora told me.

I was sick. I wanted to go to Edwin and interject my body

between his and Helena's. "I'm going to take the question up with the mayor. Shipley has some sense, even if he is a plumber," Charles told David.

Flora parceled out a few more slices, placing them precisely in the middle of paper plates. She had taken upon herself the role of comforter; I hated her for it. She made it impossible for me to believe what I wanted to believe: that what Edwin was doing was nothing. She began to sing with gusto and the rest of us joined in.

Flora began to pick up the paper plates, although some of the children had not finished eating. She ordered them to help, but except for Chrissy, who went on methodically chewing, the children took one look at Flora's face and abandoned their dessert, running off and shouting back that they were going to play tag. I had never seen Flora's will flouted before. She was biting her lips, her face grave. "Monsters," she said, stuffing trash into the basket. Charles and David began to gather up the rest. In the midst of our activity, Edwin and Helena preserved their island of calm. We flitted around them, talking, united by a pretense that nothing was amiss. Edwin's hand sat quietly on Helena's knee.

"We're going up to the house," Flora sang to no one in particular, and we trooped after her, leaving Edwin and Helena by the fire with Chrissy, who was still chewing.

In the kitchen, we all fell silent. The men piled the remains on the table and went off to the living room to look for cigarettes. "It doesn't mean anything—it never does," Flora told me, her forehead close to mine as we crammed paper plates into the garbage pail. "I'm going to give up using paper plates after this. Look at the disgusting waste. I hate to think of the trees . . ."

I was afraid that she was going to begin to cry.

Chrissy ran in, full tilt, slammed a ginger ale bottle on the table, and was nearly out the door again when I caught her arm. "Is there anything left down there by the fire?"

Headed away, she did not turn around. "Mommy and Edwin are bringing up the rest of the stuff."

The intimacy of their cleaning up together hurt me more than the aborted kiss. I knew that I had to find a place to be alone before I broke down in Flora's arms. I started for the stairs.

"Where are you going?" she called after me.

"Upstairs." For a minute, I was afraid she would follow me. Then I heard water running in the sink.

At the top of the stairs, I went into Flora's and Edwin's bedroom, a chilly little space shaped by the eaves. On their bed the telephone, the newspaper, and several piles of folded laundry lay mixed together. I moved some of the clothes in order to sit down. Edwin's faded blue undershorts were on top of one pile.

I reached for them and opened them out. The elastic in the waist was worn out, and the cotton felt thin too. I seized the material in my teeth, but the cotton did not give as easily as I had expected. I drew it into my mouth, sucking and chewing. Wet, it seemed thicker, even more resistant. I spat it out, took the pants between my hands and with all my strength, ripped them in two from the bottom of the fly to the waistband in the back. I sat holding them for a long while. The sound of the tearing lingered, and my mouth was soft and dry, like the cotton. I threw the rag on the floor and knocked it under the bed with my foot. I began to walk toward the door. Suddenly, I saw Jeff standing beside the bureau, shrinking into its shadow. In the kitchen Flora was crashing pans. After a while, I noticed Jeff slip down the stairs. I followed him to the living room.

8

Tom and Fred are walking toward the sofa. David gets up, Keith too, after a little. I look at the room as though for the last time. It is my favorite place in the house. The children used to play here while I cooked. In winter, the fireplace was lit (it always smoked; there is a dark stain under the mantel), and when the Fields came to dinner, I opened out the table with all its leaves. The big white pediments over the doors and windows, the pale yellow walls make a frame now for a picture of contentment that no longer exists.

Veering off from the sofa, Tom inspects the rest of the furniture huddled in the corner. He is checking for red tags, which mean that the object is not for sale. "The only thing in here with a tag is that loveseat," I tell him and smile at his relief. He did not believe me when I promised him that I would not be keeping most of the items. He wanted to go over the house with me to make sure. I refused. The deal almost collapsed then. I couldn't bear to sort it all out with his thick face and the stink of his beer breath over my shoulder. The few things I am keeping are not valuable. I want them because they have stories attached to them.

Of course, everything in the house has a narrative of some sort—on a rainy day at an auction we bought an old white chamber pot, porcelain, covered with roses, for a vase—but most of the stories are trivial, and a few no longer bearable. The beds for instance: I will never sleep in any of these beds again. Most of the things that my family gave me have gradually shed their meaning, losing color, except for my grandmother's loveseat, its mahogany back arched like a wave. I used to sit there, uncomfortably perched on the slippery horsehair, while she unwound her memories. Under a coating of Southern charm—brides like "lighted candles"—her reminiscing was more often about mayhem, murder and, particularly, rape. My grandmother prepared me for the ways of the world, teaching me to live with lies, rather than face the uncomfortable truth—"She died beautifully, beautifully. They never knew the cause." Better, she thought, than: "They said he shot her in the throat." But when I finally read her diary, I discovered otherwise. My grandmother never left her state, and she considered women who did gallivanting fools who deserved whatever calamity befell them. When a friend of hers was mugged in New York, she had no sympathy. "I told Matilda before she left here she was making a mistake." Some of her wisdom still clings to me, and since it protected me for most of my life, I plan to keep her loveseat, which I plan to have re-covered with brown corduroy.

Tom and Fred begin to pull the sofa toward the door. Molly comes from the parlor to watch. Her father and her brother pass her, in retreat. "Is he taking everything in here?" Molly asks.

"Everything except for Great-Grandmother's loveseat."

"Why do you want to keep that old thing?"

"I used to sit on it when Grandmother told her stories. I've told you some of them."

"Yes, that one about the woman who drowned in a cask of wine, all her blond hair going on growing."

"They were terrible stories. I loved them."

"Aunt Edna gave me my dollhouse. I should get to keep it too."

"I've told you several times, Molly, if you want to give up your bed and keep your dollhouse . . ."

David says from the hall, "Let it go, Molly. We can always buy another dollhouse."

Molly runs to him to seal the deal: my daughter who, unlike me, always knows when to press her advantage.

I try to rein in my irritation. David mutters from the doorway, "It's really too hard on her, you know."

"It's not too hard on her. Nothing is too hard on her. She's tough as nails." I stop, lining up my priorities. This is not a fight I have to win.

"I saw one in FAO Schwarz that even has an elevator," Molly says.

"Hold on there now." They begin to discuss the amount of money David is willing to pay—a large sum which will buy his daughter's allegiance for at least a week. I hear him haggling. He wants her cheap. No elevator, he decrees. They finally settle on a dollhouse that Molly has seen in a neighborhood store in the city. It has stairs and a fireplace and a porch and a chimney, but it does not have an elevator.

"What about the old dollhouse. I thought you were so fond of it," I say.

"The windows are just plastic," she says airily, and goes off with her father to the kitchen, hand in hand.

Fred and Tom begin to take the dinner table apart, stacking the leaves carefully against the wall. They push the two semicircular halves together, and the table is now small as it was when we first lived in the house. Then there was no one to eat with us.

There was a snowstorm our first Christmas. The wind blew the snow under the kitchen door while we sat at the table eating our small-family turkey. I cried after lunch because we had no family, except for the children, who were not enough, would never be enough, even if I continued to pump out a baby every two years. There was no ritual, no sustenance for me. At that point, we had no country friends. "You could have invited somebody," David reminded me, clearing away the plates. The children had hardly touched the food, which I had spent two days preparing. "I didn't want my mother to come," I said—I did not dare to want her. She was not available. Freed at last from the thankless task of raising a daughter who was neither a beauty nor a scholar but a self-defeating combination, a bright girl who only cared about love, she moved to Palm Beach, growing younger and more handsome as I frayed, thriving in her beachfront condo. She sent us all big checks at Christmas. My grandmother by then was long dead, my uncle far gone into alcoholism, and so we were left with the children. They'd all been weaned by that first Christmas in the country.

Tom rolls the table swiftly to the front door, the casters squealing. He and Fred maneuver it onto its side and push it into the doorway. It is wedged briefly, its goat legs in the air, before Fred with a grunt shoves it through. I wonder who will sit at it next, and whether the new owner's dream of a family for grownups, united by food and love and honesty, will by some wild stroke of luck be transformed into reality.

9

Long ago, in the middle of a hot week, Flora telephoned to ask me whether or not I had seen Dan, the plumber: Her septic tank was overflowing. At that point, I had never met Flora, who seemed as much in control of the contents of her septic tank as I was of Jeff's diarrhea—that is, not at all. But Flora was detached. "Isn't it too much?" she said. For me, Jeff really was too much. My eyes were swollen with fatigue, my lips dry and cracked as a nomad's. I hadn't slept through a night for almost two months. After I told Flora that I didn't know where Dan was, I realized with a pang that I had disappointed her. To make up for that, I invited her to bring her children over to swim. She replied at once that she couldn't stand swimming pools—"All that concrete"—but would be pleased to welcome me at the little pond, which Edwin had dug with a rented backhoe. There was clearly no argument, and again I felt almost embarrassed, as though Flora was a finger pointing a finer way.

At first glance, Flora's size impressed me. Standing on the edge of the little pond wearing a pastel bathing suit of the kind my mother called Dressmaker, she seemed planted to the ankle in the dirt, and I was not surprised when she did not step forward to speak to me. She waited, and I went to her and held out my hand, which she took, graciously. Her rather small blue eyes checked me over carefully, looking for a certain signal or detail. I didn't know whether or not I passed, but I knew my bikini was not appropriate for that patch of brown water. My children lingered behind me, looking askance at Flora's three who were skirmishing in the water.

"I'm sorry I couldn't find Dan," I said.

"Never mind. I've called Edwin, and he's coming up on the four o'clock train."

"Meanwhile—"

"Meanwhile—" Wrinkling her nose, she indicated the putrid stench which seemed to edge the air we shared. "Meanwhile, I suppose we will simply have to put up with the smell." She led me to a picnic bench set at an angle in the mud, as though she was leading me to a throne.

She shouted at her children so suddenly I jumped: "Get out of there!" They jumped as well, and assembled, dripping and fidgeting, a little distance from my feet. She introduced them formally—"Saul, Frank, Seth"—and I shook their slippery hands and then introduced Molly and Keith. They were small brown creatures that summer, their hair bleached white. "And the baby?" Flora asked reprovingly. Jiggling him in my arms, I pronounced his name as though for the first time.

"OK. Get back into the water," Flora ordered, and her children dove in at once, followed at a little distance by Keith and Molly, who stood in the shallows and watched while the others ostentatiously splashed and screamed.

"The noise!" Flora rolled her eyes. "Shall we go up to the house?"

"And leave them in the water? I don't generally—"

"Yours don't swim?"

"Molly doesn't, not yet, really—she's only four."

"Absolutely essential for them to learn to swim. You must take them down to the village on Monday. They give lessons at the American Legion Pond. Now, you can sit by the kitchen window and watch their every move." I followed her up the hill to the little gray house.

Inside, Flora fixed glasses of iced tea, dwelling on her dislike of the instant kind, which Frank had managed to buy behind her back at the IGA. He had slipped it into her cart at the last moment, and she had nearly missed it. "Nothing but chemicals," she said grimly. "I made him pay for it."

"Keith is the same," I said. "Always snatching candy from those racks by the cash register."

My arms were tired from holding Jeff, who was stamping up and down on my lap. "Will you hold this baby for minute?" I asked. Flora looked surprised, but she held out her hands, and I placed Jeff between them.

Jeff took one look at Flora and gave an indignant roar. She patted his back, expertly and remotely. "Gas, I expect. Is he on solids?"

"Not yet. I've nursed him for a year."

"Oh, you're one of those," she said good-naturedly, glancing at my shirt, which was stained under my left nipple by a damp patch of milk.

"I've nursed all of mine," I said, proudly.

"Edwin never would make that sacrifice."

Dismayed, I explained that I had never met her husband.

"You will presently," she said. "He'll be here a little after six to deal with this mess. Of course, he'll have to go right back to town in the morning."

"I won't be staying that long. It's only three now," I protested.

"Why don't we all have supper together? We can fix spaghetti," she said. "It would give the children a chance to make friends." Flattered, I still hesitated, thinking of my own dinner and the early evening alone, David at work in the city. "After all, we're all in this together," she went on. "There's absolutely no one to visit with up here—which is why we chose this place! To be private." She seemed to shine the word and hold it at arm's length to admire it. "But of course, the children must have friends."

In the end, I stayed till supper. The children had already begun to form alliances by the time they came up from the pool. Molly, the only girl, had been accepted as a mascot and a crybaby because Keith saved her when the others were holding her under the water. Frank, a sad, shabby nine-year-old with a fringe of wet hair in his eyes, had the distinction of his unhappiness. He was tormented by his brothers and yet respected because he was the one most apt to get into trouble. Seth, Flora's silent one, was presumed to be holding secrets. As for Keith, he was still on his guard. He stood in one corner of the kitchen and watched the other children darting to the table like swallows with their plates of spaghetti. My eldest had always been the leader at home, and I saw that he now felt too evenly matched for prestige. Still, I was delighted by the easy way Flora's three were interweaving with mine. There was material here for several summers. The weight of my concern for my children began to lift.

They all managed to crowd onto kitchen chairs around the table, dripping water as they ate. "Not on my clean floor, you beasts," Flora objected, but they refused to dry outside, shouting together as though they had practiced it. Flora rapidly spread newspaper under their feet. My baby was howling again after a brief, jerky nap, and I asked her if I could nurse him in the kitchen. She glanced at me with a startling wince of distaste. "Edwin feels very strongly that the children shouldn't be exposed to that sort of thing."

I stood up. "Then I'll go upstairs."

She began to explain rapidly, "It's not that I disapprove. Edwin feels the children are constantly stirred up and overexcited. They hardly have a chance at latency . . . Make yourself comfortable on our bed. I'll take care of supper."

Climbing the narrow stairs, my irritation died. After all, I thought, Flora was right to insist on her opinions, even if they were her husband's. So few people had convictions, it seemed to me. Yet there had been an oddly artificial tinge to Flora's voice, as though she was speaking from the book. I wondered if she often quoted Edwin. I had heard, casually, that he was a well-regarded pediatrician, and so of course it was perfectly appropriate that he should guide his children and instruct his wife. Yet the hint of shellac bothered me. I wondered if Flora had only been trying to explain her distaste.

I went into a low dim room under the eaves, still stuffed with heat from the long day. I waved the air away with one arm, making my way to the unmade double bed. The pillows were heaped up on one edge, and a pile of laundry lay across the foot. As I sat down and arranged the pillows with one hand behind my head, I suddenly realized that I had no business there. The room reeked of intimacy. It was as though each shabby and ordinary object—the telephone, the newspaper, and a broken-spined paperback—was covered with luminous fingerprints. At once I remembered the particular smell of my parents' pillows, too. On the sly, I used to bury my nose in them, learning to distinguish my mother's dry faded fragrance from my father's leathery reek. Sitting upright, I resisted the impulse to turn and sink my face into these pillows. They are strangers, I thought. Still sitting up, I unbuttoned my shirt and nursed the baby distractedly, trying to sort out the afternoon, hardly aware, for the first time, of the delicious prickling of my milk.

As the baby finished up, I heard a car turn in at the gate, and leaned over to look out of the little low window. A car door slammed. Almost at the same moment, the screen door slapped, and I saw Flora flash out. She jumped and skipped like a rabbit toward the car. I saw her hold out her arms, and then a man in a dark suit disappeared briefly in her embrace. As he emerged, I saw his smile, narrow-lipped and rather set.

They came toward the house hand in hand, Flora talking rapidly.

I buttoned my shirt, snatched up the baby, and hurried down the stairs, shouting for my children.

In the kitchen, Keith was doling out big scoops of ice cream. The younger children stood around him in a circle with their bowls. "We can't go home yet!" Molly wailed as soon as she saw me. I argued as Flora came in the door leading Edwin by the wrist. With a graceful gesture, she released him and steered him gently in my direction. He seemed dazed. He scarcely noticed me as Flora spoke my name. I held out my hand. He took it briefly and looked at me coolly. The skin of his palm under my fingertips felt rough and worn.

"I must go," I said.

"Stay and have supper with us. We'll get these monsters to bed and have some quiet time later," Flora sang. Edwin said nothing.

"But you must want to talk—"

"Plenty of time for that," Edwin said suddenly with a grin that came and went rapidly, leaving his face unchanged.

I stayed in spite of myself. The situation was ambiguous: I felt that I was wanted and not wanted about equally. That bedroom atmosphere seemed to be spreading solidly through the house. Edwin made us all whiskeys without asking our preference. He broke the ice out of the tray, took off his jacket—it had a light blue stripe—and hung it carefully on one of the cabinet knobs. That seemed to be a signal. He stretched and threw back his head to yawn. I noticed his shoulder blades as he reached his arms over his head. The shirttails fell out, and I saw the edge of his blue shorts, crumpled against the smooth skin of his back. He took a drink and smiled at me. "So you're another victim of Dan's mediocre plumbing skills? I hope he's been better with you, less of a disappointment. I expect he would try harder with a lady. I must reach him now about this mess, or should I say this stink?" With relish, he stomped away toward the telephone. As he was dialing, Seth came and hung around his waist. Edwin put down the receiver and crouched to receive the little boy's embrace. He nuzzled and squeezed Seth and then suddenly glanced at me.

"Have some spaghetti," Flora said and heaped my plate. "How are you finding your first summer in the country?"

"It's very lonely," I said and realized that was the simple truth which I had been hiding for six weeks under my lists and my chores, my gardening and my sewing and my homemade blackcap jelly.

"You must come over whenever you want. The children will amuse each other. It will make life much easier for all of us. We'll plan the summer together," she said with such warmth I was stunned.

Edwin put Seth away gently and dialed again. He began a conversation with Dan, which was very long and, apparently, very funny. He could have been listening to an old boyhood friend. I understood now why the Fields' house had been the first of the four houses to be finished.

Flora settled down across the table from me with her plate of spaghetti. Turning, she flapped the last children out of the kitchen. Then she bent her attention to me. "Have you met the Jacobis yet?"

"They have the new house on Miller Road, don't they?"

"Yes. It's just like ours—except it's a horrible shade of brown. The children are very rude about it. Jacobi is all right—Edwin knows him professionally. He's a dentist. But I don't believe I'm going to be able to tolerate his wife, Wiggy, one of those professional volunteers. It is a shame when people like that decide to move to the country. They really don't like it. They don't know what to do, and they impose themselves on their friends. Besides, any grown woman who allows herself to be called Wiggy—"

"They have a green Mercedes," Frank said, passing through with a flashlight.

"Here in the country!" Flora remarked. "Wiggy has a different enthusiasm every time I see her. First the homeless, then the blind. I'm sure it's very worthy, but it annoys me. And they will drop in without telephoning ahead."

"I hate that fat Arnold," Frank said, still hovering. "He's always breaking my models, and then he says he'll pay me for them."

"Hush. Arnold's their oldest," Flora explained, then turned to Frank: "Get out of here. Your father is trying to talk on the telephone." As Frank left, Flora said, "The boys are horrible about

Arnold. But he is really quite disgusting. They let the children eat all kinds of junk, and they have absolutely no responsibilities."

"It sounds like you'd be better off without them."

"Yes, but they will drop in. Edwin encourages them. He feels sorry for Wiggy. Apparently she's going through some kind of crisis."

"Premenopausal," Edwin said, hanging up the telephone. "A good deal pre-. Also she has nice legs. Dan says he'll be here with the pump truck in half an hour."

We both exclaimed. "How did you do it?" Flora asked.

Edwin smiled, and I saw his eyeteeth set like seeds in his mouth. "You know my charm!"

"I thought it only worked on women."

"I have my way with men too. Always have."

"Now don't be disgusting." With a rapid motion, Flora snatched all the plates off the table. "How am I going to teach the boys not to boast if you go on that way?"

"I must get them to come down with me and watch Dan. They might possibly learn something."

"Don't you want to eat first?"

"No, I don't—hardly!" He was pulling on a pair of black rubber boots, tucking up the legs of his trousers. Then he was gone; I heard him calling the children outside. I glanced at Flora. She had stopped what she was doing and was standing empty-handed at the sink, frowning at the paper towel roller. It was as though the light, which had been failing, had suddenly gone completely out of the room.

Flora snapped on the light switch. "These country evenings when it's always getting dark!" The bare bulb dangling from the ceiling was flooding us with hard light, and the night outside thickened. I heard the children yodeling away down the hill.

"Edwin is such a child," Flora said.

We began the washing up. Flora moved slowly as though suddenly exhausted. She would not let me load the dishwasher, explaining succinctly that she had her own system. She began to loosen up after a while. "Sometimes I'm positively jealous of the children. Edwin spends so much time with them—his patients, who are children, and our children. He cares enormously about them. I used to feel . . . squeezed out." She gave her shoulders a shake. "That was in the beginning when they were small. I used to watch him holding them in his arms . . . yes, it was jealousy," she said firmly. "And then how can I teach them anything when he's so impossible?"

"What do you mean?"

"Oh—he likes the naughtiness in them."

"He encourages them?"

"He certainly does." She said it with pride. "I mean, of course we agree, basically," she added. "But he lets them be little monkeys sometimes, and they love it. I'm the one who has to see to the discipline. He'd let them grow up anyhow."

A little later, we heard splashes from the direction of the pond. Flora looked at me. "You see? That's the kind of thing I mean. They were supposed to be watching the plumber."

After a while, I went out to collect my children. The thick, soft country closed around me as I moved, feeling my way down the hill toward the pond. The children were all in the shallows. I caught sight of their naked white skin as they jumped and cavorted in the headlights from the car, which Edwin had driven to the edge of the pond. Edwin was standing in the water with Molly clinging to his back, her arms around his neck, her long legs wrapped around his waist. He'd taken off his clothes too. I called to my children from the darkness, and Edwin sank quickly into the water, releasing Molly, who floated away from him like a petal. My two boys came scuttling, but it was a long time before I could draw Molly out. Finally I went to stand and scold at the edge of the pond. Edwin was swimming at the deep end by that time, enthralled with his boys.

I realized I would never be able to find the children's clothes and shoes thrown down on the grass in the dark. They huddled against me shivering, subdued. Suddenly it seemed very late, later than we had ever been out before. "It's miles past your bedtimes, and you're going to catch colds," I scolded, herding them toward the car. It seemed minor somehow to be worrying about pants and shoes when the night was so mild, and the other children were shouting with excitement and glee. My own life, and my children's, looked shrunken by comparison. It would never have occurred either to me or to David to take them skinny-dipping.

As we went to the car, Flora came hurrying behind us with an armload of towels. "Here, wrap them up in these—don't worry about their clothes! Come by in the morning and pick them up."

I got them into the back seat, covered them with towels, and started the car. As I turned out of the gates, I nearly collided with the pump truck lumbering along. The driver shouted at me, "Watch where you're going, can't you?" Smiling, I apologized, pleased that the summer was taking shape.

10

It is almost ten o'clock, and the cars are arriving steadily. Jeff and Molly are outside directing parking. Molly flashes into the house. "Eleven cars and more coming! Should they park by the barn? They must!" she shouts. "The place by the shed is all full." It is a feast, a festival—friendly strangers milling about on this warm, high-skied day. The shadows are short now, the grass has dried, and the sun is hot without the damp of August. This day is the culmination of my planning and perseverance; I am determined to enjoy it. Snatching at Molly as she flies by, I ask, "The Fields— where are they sitting?"

She deflates suddenly, comes to a dead standstill. "At the back. Saul wouldn't say hello to me." She is off at once, wriggling out of my grip. I fight hard for a minute against the rage her rejection inspires, and then suddenly I can't help myself. The Fields shouldn't be making our children suffer. We have not spoken in public since Easter. The solid link between our two families, forged out of so many weekends and holidays spent together, broke in March when I asked Edwin to leave Flora. Edwin, hard-pressed at last by a devotion he didn't want, was trying in any way he could find to reject me without words, and I was determined to hold on. My proposition revealed that I understood nothing about him. I was blinded by my own need. How could I have imagined that he would leave Flora for me? Flora knew what I'd done in a day, David in a week. No one mentioned it out loud, of course, but we all began at once to avoid each other. Meanwhile our children continued to telephone back and forth, arranging visits with one parent or another dropping them off at the gate.

I began to telephone Edwin after he refused me. I called him at his office every day, every week, sweating with shame and anxiety. I had to change my clothes afterward to get rid of the stink. I gave businesslike messages to his receptionist or, on bad days, hung up in terror when the woman answered. Edwin did not return my calls, no matter how I worded the message. Finally I began to write him letters, which I hope I will never again have to read. So much pleading and explaining—he did not answer them either. I sometimes drove by their house and saw the smoke drifting out of the chimney and the dog nosing around the geraniums and the children's bikes sprawled on the grass—the daily routine unaltered by my anguish. I would not descend to tracking him down in the supermarket in the presence of his wife and children. In the end, my frustration and rage became all I had to offer, and I wanted to force him to accept them—but he was afraid, he kept his distance.

I notice David standing in the shadow by the living room window, watching people arrive. "It looks like a big crowd," I say to him, my anger elevating those colorless friendly exchanges which have taken up so much of our lives. His refusal to notice has kept us together for four or five years after our marriage was effectively dead. Now I need him, my fellow conspirator, my confrère peering through the window at the scene outside. I go on, "Molly says the Fields are sitting in the back. Saul wouldn't say hello to her."

David inches his head forward. "Coming here takes some nerve."

"I suppose they want a souvenir, a plate, or something to show for all those Thanksgivings and Christmases and Saturday nights together."

"Maybe they just came, you know, on their way back from town." He goes on hurriedly, "I see Mary Cassaday and Eddy and Parker have arrived."

"Good! I mentioned it to all of them, but I wasn't sure they'd come. I thought embarrassment might hold them back."

"Embarrassment?"

"Picking over the relics. Some people might be ashamed. I see Helena in front, but I don't see Charles."

"You said you wanted them all to come."

"Yes, but there's still the question of embarrassment."

"Yours?"

"I'm trying to look past that."

The tent is open on our side, its flaps propped up, and I can see rows of rickety church-supper chairs. About half of them are occupied. Mrs. Pultz, the checker at the Grand Union, sits alone in the front row, as imposing as a duchess, an enormous pocketbook clasped in her lap. The Knoors, a tiny old couple who run the antique shop on the highway, are sitting tentatively on the edges of their chairs. They are worrying that I will assume they have come to buy things for their shop. I wish them good bargains. Our children used to drop by their little antique store and handle everything and ask for old horse paraphernalia or ancient cameras. Tom Goldsmith, who hayed our fields, is sitting in the middle wearing his gray sweat-stained fatigues next to his pretty wife and a row of squirming children. There's George, the handsome kid from the gas station—I am surprised to see him. I didn't think he even knew our name. He is looking across the aisle at Helena, in her best blue jean jacket with the daisies on the lapels. Parker and Eddy are further down, as discreet as a pair of mice, their hands folded on their laps. Winty has not come. Mary Cassaday's face is strangely severe. I have never seen it before without its decoration of smiles.

I am pleased by the size of the crowd. It seems to me that they have come here to honor me as well as pick over our possessions. Their presence means that there is something of mine they wish to keep after I am gone and the house is sold. The auction is oddly cheerful. I wonder what ornament or piece of furniture each of these people will choose and imagine them saying years from now, "Yes, that came from those city people who had to leave, the ones who had the house on Shultz Hill." I hope they will choose well and go home satisfied.

Tom has climbed onto the front steps and is holding up a pair of David's prints—two views from West Point. The auctioneer's rattle fills the room. "Five? Do I hear five? Five? Five? All right, we'll start at three-fifty."

"I'm not going to lurk in here all morning," I tell David. "I wish there were a mountain to climb or a sea to swim. I could have avoided all this, but I cannot hang indoors any longer. They'll think that I'm afraid."

He looks at me sideways, dubiously. "I don't think you ought to go out there."

"I need to go out there. I need to see what those people choose."

He shrugs. "Well, then, go."

I equivocate. "I'm curious to see what they think our things are worth."

He says heavily, "They probably won't even bid."

"Oh, no, they'll take something home. I'm sure of that." Still, I hesitate. Fred barges in.

"We need a few small things to get them started," he says, a little feverish himself. Glancing around the room he notices the silver candlesticks on the mantel and reaches for them. David stretches out his hand. "Not those."

"She said—" Fred stops at the look on David's face, a terrible look, as though he is guarding his only child.

"Not your grandmother's candlesticks," David tells me, glaring.

"I don't want them anymore."

"For the children."

"They don't care about those candlesticks. They never even knew her. They mean a lot to you—they're very fine." David in fact has looked them up in one of his silver-mark books. He is delighted by anything rare or old. "If you want them, you can bid on them when they come up."

Fred backs off hastily and snatches up an inoffensive blue pottery bowl on his way out.

"I'm not going to bid for those candlesticks." For the first time David is implacable.

He reaches for them. He won't descend to force, although he may be tempted. "I told you I wouldn't let you take anything at the last minute. I need every penny I can get. Besides, it wouldn't be fair to Tom," I explain.

"I don't care about Tom. You're getting rid of the past."

"That's what I want to do," I remind him.

"Adolescent," he snaps.

"You never wanted me, even at the start. You wanted what I stood for, and I put up with that: a pair of beautiful old Georgian silver candlesticks. Sterling at that."

"Don't be ridiculous. I love you. I always have. I am very proud of you."

"Yes, I made a good catch, trailing money, possessions, relatives."

"Believe what you want to believe. It has nothing to do with those candlesticks."

I grab one candlestick and reach for the other. "I used to think you married me for my money, but now I know it was pure snobbery. Great-Grandfather's letters from the Battle of Bull Run, Grandfather's Legion of Honor, Grandmother's stories of the old days—all so laughable, so desirable."

"I want Molly and Jeff," he says suddenly.

I do not understand him; I look charming and baffled.

"I want Molly and Jeff," he repeats.

I laugh and push the candlesticks in his direction. "Here. You can have them."

"I don't really want those," he says, his voice level. "I have plenty of that kind of thing. I want Molly and Jeff."

"You have Keith—we agreed on that. You can't have Molly and Jeff. It's just not possible—you know that."

"I believe they would be better off with me."

"I won't permit it, David. It's unthinkable."

"My lawyer says I have a fairly strong case," he says flatly.

"You've been gathering evidence—that yellow pad. Shit, you bastard. Here in my own house, under my own roof."

"It is our house," he says.

"Was it ever? Did you ever make a fire here, or cook a meal, or get up in the night with a child?"

"I paid the mortgage installments," he says dryly. "The other things I might have done as well."

"If what—?"

"You never made it easy for me, Ann. You jumped to do everything yourself. With the children especially. You never made me feel it mattered what I did or didn't do. The children sensed that too. You erased me."

"'Erase you?' You un-erasable you?" I sing, my inappropriate humor spreading like a sail.

"And then, with Edwin. Even the children knew what was going on. Locking yourself in the guest room with him the day after Thanksgiving, with the kids in the next room. You haven't been very careful."

"No court is going to declare me an unfit mother."

"That isn't necessary anymore. They may ask the children what they want. Their opinions at least will be taken into account. And I can support them."

"All the money you saved from the years when I was shelling it out."

"I don't mean money," he says with dignity.

"But the money will mean something to a judge. The money you saved will buy them what I can't afford to buy them now— vacations, a handsome apartment, all the lovely little extras."

"The only thing that really matters is what the children want," he says with lofty assurance.

I think of Molly's perpetual whining, Jeff's small frown. "You'll destroy them. Why don't you beat me instead, tear me limb from limb—"

"I don't want to hurt you. I never have. I've never been angry at you. I know you simply couldn't help yourself. I just believe the children will be happier with me. They're going to need stability, routine. You said yourself you were going to change your life. You said you might want to travel."

"What has that got to do with it?"

David waits while Fred comes in and goes out with a carton of books. "It has a lot to do with it. They need security. I want them to live in one place, quietly, with a good housekeeper, friends, school, a calm emotional atmosphere."

"And you can provide all that?"

"I can try."

"You're talking like a daddy at last."

"Your emotional swings were hard enough for them to take before, when I was around. Now they'll be entirely exposed to your bad temper, your depressions. Think of them, Ann, not just yourself."

"I'm not crazy, David. You'll never convince anyone of that."

"No one is thinking that. No one is trying to prove anything."

Yet the word "crazy" is out there, vigorous, with a life of its own.

"That's a lie, and you know it. You are going to try to prove that I'm incompetent. That was always your way of dealing with me—explain my feelings away as some kind of aberration." I do not add that over the years he has half convinced me.

"All that is in the past now," he says.

"Yes, but it's because of the past, or your version of the past, that you're trying this. It won't do, David. What's more, it won't work. You can't have Molly and Jeff."

"You never should have told me about Edwin," he says calmly. "You exposed yourself."

"You and I were trying to work things out then! We were trying to be honest and humane—to understand. We weren't enemies;
we weren't storing up ammunition—"

"Still, you exposed yourself."

"But you condoned it."

"Not legally. And besides, that has nothing to do with the
welfare of the children."

Molly runs in. "Eric from riding school is here. Can I take out
some peanut butter cookies?"

"Go ahead," I tell her, my mouth dry.

Stalling for time, I turn my back on David and watch my
daughter dart into the kitchen. All my little ones. Surely the
months I carried them in my belly must count for something—
the months I spent nursing them, the interminable procession of
interrupted sleep.

"Eric might want something to drink," Molly says, flying by
with the cookies.

David goes on, "Ann, believe it or not, I'm trying to spare
you. I'm not telling you things I feel you can't tolerate. Just the
broad outlines. I know how hard this is for you. But believe me,
it will be best for everyone in the long run. You'll be able to have
your own life—"

"I have my own life. My life is not something you can give
me, or take away."

"You'll have your independence. I know how much that has
always meant to you."

"Go to hell. Go to hell, you bastard, you stinking shit."

"If you wanted to keep the children, you should have behaved
differently. You should have been more careful. You could have
avoided allowing them to see you with Edwin—"

"They never saw me!"

"I don't mean actually in bed," he says. "They were certainly parties to your intimacy."

"They loved it. The meals and the days we had together. The best fun of their lives."

David clasps his hands. They are trembling. "You let them know exactly what was happening. That was why Keith couldn't stand the idea of living with you, without me. He thought it would be more of the same."

"So that is what you two have been discussing."

"I answered his questions, Ann. I couldn't very well avoid them."

"You could have told me, at least."

"I didn't want to upset you," he says.

"I won't accept that. I won't accept your version of the truth, or your kindness. You've taken Keith for vengeance, and now you want to take the others for the same reason—to break me. It has nothing to do with the children or their welfare. It has to do with your rage. You've seen me growing stronger since you moved out, since you stopped living on me, and now you want to punish me for that, to break me by taking my children."

"Be quiet, Ann. They'll hear you."

In the silence I hear Tom's voice drumming outside the window. "You can't have them," I say. I am suddenly so tired my eyelids ache.

"We'll see about that." He makes a bracket with his hands, enclosing the case. "My lawyer will be in touch with yours next week. You made your choice, Ann. You made it a long time ago, whether you knew it or not."

Watching him, I feel a vacuum opening in front of me. David's self-assurance will win the case before he even needs to make use of his evidence. I see myself sniveling in the dock, a bad mother, a self-confessed adulteress.

I tell David, "I'm going to fight you on this one. I'm going to fight you, and you are not going to win."

He disappears into the living room.

I rush into the kitchen, bang through the cabinets, open the refrigerator. I stand there staring, remembering when it was crowded with food, remembering its little light at two in the morning when I couldn't sleep. Surely the pleasures of touching and kissing cannot lead to this catastrophe. We were hardly innocent, yet our lust for each other had a kind of innocence—the way my babies once grabbed my breast.

The children are not my life, but they are my ties to the world, the channels through which my energy runs. Without them, I will lose the part of myself that functions socially. Otherwise, I'll lapse into the isolation of my childhood. Then, there was always an escape hatch—growing up. This time there will be no escape.

I spot four bottles of champagne in the fridge and announce in a forced, girlish tone, "We are going to drink this champagne!" I expect to hear a protest, my children doubting, David doubling himself up to repress his irritation, but the kitchen is large and empty, as empty as it will be tomorrow when we are all gone.

The glasses have already been removed, but there is still a stack of paper cups by the sink. I pile the cups on the tray, arrange the bottles, and find a corkscrew in the muddled drawer of leftovers. Then I lift the unwieldy tray and make for the front door. David looks up at me with astonishment from his post in the parlor.

"Where are you going with that?"

"I am going to offer our friends some champagne."

"That's very foolish," he hisses as I pass.

I open the front door with one hand and step out. Tom is on the steps. I edge my way around him. A bottle slides and threatens to fall; I stop and right it. There are rows of faces before me—no one I now recognize. I'm blinkered, staring at my tray. I carry it to the back of the tent where Mrs. Porter has set up her stand selling coffee and doughnuts. She peers at me through her blue-framed glasses. I set the tray down on the trampled grass.

The Fields are sitting in the very last row. Saul turns hastily to catch a glimpse of me, then jerks his head back around. I see Flora's heels in her old sandals, crusty and small. Edwin is wearing sneakers with holes. The children's feet perch like birds on the chair rungs.

I begin to unwrap the foil on the top of the first bottle of champagne.

Suddenly Edwin rises and climbs across his children's knees. He comes toward me, his face averted. He crouches beside me, "You don't use a corkscrew for champagne."

"Let me handle this myself," I say.

"No. Let me help you," he says for the first time and last time.

I watch him fumble with the foil. He is working very slowly and methodically, making his task more complicated. I remember his hands on the chainsaw, his hands setting the logs for the fire, his hands on my thighs. He lays aside the foil and begins to uncoil the harness of wires underneath. "Will it pop?" he asks.

"Yes, it will pop."

He aims the bottle away from me and pulls the cork. It leaps out with a small explosion, the champagne foaming over his hand. We grin at each other, briefly. "An embarrassment of riches," he says. Then he begins to fill a row of paper cups. I set them up one by one, and he tips the bottle, filling each cup halfway, twisting the neck of the bottle so that it will not drip as he passes it along to the next. How deft he is, what magic there is, even in the sight of his hands.

"Start passing them," he says, and I take a cup and pass it to Flora, over her shoulder.She flips her head around, glares at me, then glances at the cups. She has grown older, the lines in her face spreading across her forehead. "What's this?" she asks in her familiar tone, grudgingly.

"Champagne, or poison."

"Can I have some?" It is Saul, the intractable. I settle one cup in Flora's fingers and hand Saul another. Flora snatches it from him. She holds the cups over her head out of reach.

I give another cup to Frank, who takes it without a word. Then I go back to Edwin. He is about to open the second bottle. I hear the pop as I pass along the rows. Smiling, bowing, I am as cautious as a churchwarden passing the plate. I thrust the cups into their hands. I do not see anyone take a sip. It doesn't matter. They've got their champagne.

On my way back to Edwin, I see Saul snatch a cup from Flora's hand. She whispers to him fiercely. He grasps the cup so tightly he crushes its edges. Champagne leaks down his hand; "I just wanted to try it," he whines, and looks back at me—I am his excuse for naughtiness now.

Now I hear Tom auctioning off the fire screen where the children hung their Christmas stockings. Bidding is sparse. Perhaps I'm distracting attention from Tom by handing out drinks. "This is to celebrate," I say, raising a cup to Mary Cassaday.

I hand over a cup to Helena from the last batch. She takes it with a grimace. "Ann," she whispers across her staring neighbor, "you must be terribly upset. This is all so difficult. Can you have lunch next Tuesday?"

"No more lunches," I tell her with a smile to take the edge off. "No more feasting on my bones."

"Why, Ann, you know perfectly well—"

I turn away. I will miss her. I will miss all of them.

I hurry back to Edwin, who is still crouching on the matted grass, filling cups from the last bottle. "That's it," he says.

"You take this cup."

He rubs the cheap paper. "A great idea, Ann," he says in a flat tone.

"Will you go on again now, the same way?"

"What do you mean?"

"Taking women . . ."

"Edwin," Flora's voice cracks over the children's heads. She's beckoning.

"Goodbye," he says, placing the untasted champagne in the center of the tray, then settling down next to Flora.

Now Tom brings out the rocker. Frank raises his hand to bid, startling me. Flora, her face set dead ahead, seems unaware of what he is doing. Tom hesitates, then accepts his bid of fifteen dollars. I wonder where he will get the money to pay for it. Flora always wanted that rocker. I used to sit in it to sew beside the fire.

Fred brings the rocker down the aisle and sets it at the end of the Fields' row. It moves gently back and forth on the grass. The sight of the rocker beside them is more than I can bear. Now Fred comes out of the house with the box of Christmas tree ornaments. "What am I bid for this box of balls and things? Some strings of lights. Nice. Nothing broken as far as I can see."

Saul's hand shoots up.

"No," Flora hisses, batting at his hand across Edwin.

The child whines, "I want that angel!" His hand is still up avoiding hers.

"Make him stop!" Flora orders Edwin. She reaches in front of him to slap Saul's hand, but Tom has already accepted the bid.

"Sold for two dollars to the little fellow in the back."

I do not want my angel to hang at the top of their tree.

I duck out of the tent, realizing as I bend over that my neck is stiff-to-cracking. I walk across the grass toward the covey of cars.

Molly runs up behind me. "Where are you going?"

"For a little drive."

"I want to come. It's boring here."

"Life is boring, Molly. Boring or painful."

"I want to come with you anyhow."

"Better not," I say, to myself.

"Why better not?" I do not answer. "Tom is beginning to auction what's left."

She is pleading, and I'm sorry for her. I cannot bear to see her face fall. "All right, you can come," I say.

She scurries along beside me. As we walk to the car, I hear far-off thunder. I remember the big summer storms rolling up the valley from the river, churning the air ahead.

"Daddy says he'll buy me a bed with four posts when I come to live with him," Molly says, running to keep up.

"You're not going to live with him, my pet."

She doesn't respond, avoiding trouble. She runs ahead of me, ferreting through the cars, shouting when she spots our station wagon. She is sitting very straight in the front seat when I arrive.

"Where are we going?" she asks, bouncing as though we are heading out for a picnic.

I fasten my seatbelt and twist the key in the ignition. "We're going for a drive. Put on your seatbelt. You must do exactly as I say."

She stares at me. I have never spoken so firmly.

I turn the car onto the highway and pick up speed. The highway is deserted. I press the accelerator down to the floor, and the battered car leaps. Along the road, the trees have turned color, blazing, then fading to dusty reds and browns. There are For Sale signs in another of the old fields. Our own pasture has been sold to a developer; he will put up twenty little boxes.

"Where are we going?" Molly asks again. "You're driving terribly fast."

I slow down and wonder if David has noted my carelessness on his yellow pad: unsafe at any speed.

"Don't worry, I'm not going to wreck us," and I feel her relax beside me, reassured as always because of my confidence.

We turn onto the humped tree-hung side road. She looks out the window and says nothing. She knows where we are going. Over the bump which used to make her giggle when she was tiny, strapped in her car seat and bouncing high. The car hangs suspended in the air for a moment and comes down with a wrenching thud. "Daddy says it's bad for the springs," she remarks. She is smiling, my partner in crime.

Fuck Daddy. Fuck all daddies, and their wives.

I drive through the Fields' gate, past the shed where Edwin keeps his car. The door is open. I slide the car inside to evade the neighbor's notice. "You stay here in the car with the door closed," I tell Molly and reach across her to roll up the window. "I'll be back in a few minutes."

"What are you going to do?"

"Never mind. I'll be back in a few minutes."

I would like to lock her in, but I relent when I see her peaked face; she is frightened enough already. "You stay here," I repeat with the full weight of my new authority. She sits very still to impress me, as though welded to her seat.

I slam the door and walk around to the front of the car. Edwin's power mower is standing in the corner next to his gardening tools. Everything he touched bears his mark: the smoothly worn handles are circled with bands of invisible fingerprints. I see the red gasoline can and approach it cautiously, leaning down to lift it by the handle. I sigh with mixed relief. It is nearly full.

Molly is watching me through the car window. I wave at her, then hoist the can and walk out of the shed.

I start down the path toward the house. A little smoke is climbing out of the chimney from Edwin's early-morning fire, left banked against their return. How fragile the house looks, how defenseless and pretty with its green shutters and dormer windows. It is like an illustration in a children's book, a house of rabbits—all Edwin's handiwork. There's the terrace he laid himself next to the front door, the flower bed he dug for Flora, the window boxes he hammered together so that she could have her petunias. They are thriving still, falling over the edges of the boxes in long white and purple sprays.

I walk around the north side of the house where I am out of sight of the road. The handle of the gasoline can is cutting into my fingers. I set it down on the grass and unscrew the top, then realize I have no matches.

Leaving the gasoline can, I slide open the porch door and step inside. There's the familiar chaos and smell of burnt bacon. Tennis rackets and children's boots are heaped on the floor. I hear the tap dripping on plates in the kitchen sink. The table is covered with the remains of their breakfast, chairs pushed back as though they all rushed out on impulse in the midst of toast and tea. Flora's heart-shaped silver tea strainer is winking in the sun.

I know she keeps her matches in the drawer next to the stove. I take the box.

Out through the kitchen where we made fruitcake three Novembers running, Edwin giving us each a boiled dime to drop into the big bowl of batter: we were all his children then.

Out through the porch. I stumble on Frank's knapsack bulging with books.

Down the steps to the gasoline can, shining red in the sun. Tipping the can, I sprinkle the geraniums growing along the house. Their fleshy leaves do not absorb the gasoline; it spatters, staining the paint. The acrid smell overwhelms the citrusy scent of the geraniums blooming in the sun.

I tip the can up again and soak the leaves and the grass. Cool air touches my cheek like a set of fingers, and I look up the hill and see the bright trees behind the children's swing. It is a beautiful day.

I strike a match against the strip of sand paper, throw it into the geraniums, and jump back. With a gush, a big flame flares up.

Molly sounds the car horn.

Stepping back, I watch the flame consume a tuft of dried grass leaning against the side of the house. Edwin, trimming with his shears, missed that one. I watch the flame leap up the wall, the paint wrinkling. Another flame, spurting up a separate stalk, follows the first one onto the wall.

Molly sounds the horn, two short and one long. I watch the first flame feeling for a foothold a little higher up the wall. It finds a blister and lays hold. The second flame is quick behind it. The grass near my feet is crackling, and a pungent smoke rises. The first flame climbs the wall, reaching for the open kitchen window. I see Flora's gingham curtains suddenly sucked in. The flame touches the white window frame and turns it brown.

The second flame fans out further down the wall, and the paint crackles and sears. The first flame is mounting the window frame, edging it like a vine.

A scorching, darkening stain is spreading across the north wall of the house, board by board, above the kitchen window.

Molly sounds the horn.

The top of the window frame pops and cracks. The second flame, spreading, reaches up. The first and second flames join together. Together, they race for the roof line.

My God, it is burning. The house is burning.

Treason

A Play

Time passes and pisses on us all.

—WILLIAM CARLOS WILLIAMS

CHARACTERS

EZRA POUND

midsixties to late seventies

DOROTHY (Shakespear) POUND

his wife of thirty years, English, midfifties to sixties

OLGA RUDGE

his mistress of twenty years, ten years younger, American,
raised in England, light accent, midforties to fifties

SGT. PAUL WHITESIDE

US Army, African American, thirty-five

DR. OVERHOLSER

Chief Psychiatrist at St. Elizabeths, fifties

SHERI MARTINELLI

a painter, early twenties

MARCELLA SPANN

a teacher, late twenties

JOHN KASPER

New Jersey–based anti-integrationist, white supremacist, thirties

MARY RUDGE

Olga and Ezra's daughter, brought up in the Tyrol, light Swiss-
German accent, early twenties to midthirties

ELDER LIGHTFOOT SOLOMON MICHAUX
African American evangelist,
minister of the Radio Church of God

TIME: The action of the play takes place between 1941 and 1965,
in Italy, the Tyrol, and Washington, DC.

Act I

SCENE 1

Setting: At home in Rapallo and broadcasts from Rome.

November/ December 1941

(As the audience enters, we see documentary footage of Mussolini's Italy and the Allied invasion. As the stage fades to black, we begin to hear static from a radio trying to tune in a shortwave station. Out of the darkness we hear three voices.)

DOROTHY

You and I, Olga.

OLGA

Yes—you and I, Dorothy, sitting here in the dark, to save electricity.

EZRA'S VOICE
(Radio broadcast)

Ezra Pound speaking . . .

(Dissipates into static)

OLGA

Over the static . . .

DOROTHY

Even over our static.

OLGA (*Flaring*)

Our static!

(*Radio static becomes louder, then suddenly a spotlight on* EZRA, *at a broadcast studio in Rome. He is flamboyantly dressed in cape, sombrero, flowing cravat, ruffled shirt. Incongruously, he wears heavy old hiking boots, mud-caked, that are clearly too big for him.*)

EZRA

(*Radio broadcast*)

Kike Rosenfelt that snotty barbarian. . . . The profits of usurers. . . . If ever a nation produced efficient bureaucracy it has been in Germany. . . . Eliminate Roosevelt and his Jews or the Jews and their Roosevelt. . . . Which of you is free of Jew influence, from Jew control . . .

(*As he speaks, light slowly expands to include* DOROTHY, *who is sketching by candlelight. She is in* OLGA'*s living room at Rapallo, which is very simply furnished: a table with type-writer, several chairs, kitchen nook.*)

DOROTHY

I know how difficult this arrangement has been for you.

OLGA

I wanted it just the way it was, here—white, empty. No junk, no clutter, only candlelight. Now

(*Gesturing*)

your trunks, your boxes, overflowing everywhere . . . the three of us here—mess, disorder . . .

(*Static again*)

EZRA

(*Radio broadcast*)

Europe calling, Ezry Pound speaking. . . . You 'Mercuns would not listen, you would not listen, nothing would make you take the faintest trace of a half-possible interest in Hitler's warnings. This war was made to make debts, it was made to impose the gold standard—for manipulation by kikes. You don't want to hear this, you turn off your radio, you go back to sleep. . . . When this war is over, everything will be just as it was before—until the next one gets going—and you will have killed off some women and children and you'll feel proud.

All we've got now—it cost us three years of war—is a revelation of hoaxes, designed by the London *Times* and the rest of the press swine, to conceal the basic issue, which is economic—always economic: world usury, the creation of wars by an international band of Yid bankers.

OLGA

And never, ever any money, except what I could earn—playing my violin every chance I get, down in the village, then climbing back up here in my evening dress, the violin over my shoulder . . . I've hidden an old pair of espadrilles under the steps down below, for the climb—alone, in the middle of the night.

EZRA

(*Radio broadcast*)

Of the three murderers, Churchill, Roosevelt, and Stalin, Stalin is the most open. He's never tried to deny his hand in mass murders, assassinations. He'd argue it's just part of his business. Roosevelt would say that a murder today is committed solely in the hope of preventing murder by his great-grandchildren.

DOROTHY

I've understood from the beginning what Ezra needs: perfect peace and quiet.

EZRA

(*Radio broadcast*)

Mr. Churchill who is an arrant coward and a clever sceneshifter has never faced Mencius's question: Is there any difference between killing a man with a sword and killing him with a system of government? Oh yes, I want this war to stop. I'd like to conserve a few art works, a few mosaics, a few printed volumes—what's left of the world's cultural heritage.

FDR

(*Radio broadcast*)

Yesterday, December 7th, 1941, a day which will live in infamy, the United States of America was suddenly and deliberately attacked by the naval and air forces of the Empire of Japan.

OLGA

The United States will come into the war now—no more excuse for neutrality.

DOROTHY

The Allies will crush us.

(*To* OLGA)

We must help each other now.

EZRA

(*Radio broadcast*)

On Arbour Day, Pearl Arbour Day, at twelve o'clock noon, I retired from the capitol of the old Roman empire to Rapallo to seek wisdom from the ancients. I wanted to figure things out. I had a perfectly good alibi, if I wanted to play things safe. I was translating the Analects of Confucius . . .

SCENE 2

Setting: Next day, the living room at Rapallo.

(OLGA *is sitting on a small sofa, copying music. She holds the papers in her lap.* DOROTHY, *at the other end of the sofa, is working on a small watercolor.* EZRA *sits at a table covered with books and papers. There is no other furniture in the room. For a beat, all work in silence.*)

EZRA

(*Looking up*)

What is the answer to the philosopher's question?

(*Both women look up. It's not clear which one* EZRA *is addressing.*)

Confucius asked his disciples, "You think I've learned a great deal, and kept all of it in my memory?" Dorothy?

DOROTHY
(*Continuing to paint*)

Your memory is phenomenal, Mao.

OLGA
(*Checking watch, getting up*)

My English student will be waiting.
(*She rises, puts on coat.*)

EZRA

Wait, Olga. Your answer.

OLGA (*Irony*)

You know everything, Ezra.

EZRA
(*Quoting from his manuscript*)

"It is not so. I have reduced it all to one principle."

DOROTHY
(*To* EZRA)

It's almost time for you to leave for Rome, you don't want to be late for your broadcast—again. I'll make you a sandwich for the train.
(*Rising*)

We have a tomato, I believe.

(*She goes to a shelf, takes down a tomato, bread, and cheese, makes sandwich, wraps it.*)

EZRA

Soggy, long before Rome. Is nobody going to ask me what the principle is?

DOROTHY

What is the principle, Mao?

EZRA

I will tell you. Rapacity—the main force of our times.

(*He picks up his manuscript.*)

If a book contains this wisdom, it's impossible to force any publisher to print it . . .

OLGA

And so we can't pay the rent, even for one establishment.

EZRA

(*Ignoring this*)

My usual publishers refused my last Confucius. What hope do I have for my translation of the whole Analects?

DOROTHY

None, I'm afraid. It was different in London, before the war, when everyone was saying you were the greatest poet of the twentieth century . . .

EZRA

. . . my photograph was even published in Australia!

DOROTHY

In your little green jacket.

EZRA

William Butler Yeats called me "a solitary volcano"!

OLGA

(*At the exit*)

I must go—my student pays me today.

EZRA

And I must catch my train—with or without my sandwich. I may have to eat my boots.

DOROTHY

Be careful, Mao. The Americans have been bombing the tracks out of Milan. They're saying the Rome line will be next.

OLGA

(*To* DOROTHY)

Fuss, and more fuss. He'll go anyway, as you know—he always does. Rome Radio, for three years, twice a week, regular as a clock, but who, may I ask you, listens?

DOROTHY

You and I, Olga.

EZRA

All the English-speaking world! And don't forget—three hundred and fifty lire, each broadcast—for getting the truth out, to a
world gone mad.

(*He begins to assemble papers etc.*)

OLGA

(*To* DOROTHY)

He doesn't even read you his scripts anymore.

DOROTHY

There are jumps in them I can't follow.

EZRA

I saw it all coming, after the First War—the War to End All Wars.

DOROTHY

Did you find anything other than a tomato for his sandwich?

OLGA

Bit of cheese. I was down to the market by six.

DOROTHY

I heard you.

(*Attempt at humor*)

Herd of wild elephants on the stairs.

OLGA

YOU could go.

DOROTHY

Your Italian is better.

OLGA

You could have learned! Sixteen months trapped here together—

EZRA

Birds in their little nest must agree!

OLGA

(*To* DOROTHY)

I never invited you to move in here.

DOROTHY

Ezra did. I had no choice; my apartment was requisitioned—

OLGA

It's convenient, for you—but what about me—my feelings, my convenience—forced to live together, the three of us, after all these years. Before, at least, when you lived down the hill, I didn't have to confront, every day—

EZRA

(*Interrupting her*)

The facts, Ma'am, just the facts. You, Olga, *mia amorata*; Mao here, La Signora Pound.

(*Quoting Confucius*)

"If the terminology be not exact, if it fit not the thing, government instructions will not be explicit, and business cannot be conducted properly . . ."

OLGA

Stop it, Ezra! The sayings of Confucius can't be made to fit every situation!

EZRA

"If business is not properly run, rites and music will not be honored . . ."

OLGA

How am I supposed to get on with my life? I've completely stopped practicing my violin!

DOROTHY

I hardly see how I am preventing you.

OLGA

You LISTEN!

DOROTHY

This apartment is very small.

OLGA

I'll just give my violin away, then—too fine an instrument to let go to waste!

DOROTHY

Here, Mao—for the train.

(*Gives him the sandwich*)

EZRA

(*Examining it*)

Cucumbers and watercress?

DOROTHY

We ate our last cucumber a week ago, and since the war the villagers don't gather watercress—the English who loved it are all gone away.

EZRA

(*Puts sandwich in his pocket*)

There are some crimes that nothing will whitewash.

SCENE 3

Setting: Radio studio in Rome. May, 1945.

(*On a darkened stage, spotlight on* EZRA *with microphone.*)

EZRA

The United States has declared war ILLEGALLY through what I consider to be the criminal acts of a president—Stinky Roosenfeld —whose mental condition is NOT, as far as I can see, all that could be desired of a man in so responsible a position . . .

He has broken his promises to the electorate; he has to my mind violated his oath of office—and his oath of allegiance to the US Constitution. After Pearl Harbor I spent a month trying to figure things out. I consulted Confucius and Aristotle, both of whom had seen empires fall—and decided I had to return to these airwaves to talk to you again.

What sort of old age do you picture for the boy who is sent

off to machine-gun women and children? And what sort of bill is the American people expected to foot for this attempt to control the world? If you want a permanent garrison in Europe—just how large a garrison would it require, and WHAT would be the annual costs to taxpayers in Kansas and Californy?

(*The Pisan prison cage begins to rise around him.*)

The United States has been MISinformed. I don't think it's the function of the commander in chief of the United States American Army to dictate this citizen's politics. Free speech without free radio is a mockery! I am only exercising my rights as a loyal American . . .

BLACKOUT

SCENE 4

Setting: The Cage, Disciplinary Training Center, Pisa.

May, 1945

(*The cage is now complete.* EZRA *gets down on his hands and knees to examine the sharp spikes at the bottom of the cage wires.* SGT. WHITESIDE, *an African American, enters, carrying a bedroll, latrine can, packing case, etc.*)

EZRA

Who are you?

SGT. WHITESIDE

(*Coming to attention*)

Sergeant Paul Whiteside, US Army, Disciplinary Training Center, Pisa.

(*He salutes.* EZRA *responds with the fascist salute.*)
Not in here, Mr. Pound. There are rapists and murderers out there in all those other cages—patriots all—you wouldn't want them to . . . misunderstand.

EZRA

Whiteside. Good old 'Mercun name. Grandparents born in slavery? Virginia, from your accent?

SGT. WHITESIDE

North Carolina.

EZRA

Mother octoroon?

(*No response*)

Quadroon?

SGT. WHITESIDE

My mother is half white.

EZRA

Old Massa hisself, pretty black slave his concubine, half-tone pickaninnies running all round the plantation!

SGT. WHITESIDE

(*Ignoring this*)

This is your latrine. It'll be emptied every other day.

EZRA

You read poetry, Whiteside?

SGT. WHITESIDE

I read Countee Cullen, Langston Hughes . . .

EZRA

Good man, old Hughes! I wrote him years ago re what classics should be taught at those nigger universities. Old Hughes wrote me back, "We are unfortunately not yet up to that standard."
                    (*No response*)
My grandfather, Thaddeus Pound, was an abolitionist. I understand the black heart of American history—rape, miscegenation . . .

SGT. WHITESIDE

Latrine there,
                    (*Indicates bucket*)
sleep here. Reveille at 0700.

EZRA

Why do you want to speak like a Havud sophomore? One race and one race only—YOURS—has fostered a speech mellow and full—in charm not inferior to that of the eighteenth century.

SGT. WHITESIDE

Belt. Shoelaces.
        (SGT. WHITESIDE *removes* EZRA*'s belt and shoelaces.*)

EZRA

My shoelaces?

SGT. WHITESIDE

The Army doesn't want you to hang yourself.

EZRA

(*Going to the spikes*)

They want me to slit my wrists—save them the trouble.

(*He leans down as though to slice his wrists.* SGT. WHITE-
SIDE *intervenes. There is a moment of closeness.*)

If I am not hung for treason, I think I have a good chance of seeing
the president. I could have stopped this war.

SGT. WHITESIDE

It's late. Go to sleep, Old Man.

(*Harsh blue lights bathe the cage as* EZRA *begins to take
off his boots.*)

EZRA

Turn out those lights!

SGT. WHITESIDE

You're considered dangerous. Mr. Pound. We've got to watch you.
Twenty-four hours a day.

(SGT. WHITESIDE *leaves the cage, locks it.*)

EZRA

You don't know who I am.

(*He finishes taking off boots, examines his feet.*)

Blisters big as marbles. I borrowed these boots in Rome—two
sizes too small. The Americans were marching north, Mussolini
in hiding, the Italian Army fleeing. I told the hellcats in Rapallo, "I
have to see the Leoncina—Mary—my daughter, with her peasant

family in the Tyrol." They didn't want it—the hellcats—the two of them, united front, for once, telling me, "Don't make more trouble." Trouble's my middle name.

The Leoncina deserves to hear the truth—finally. Maybe my last chance to explain. I started walking north. Two days on the road . . .

BLACKOUT

SCENE 5

Setting: Memory of the Italian Tyrol.

A few years earlier, in September 1943

(*Newsreel shots of Italy during the* 1943 *invasion, smoking ruins at Monte Cassino, Italian soldiers surrendering.*

MARY *enters, wearing Tyrolean costume, carrying a basket. Lights indicate this is in* EZRA's *memory.* EZRA *enters.*)

MARY

Babbo—you're limping!

EZRA

Boots two sizes too small—I walked all the way from Rome.

MARY

(*As* EZRA *limps toward* MARY.)

We heard on the radio this morning—Mussolini's been liberated by the Germans!

EZRA

Impossible!

MARY

No, it's true—flown to Berlin to meet with Hitler. But how did you get here, Babbo?

EZRA

Slept on a bench one night, under a haystack the next. Had to come all the way to see my only daughter.

MARY

My real family is here, Babbo. They raised me. Have you forgotten?

EZRA

Well, I had no choice. Olga wrote me from the hospital, two days after you wuz born, said, "I can't look after it, having no talent that way. But, there's a Swiss peasant woman here, from Gais—her child has died—she's agreed to nurse it, take it in . . ."

MARY

You mean me?

EZRA

Olga called you "it" for a while.

MARY

She frightens me.

EZRA

I know the feeling.

MARY

But you wanted me, Babbo?

EZRA

Tried to have you live with us, in Venice, but only visits permitted. Olga was adamant! Her violin, you know. Needed peace and quiet.

MARY

And when I did visit, those terrible afternoons when she tried to teach me Italian, reading to me and making me translate. I never could do it. I only spoke German, then.

EZRA

She wanted to "form" you.

MARY

But not live with me, not love me. But you, Babbo . . .

EZRA

The American bar, in Venice. You used to love their cheese sandwiches.

MARY

And afterward, always ice cream—gelato *cioccolata*. That much Italian I could say. Then you'd take us swimming at the Lido . . .

EZRA

Where you told me that you missed your "family" and wanted to
go back to Gais.

MARY

Well, you asked me.

EZRA

You wanted to go "home."

MARY

That was the only time I ever saw Olga cry. You set us both on
your knees, tried to comfort us. I was crying, too, because I knew
I shouldn't want Gais, shouldn't want my family here—

EZRA

I wanted to tell you then, but she wouldn't let me—never the
right time.

MARY

Tell me what?

EZRA

(*With difficulty*)

To tell you . . . I came here to tell you . . . my other family. My . . .
wife.

MARY

Your other family? Your wife!

EZRA

Dorothy. Dorothy Shakespear—no relation to . . . her mother was Yeats's lover: It happened a long time ago, in England. I was a young, penniless 'Mercun poet. Dorothy came complete with two hundred pounds a year—"So, a bargain says the Jew."

MARY

That woman who tried to talk to me in the street in Rapallo . . .

EZRA

Yes, Dorothy. She has a son.

MARY

Yours?

EZRA

A year younger than you—Omar.
(*Attempt at humor*)
I named him that so he could never be a poet.

MARY

Oh Babbo—

EZRA

Dorothy insisted on it, after you were born. What Olga has, Dorothy must have. So we had a son.
(*Silence*—MARY *unable to speak*)
Best to say nothing. Our secret. Like the gelato.

MARY

But it's not a secret. Everybody must know.

EZRA

No one wanted me to tell you. Sordid complications, they said . . . Leoncina, you must have guessed . . .

MARY

No. Never. Olga never said anything.

EZRA

You must have wondered why I was only with you and Olga on Tuesdays and Wednesdays, and the occasional Thursday.

MARY

(*Near tears*)

I thought you were away working.

EZRA

You were better off, in Gais, learning how to farm. Do you still keep the accounts? The way I taught you?

MARY

It's not a farm now. We had to eat the sheep early in the war.

EZRA

I gave you a real account book—you no more than fifteen, but good at figgering! Staked you to your first breeding ewe. A man must work with his head, or with his hands.

MARY

You taught me so much, Babbo. Still the most fascinating man I know.

(*She takes his hands.*)

EZRA

What's this your Ma tells me about a boyfriend?

MARY

Oh, just Boris—he kissed me, once, in Rome.

EZRA

(*Gently mocking*)

I hear he's a "Prince."

MARY

I didn't know anything about his title, then. Neither did he. I just thought he was the most interesting man I'd ever met—except for you, Babbo.

EZRA

You're not going to marry him, Leoncina? The torments of hell! Get back to your sheep.

MARY

We ate the sheep. And anyway, this is not the time for me to get married. Olga wants me to get "culture" first.

EZRA

You know enough to help me with my translations—that's a pretty thorough education. And you've read Shakespeare . . .

MARY

I was rereading *The Merchant of Venice* the last time I was in Venice.
(*Quoting*)
"I have a father, you a daughter, lost."
(MARY *exits. Light changes.* EZRA *wraps himself in the bedroll, lies down. Lights intensely bright and blue. He rubs his eyes.*)

EZRA

(*Quoting*)
"There is some ill a-brewing towards my rest . . ."
(*Shouting*)
Turn off the goddamned lights!
(*Intense light*)

BLACKOUT

SCENE 6

Setting: The Cage, Disciplinary Training Center.

Morning, May, 1945

(*The packing crate now has a board nailed across it to make a desk, with papers, books, etc.* EZRA, *in army fatigues, is asleep.* ELDER MICHAUX *is heard over the camp speakers* . . .)

EZRA

Cat piss and porcupines!

(*He rises, turns, and urinates into the can. Lights up on a distant view of farmlands toward Pisa.* EZRA *grips the bars, looking out.* SGT. WHITESIDE *enters with a magazine, which he takes into the cage.*)

SGT. WHITESIDE

Morning, Mr. Pound.

EZRA

What's that caterwauling?

SGT. WHITESIDE

Elder Solomon Lightfoot Michaux's Radio Church of God. Every Sunday. It'll be over soon.

EZRA

Mussolini wouldn't even let the Pope broadcast. He drained the swamps, made the trains finally run on schedule. . . . Il Duce said

every man a house of his own in eighty years . Didn't have eight
years to get it done. . . . "Shoot me in the chest!" he said—hung
up by the heels in Milano, with La Clara.

SGT. WHITESIDE

New issue of *Time* just came.

EZRA

(*Eagerly scanning magazine*)

Baseball. Now I know the war's over. Thanks! And thanks for this
"table" ex packing box.

SGT. WHITESIDE

You're the only man in the DTC, Mr. Pound, who knows the poetry
of Langston Hughes.

(*He turns to go.*)

EZRA

I set old Hughes on the right path—same as Fordie did me, same
as I did Eliot! Told Hughes he finally got the authentic nigger talk
in that poem of his called "Harlem."

SGT. WHITESIDE

"What happens to a dream deferred?"

EZRA

(*Taking up the recitation*)

"Does it dry up
like a raisin in the sun?

Does it stink like rotten meat?"

(SGT. WHITESIDE *joins in on the final lines.*)

"Maybe it just sags

Like a heavy load

OR DOES IT EXPLODE?"

SGT. WHITESIDE

It might . . . here's some Countee Cullen you might not be familiar
with.

"Once riding in old Baltimore,

Heart-filled, head-filled with glee,

I saw a Baltimorean

Keep looking straight at me.

Now I was eight and very small,

And he was no whit bigger,

And so, I smiled, but he poked out

His tongue, and called me, 'Nigger.'

I saw the whole of Baltimore

From May until December;

Of all the things that happened there

That's all that I remember."

EZRA

You got an opinion on the Civil War, Whiteside?

SGT. WHITESIDE

The right side won.

EZRA

I know what you THINK. I know what you've been TOLD. But you're wrong. Economic—all economic! The South was in debt to the Jew North. That started the Civil War! You got any opinion on the Ku Klux Klan?

SGT. WHITESIDE

I've got an opinion. My father was a sharecropper—burnt out, in Virginia. Lost everything he had—except his life. And not because they didn't try to take that too.

EZRA

American lynch law had its origins in the deliberate ruin of the American South. The Ku Klux once had a reason . . .

SGT. WHITESIDE

You in favor of the ovens, too?
(EZRA *appears not to understand.*)
The ovens we found in Germany, Poland, Czechoslovakia?

EZRA

As to the Hitler program, it was—what we all know, and do nothing about—that the breeding of human beings deserves more care and attention than the breeding of horses and sheep. That's point one of the Nazi program. Breed GOOD, and preserve the race.

SGT. WHITESIDE

You talk some dangerous shit for a man in a cage.
(SGT. WHITESIDE *exits.*)

TREASON

EZRA

Whiteside!

(*He finds what he is looking for in a manuscript.*)
"A white ox on the road toward Pisa,
as if facing the tower,
dark sheep in the drill field and on wet days were clouds
in the mountain as if under the guard roosts."
(*He sees something, drops to his knees.*)
"A lizard upheld me . . ."
(*Takes lizard in his hand as* DOROTHY *and* OLGA *enter. He
puts it down carefully as he sees them. They stand on either
side of the cage, holding the bars, looking in.* EZRA, *seeing
them, raises his arms in silent greeting and exultation.*)

OLGA

It's hard writing into the blue, never knowing whether you get it
and having no answer. If I could only do something for you . . .
(EZRA *grabs her hand through the bars.*)
I expect you'll be out waving your wild tail before long, outside
the barbed wire of the DTC and INSIDE the domestic cage . . .
(*He grabs manuscript from the table, reads from it.*)

EZRA

"O white-chested martin, God damn it
as no one will carry a message
Say to La Cara: amo."

(*To* DOROTHY)
Please see that Olga has money.

DOROTHY

I sent her one of the thousand-lire notes I found in your room soon after you were taken away. I wrote her, "This, as you may remember, was HIS money, not mine. . . ." I was not thanked.

OLGA

(*To* DOROTHY)

I've never taken Ezra's money. All I have, now, are the few lire my students pay for their piano lessons.

EZRA

(*Taking* DOROTHY*'s hand through the bars. He is now holding both women's hands, which means they must stand close together. He speaks to* DOROTHY *as though they are alone.*)
You have given me thirty years of peace clear as blue feldspar and I am grateful. Do you remember Sirmione?

DOROTHY

Where I first saw color. My life began then.

EZRA

The little temple over the lake where we lay on the grass—with your glorious mother.
    "If, at Sirmio,
    My soul, I meet thee, when this life's outrun . . ."

DOROTHY

    "Thank you, whatever comes. . . . Nay, whatever comes
    One hour was sunlit . . ."
Dear Mao—are you able to work here?

EZRA

I have my Confucius, a Chinese dictionary, paper—

(*He picks up papers to show them.*)

for these new Cantos I need the ideogram "chang": constant, usual.

DOROTHY

(*Taking pages through the bars*)

I'll find it, send it to you.

(*Privately*)

Pazienza!

OLGA

Give me the drafts, I'll type them up.

(*She reaches for the papers.* DOROTHY *does not give them to her.*)

EZRA

(*To* OLGA)

Tell Mary I bless the day I first saw you for all the happiness you have brought me.

(*To himself*)

But first I must go this road to hell.

OLGA

(*Realizing she won't get the papers*)

Mary always exhorts me to be a good loser, reminds me of Violet Hunt, how you counseled her when Fordie left her, "Never mind, you'll be old soon, and then you won't care."

DOROTHY

All our friends send messages.

EZRA

The First War took our best. Age has got the rest of 'em. Willy Yeats and Fordie Madox Ford that once was Hueffer, and Jimmy Joyce that made a new language—I helped him publish that gawddarned *Ulysses*—and other men, many others—the best of the best. I don't see them now, the ones that are left, don't hear from 'em. . . . When Willy Yeats came to Rapallo to show me his new work, I wrote "Putrid" across it, can't remember now rightly why . . . — no more letters, now.

DOROTHY

(*She pockets the papers, takes out notes, begins to read from one of them.*)
"A good man, so kind, he never did anything wrong."
And here are some from our friends in England.
(*Hands him letters through the bars.*)

EZRA

(*Reaching through bars for the notes*)
O Mao! Tell me everything—all the news. Personal gossip, anything. Tom Elliot, Willy Yeats—
(DOROTHY *strokes his wrist.*)

OLGA

Mary sends her love. She longs to visit—

DOROTHY

Your mother wants to hear from you. I moved down the hill to be with her as soon as you left. The old lady's well, though a nuisance. Talk, talk, talk.

(*Quietly*)

You may imagine that I'm thinking of you all the time; but I do not worry all the time. I only hope captivity is not proving bad for your health—

EZRA

The army feeds me very solid.

(*Pounds his stomach*)

Back to 166 pounds, but nothing like the prewar bulge. Tell me more—

OLGA

Mary's quit her hospital work, gone back to Gais, now the war is over. I asked her to stay with me, but she wouldn't. She told me she couldn't do anything to make me happy. Left me that quote from *The Merchant of Venice* about losing a daughter. She underlined it three times.

EZRA

Loves the mountains, that girl—fat as a cat full of cream.

DOROTHY

Omar's quite happy in the army. He just heard his first *Magic Flute*.

EZRA

How old was he when I . . . ?

(DOROTHY *doesn't understand.*)

How old was my son—when I first . . .

EZRA

DOROTHY

When you first "met" him? He was twelve, on vacation from boarding school, staying with my mother in London. You came for one day.

EZRA

Dorothy . . .

DOROTHY

Your son is very proud of you. Pray God he survives this war.

EZRA

I could have stopped it in '39, when I went back to the States to speak to Stinky Roosenfeld . He wouldn't see me, too busy talking to his Jew banker friends—palmed me off on that old fool congressman from Idaho. "I'm sure I don't know what a man like you would find to do in Washington." Waall, they'll hear from me now—if they try me, I'm prepared to defend myself.

OLGA

Oh no, Ezra.

DOROTHY

You always have too many ideas, you'll go over the edge, exhaust everyone.

EZRA

I have no choice. It would take a superman to defend me.

DOROTHY

I'm prepared to spend my last penny—

OLGA

I'll start a petition—
(SGT. WHITESIDE *enters.*)

SGT. WHITESIDE

Time's up, ladies.

EZRA

(*Holding their hands*)
Write me. Anything. A scribble. Tell the others—

OLGA

I'll come again as soon as they'll let me, even if I have to walk. . . .

DOROTHY

Thank you, whatever comes.

SGT. WHITESIDE

That's it, folks.
(*He escorts* DOROTHY *and* OLGA *off,* OLGA *protesting.*)

EZRA

(*Hanging onto the bars, looking after them*)
Trees die & the dream remains.

"UBI AMOR IBI OCULUS EST.

Where love is, there is the eye."

(*As* OLGA's *protests die away*)

The female is a chaos. . . .

SGT. WHITESIDE

I'll have to take those letters.

(*He unlocks cage, enters, takes letters.*)

EZRA

(*As he's doing this*)

Just little words of friendship, encouragement.

SGT. WHITESIDE

Sorry. Regulations.

(*He takes letters, leaves cage.* EZRA *appears devastated.*)

EZRA (*Shouting*)

Twenty minutes with Stalin is all I ask—WHITESIDE!

SGT. WHITESIDE

What do you want now?

EZRA

Come here.

SGT. WHITESIDE (*Approaching*)

What've you got up your pants this time?

                           EZRA

Not much. Hand me that broom.

        (*He indicates a broom lying outside the cage.*)

                    SGT. WHITESIDE

Now, you know . . .

                           EZRA

No rule against brooms.

                    SGT. WHITESIDE

What do you want it for?

                           EZRA

Fourteen days in this gorilla cage. What I need is exercise. So hand
it to me.

                    SGT. WHITESIDE

Sorry. The answer is no.

                           EZRA

        (EZRA *now works the wire handle off the latrine bucket into*
        a hook. He uses this to reach through the cage bars and hook
        the broom, drawing it in. Dramatic stabs and flourishes
        with the broom.)

Billy Yeats and I, reading all day in the stone cottage in Sussex,
then going out after dark with our foils. Dorothy was supposed to
cook for the three of us—our honeymoon.

"Some cook, some do not cook. Some things cannot be altered."

(*Using the broom as a tennis racket*)

I won all my games, that last winter at Rapallo—told Olga my scores. She didn't want me to talk about tennis. She wanted me to talk about love.

(*Drops the broom, gets down on his hands and knees*)

"What thou lovest well remains . . ."

SGT. WHITESIDE

Get some rest, Mr. Pound. Be careful not to overdo your exercise.

(*Exits*)

EZRA

(*Shields eyes from light, strikes a pose*)

"Put out the light, and then put out the light."

Margaret Cravens slit her throat the afternoon before her tea party, left me a note on the piano—I'd told her thanks so much for the money—a thousand a year—but no, I won't marry her. Shouldn't-a taken it personal; shoulda known I'm agin marryin'. François Villon said, "Absolve, may you absolve us all."

(*He is grasping the bars.*)

"I have tried to write Paradise.

Do not move.

Let the wind speak

That is paradise.

Let the Gods forgive what I

Have made

Let those I love try to forgive

What I have made."

(*Brilliant blue light bathes the cage. He covers his eyes. Lights burn with increasing intensity as* EZRA *begins to tear off his clothes.*)

Hot . . . hot . . . burning . . .

>(*He grabs his head with both hands.*)

WHITESIDE!

>(SGT. WHITESIDE *enters.*)

>SGT. WHITESIDE

What's wrong?

>EZRA

My head.

>SGT. WHITESIDE

What's wrong with your head?

>EZRA

Bursting.

>(*He crawls to the waste can, appears to vomit.*)

>SGT. WHITESIDE

Hold on . . .

>EZRA (*Desperate*)

Nothing remains.

>(SGT. WHITESIDE *unlocks the cage.* EZRA *cowers in the corner, does not exit.* SGT. WHITESIDE *takes him by the arm to lead him out. He crawls to the table, drags off book, notes.*)

I do not believe I will be shot for treason. If I am not shot I think

my chances of seeing Truman are good. I rely on the American
sense of justice.

(*Begins to howl*)

The world is falling in on me, the world is falling—

SGT. WHITESIDE

(*Alarmed, leading him*)

I'm taking you to the infirmary.

EZRA

Mr. President—members of Congress—what are you doing in this
war at all? What are you doing in Africa? Who amongst you has
the nerve or the sense to do something that would be conducive to
getting out before you are mortgaged up to the neck and over it?

(*As* SGT. WHITESIDE *tries to lead him off*)

Take me to the president! Stinky Rosenfeld! Give me twenty
minutes—

SGT. WHITESIDE

Mr. Pound . . . you're going to the infirmary. Now. Have one of the
shrinks take a look at you.

EZRA

(*Shaking off* WHITESIDE)

America has been up Freud's asshole for fifty years.

SGT. WHITESIDE

Is this one of your goddamned tricks, Pound?

EZRA

(*Smiling, puts on a shirt*)

Do you favor putting men in cages, WHITESIDE?

SGT. WHITESIDE

Come along, Mr. Pound.

(*Begins again to lead him off*)

EZRA (*Kindly*)

Out there's the Via Aurelia, Whiteside. Named for Marcus Aurelius—he said, "If anyone can show me, and prove to me, that I am wrong in thought or deed, I will gladly change. I seek the truth, which never yet hurt anybody."

SGT. WHITESIDE

Like hell . . .

EZRA

Hemingway and I and his wife—which one, was it Martha?— passed this way on our walking tour looking for the fifteenth-century battlegrounds of the Malatesta—lunched on cheese and wine under those olive trees.

"We will see those old roads again . . ."

Possibly, but nothing appears less likely.

(SGT. WHITESIDE *drags* EZRA *off*.)

BLACKOUT

SCENE 7

(In the blackout, a spotlight on DOROTHY. *She is writing to* EZRA.*)*

DOROTHY

"Black huts
dark tents behind
Leveled & arid flatness—
Camp EM Tousa
Disciplinary Training Center.
A great draught pushed from the heavy mountains
Sweeping over the walks.
All washed out
curtained
obliterated by the quick clasp
and sudden glow of intimacy
Ourselves joined again
after five months of half-life.
Ming Mao, bright-haired one.

For five days I was undivided from you
  Smoothing your wrist & ankle—
  Apollo
  O Apollo
  accept the olibanum
  look after your own."
   (Looking up, as though to EZRA*)*

Did you ever get my letter—with my poem? Well, not really a poem . . .

BLACKOUT

SCENE 8

Setting: Infirmary, Disciplinary Training Center.

Several months after events of Scene 6, 1945

(*Spotlight on* EZRA, *typing at a table in the infirmary. He types with vigor, shaking the table, humming and singing to himself.*)

SGT. WHITESIDE
(*Enters with a document*)
I've got something for you.

EZRA

Not now. Too busy. Got to write this letter for Ed Page—his execution's tomorrow, don't want me to tell his Ma anything about that . . .

(*He ponders, begins to write.*)

He murdered a man in a café in Milan, drunken as a skunk, Old Ed's a quick man with a knife. Learned that when he was cuttin' his way up from the beachhead at Salerno and the ammunition give out. Guess nobody told him to stop that cuttin' once the armistice was signed.

(*Goes back to writing and reading*)

"Things here in the DTC are tolerable, three squares a day, they don't work us too hard . . ."

SGT. WHITESIDE

Mr. Pound . . .

EZRA

(*Hastily finishing letter*)

Take this to Ed Page in Cell 19, tell him to put his mark on it, there.

SGT. WHITESIDE

Your orders have come through. They're flying you out tonight.

EZRA

(*Jumping up*)

To Washington?

SGT. WHITESIDE

Yes. To stand trial.

EZRA

(*Ignoring this*)

Across the ocean! My first time! Flying, Whiteside. Do you know what that means? Icarus when his wings were first put on his shoulders, soaring, before the wax began to melt . . .

SGT. WHITESIDE

You've been charged, Mr. Pound. Nineteen counts. Treason.

(*Tries to show the document to* EZRA)

EZRA

The bullet has yet to be made that will kill me.

Lights crossfade to SGT. WHITESIDE)

SGT. WHITESIDE

(Reading from the official report)

"Mr. Pound accepted employment from the Kingdom of Italy in the capacity of a radio propagandist, broadcasting over shortwave radio audible in the United States in order to provide aid and counsel to the Kingdom of Italy. These activities were intended to persuade citizens and residents of the United States to decline to support the United States in the conduct of the War, to weaken or destroy confidence in the Government of the United States and to increase the morale of the subjects of the Kingdom of Italy."

BLACKOUT

SCENE 9

Setting: A room in Howard Hall for the Criminally Insane, St. Elizabeths Hospital, Washington, DC.

February 1946

(The small room is simply furnished: a bed, table, lamp, closet, window with drawn curtain. It is late afternoon. From time to time, shrieks and moans are heard from the hall. EZRA lies on the bed, propped up on a pillow. He is dressed in baggy pants, shirt, sweater, bare feet. He is holding notes. DR. OVERHOLSER, in white coat, sits in a chair at the foot of the bed.)

EZRA *(Reading)*

"I obtained the concession to broadcast over Rome Radio with the following proviso. Namely that nothing would be asked of me contrary to my conscience or contrary to my duties as an American citizen."

DR. OVERHOLSER

Mr. Pound . . .

EZRA

"These conditions were adhered to . . . I believe in the free expression of opinion for those qualified to have an opinion."

DR. OVERHOLSER

Mr. Pound . . .

EZRA

(*Holding up a hand to stop him*)

"I have not spoken in regard to war, but in protest against a system which creates one war after another. I have not spoken to the troops and have not suggested that the troops should mutiny or revolt."

DR. OVERHOLSER

Mr. Pound—I must insist. Your letter of explanation to the attorney general is for your lawyer, not for me. What I need to know is: Do you understand that you are under indictment for treason?

EZRA

Nineteen counts.

DR. OVERHOLSER

It is my responsibility, as the psychiatrist in charge of your case, to make the determination as to whether or not you are competent to stand trial.

EZRA

Very difficult for me to concentrate.

DR. OVERHOLSER

And yet you are still a noted poet, editor, translator—and continuing your work, by the look of things.

EZRA

I broke my head. I'm all right when I'm rested, but when I'm not rested it goes beat, beat, beat in the back of my neck.

(*He gestures.*)

DR. OVERHOLSER

(*Making a note*)

What goes beat, beat, beat?

EZRA

I told them in Pisa the main spring had busted.

DR. OVERHOLSER

What do you mean by "the main spring"?

EZRA

At the vortex of my skull.

DR. OVERHOLSER

The report from the psychiatrist at Pisa is that you are mentally fit and fully aware of your actions and their consequences.

EZRA

(*He puts his hand to his head, dramatically.*)

Memory gaps. Exhausted.

(*He rolls off the bed and lies on the floor.*)

DR. OVERHOLSER

Mr . Pound, I can't interview you on the floor.

EZRA

Can't get flat enough.

(DR. OVERHOLSER *leans forward in order to hear him better, continues to take notes.*)

DR. OVERHOLSER

You will have to get up.

EZRA

(EZRA *doesn't move.*)

Can't . . . can't . . .

DR. OVERHOLSER

Let me ask you—in your opinion—do you think you're insane?

EZRA

(*Propping himself up on his elbow*)

No, in my opinion I don't think I'm insane—but I'm shot to pieces—would take me years, now, to write a sensible piece of prose. I am absolutely unfit to conduct any . . . business.

DR. OVERHOLSER

But I understand you mean to assist in your own defense?

EZRA

I wanted to represent myself, but the females prevented it . . .

DR. OVERHOLSER

Do you understand what the consequences could be if the trial is allowed to go forward?

EZRA

Two witnesses—two witnesses to an act before it can be called treason. Those radio technicians they flew in from Rome to testify against me don't even speak English! They have no idea what I said in those broadcasts.

(*Suddenly collapsing, hands to head*)

My mistake was to go on after Pearl Harbor.

DR. OVERHOLSER

(*Pausing in note-taking*)

What did you say?

EZRA

I can't work here, can't sleep. Terrible pain in my head.

(*He begins to groan.*)

DR. OVERHOLSER

When did this start?

EZRA

Fifty hours in the airplane, from Rome. They moved an ambassador and his wife so I could have a seat! I told him of at least forty instances I know of, proof positive, where the tax dollars of United States citizens were used to improve the position of Jews in Europe or America—four billion dollars, proof positive—diverted to the profit of individuals, most of them Jews.

DR. OVERHOLSER

What is your proof?

EZRA

Socrates opposed his own country when it was at war. I am being guided by an interior light, my ideas are above warring factions. Are you a Jew?

DR. OVERHOLSER

No.

EZRA

Are you sure?

DR. OVERHOLSER

Yes.

EZRA

Don't start a pogrom. The problem, the Jewish problem, is not insoluble. Don't start a pogrom! Sell 'em Australia . . . don't give 'em a national country if they'll buy it.

(*Assuming his Shylock accent*)

"Of course, you'll have to bargain with them, make them think they're getting it at cut rates, offer them long-term credit. . . ."

(*Returning to his normal voice*)

This country is overpopulated. I mean, especially after the war, with the loss of tonnage and the loss of your markets, you will have to thin out the population. Sell 'em Australia!

DR. OVERHOLSER

You're not insane. You're just another fascist anti-Semite . . .

EZRA

(*Leaping up*)

I am the Defender of the Constitution! You think that snotty barbarian, ignorant of T'ang history . . .

(*Breaks off*)

DR. OVERHOLSER

Who in the world do you mean?

EZRA

Why, Stinky Roosenfelt. I came back here to Washington in '39 to advise him.

DR. OVERHOLSER

The president?

EZRA

Don't shoot him, don't shoot him, don't shoot the president. Assassins deserve worse, but don't shoot him. Diagnose him, diagnose him. It is your bound duty as an American citizen.

DR. OVERHOLSER

President Roosevelt died in April, Mr. Pound.

EZRA

If some man has a stroke of genius and could start a pogrom at the top . . .

DR. OVERHOLSER

Have you been following the Nuremberg trials?
(EZRA *mutters something, lies down on the floor.*)

EZRA

Benito never enforced those laws.

DR. OVERHOLSER

But after his defeat—

EZRA

Hung up by the heels in Milano, with La Clara. Christ was crucified once, Benito twice.
(*Quickly*)
The Jew is a savage.

DR. OVERHOLSER

From the Venice ghetto alone, thousands to the crematoriums. How could you not have known?

EZRA

I was in Rapallo. No Jews in Rapallo.

(*Rapidly changing the subject*)

I never told American soldiers to revolt.

DR. OVERHOLSER

Is it possible that you are prepared to plead . . .

EZRA

Innocent! Innocent! Innocent!

(*Pause*)

I do not believe the simple fact of speaking over the radio can in itself constitute treason. I think that must depend on what is said, and on the motives for speaking.

DR. OVERHOLSER

Quisling in Norway, Lord Haw-Haw in England, Tokyo Rose in America—they've been shown no mercy. Quisling and Haw-Haw—an American, by the way—will hang. Tokyo Rose goes to prison.

EZRA

A country is judged by how it treats its poets. And its critics.

DR. OVERHOLSER

And its traitors.

EZRA (*Shouting*)

Two witnesses! Two witnesses to an act before it can be called treason!

DR. OVERHOLSER

Your lawyer will discuss that with you, Mr . Pound. I am here to formulate a diagnosis.

EZRA

Then my goose is cooked.

DR. OVERHOLSER

You and I understand, I believe, that between the fully normal and the grossly abnormal lies a no-man's-land of deviations. There is no logic in the assumption that a man is either "sane" or "insane." Do you follow me? I have spent the last five years writing on the difference between genius, like that of a poet, and insanity, like that of a Mussolini. I've found that the individual with special gifts is always abnormal, but that is quite different from saying he is psychotic or mentally deranged . . .

EZRA

It's all one, in the world's eyes—genius, insanity.

DR. OVERHOLSER

Some appear to know the difference. We've been receiving a good deal of mail on your behalf.
(*He pulls letters from his pocket;* EZRA *eagerly examines them.*)
"I never thought Ezra was insane unless a ludicrous egotism qualifies. His lawyer should try the case on the freedom of speech issue."

EZRA

Good old Archie MacLeish!

DR. OVERHOLSER

You know his "Ars Poetica"?

EZRA (*Disparagingly*)

Waall . . .

DR. OVERHOLSER

"A poem should be equal to:

Not true."

EZRA

(*Looking at another letter*)

Bill Williams.

(*Reading*)

"I have made up my mind to defend him if I am ever called as a witness in his trial."

(*He leaps up, cavorts with pleasure.*)

DR. OVERHOLSER

(*Recalling him*)

Here's one from Robert Frost. Wasn't he nominated for the Pulitzer?

EZRA (*Offended*)

How would I know? I don't keep up with that kind of thing.

(*He takes the letter, starts to read.*)

EZRA

"As you know better than I, nations are judged in the perspective of history by the way they treat their poets, philosophers, artists, and teachers."

I helped him get his first book published—he was a country boy, lost in London.

DR. OVERHOLSER

"Two roads diverged in a yellow wood, and I—
I took the one less traveled by . . ."

EZRA (*Impatient*)

Yes, yes. Anything from Old Possum?

DR. OVERHOLSER
(*Not understanding*)

Excuse me?

EZRA

Eliot! T. S. Eliot!

DR. OVERHOLSER

I think so . . .

EZRA

(EZRA *grabs the letter, examines the signature. He reads
from the letter.*)

"A man does not have to agree with Pound to acknowledge the excellence of what he has written."

I always knew I should have gone to Harvard.

(DR. OVERHOLSER *laughs.*)

EZRA

There's something I've been meaning to ask. By any chance is Willis A. Overholser a relative?

DR. OVERHOLSER

A distant one . . .

EZRA

His book is brilliant! I've read it three times—absolutely brilliant THAT Overholser understood the need for monetary reform. Each unit of currency must represent a unit of labor—the end of inflation, manipulation. Mussolini understood that—he understood everything—"*Multo divertimenti*," he said when he'd read my Cantos.

DR. OVERHOLSER

This may interest you, Mr. Pound—your friend the Duce's brain was sent here to St. Elizabeths to be studied after the war—I was the doctor in charge. The government was hoping to prove a physical reason for Mussolini's actions. But in fact, I've just published a paper on the absence of structural defects in Mussolini's brain.

EZRA

Brilliant mind—hanged by the heels at Milano. Have you read my *Jefferson and/or Mussolini* ?

DR. OVERHOLSER

Well, I can't say that I . . .

EZRA

(Scrabbles through papers, muttering to himself, finds a small book, begins to read)

"If you are hunting up bonds of sympathy between Jefferson and the Duce, put it first that they both hate the idea of cooping up men and making 'em into UNITS, unit production, denting in the individual man, reducing him to a mere amalgam . . ."

I assume you spell your name as he does—with an S not a Z. *(He inscribes the book, hands it with a flourish to DR. OVERHOLSER.)*

DR. OVERHOLSER
(Accepting the book)

Thank you.

(DR. OVERHOLSER then reads from the notes he has been writing during the conference.)

"At the present time Pound exhibits extremely poor judgment as to the seriousness of his situation. He insists that his broadcasts were not treasonable because he was 'saving the Constitution.' He is abnormally grandiose, expansive and exuberant in manner. He is now suffering from a paranoid state which renders him mentally unfit to advise with counsel or to participate intelligently and reasonably in his own defense. He is, in a clinical sense, insane."

Welcome to your new home, Mr. Pound.

(Exits)

EZRA
(In spotlight)

Possum said the world would end not with a bang but with a whimper. I said, "With a bang. . . ." I lost my nerve.

(As lights fade, we see images indicating a passage of nine

TREASON

years to 1955. DR. OVERHOLSER *appears, giving his court testimony in an early release hearing.*)

DR. OVERHOLSER

If called to testify at a hearing in respect to dismissal of the pending criminal indictment against Ezra Pound, I will testify and state under oath that Ezra Pound is, and since December 4, 1945, has continuously been, insane and mentally unfit for trial. There is no likelihood, and in my considered opinion no possibility, that the indictment against Ezra Pound can ever be tried.

CURTAIN

SCENE 10

Setting: EZRA's room, St. Elizabeths Hospital
for the Criminally Insane.

(*The small room is jammed with papers, books, clippings, food remnants, etc.* SHERI's *paintings hang on the wall.* EZRA *is thinner, older; his beard and hair have turned white.* DOROTHY, *older but still elegant, sits in a chair, working on her needlepoint.*)

EZRA (*Pacing*)

Had to wait till nine a.m. this morning for them to unlock me—thought my bladder would bust! And then, for breakfast, cornflakes! Ten solid years of cornflakes!

DOROTHY

Try to be grateful, Mao. Remember the alternative.

EZRA

They'll never let me out of here now. YOU prevented it, in 1948.

DOROTHY

I stopped the habeus corpus appeal because I feared for your life if you were released. America was too dangerous for you then, Mao.

EZRA

Instead ten years in St. Liz with the real crazies!

DOROTHY

You've transformed this room, Mao—the atmosphere reminds me of a London drawing room, circa 1910.

EZRA

A little lacking in the amenities!

DOROTHY

Oh well, of course! No brocade curtains, no mahogany highboys, crumpets with butter and strawberry jam, silver tea service! And no little velvet jacket for you to wear when you read one of your new poems to the admiring throng.

(*She quotes complaisantly.*)

  "Like a skein of loose silk blown against a wall

  She walks by the railing of a path in Kensington Gardens . . ."

    I always rather thought that referred to me.

EZRA

You've forgotten the rest of it.

(*Quoting*)

"And she is dying piece-meal .
of a sort of emotional anemia."

DOROTHY

My parents were keeping us apart—you had no money.

EZRA

(*Continuing to quote*)

"In her is the end of breeding.
Her boredom is exquisite and excessive.
She would like some one to speak to her
And is almost afraid that I
will commit that indiscretion."

DOROTHY

You never lacked for impertinence, Mao.

EZRA

Essential weapon for a poet!

DOROTHY

I'm working on a new poem.
(*No response. She takes out a paper.* EZRA *shows no interest.*
She reads.)

"Because of your manhood
I am enriched with
'happiness forever & ever'
So, there be peace between us
And a new serenity."

(*No response*)

At least now I always know where you're sleeping.

EZRA

Waall now . . .

DOROTHY

(*Taking chocolates out of her purse*)

I brought you some of those chocolates you adore.

(*As* EZRA *takes them and bites one*)

Don't spoil your lunch—the hospital generally serves something
fairly decent on Thursdays.

EZRA

Tuna fish—canned!

(*Eating chocolates*)

Sheri Martinelli's coming over later, she'll bring me lunch. I've got
her started reading Greek—in translation, of course.

DOROTHY

I've told Dr. Overholser she can take you out to the lawn, next
week when I'm away.

EZRA

I'll hold classes under the trees. Best students, best shade and grass,
best TEAS! I hear some bigwigs are trying to get me sprung.

DOROTHY

I know.

EZRA

Don't let 'em. They feed me, here, no expenses, first time in my
life no money worries, I've started writing, again—

DOROTHY

After seven years—inspiration, as in the old days.

EZRA

From under the rubble . . . you're in charge of me, now, Dorothy—
you're my "Committee." Stop them from trying to get me out.

DOROTHY

Mr. MacLeish and Mr. Frost haven't exactly asked my permission.

EZRA

Waall, I'm not going—I'm going to come out of here only with
flying colors and a personal apology from the president!
(*Enter* SHERI. *She is dressed in bobby sox, a gingham
blouse, blue jeans, saddle shoes and socks. Her hair is dyed
a brilliant red.*)

DOROTHY (*Appreciatively*)

Here comes family! Good morning, Sheri.

EZRA

La Martinelli! Undine!
(*He embraces her, runs his hands through her hair.*)
What's this? Another transformation?

SHERI

You placed your hand on my head yesterday, and when Ezra Pound
puts his hand on one's hair it turns crimson.

DOROTHY

Very becoming!

EZRA

A laying on of hands! I believe your eyes have changed color, too.
(*He looks at her eyes.*)
Pervenche—violet blue . . .

SHERI

My eyes are periwinkle . . .

DOROTHY

"Pervenche" means periwinkle.

EZRA

I wrote the first section of a new Canto last night.
(*Reciting*)
"That the body of light come forth
From the Body of Fire
And that your eyes come to the surface
From the deep where they were sunken
APHRODITE!—"
Moved, as I haven't been moved . . .

SHERI

By your spirit of Love.

DOROTHY

So it would seem.

EZRA

(*Grabbing papers from the typewriter*)
"Sibylla,
from under the rock heap
m'elevasti—you lift me up,
from the dulled edge beyond pain,
m'elevasti . . ."

SHERI (*Coy*)

Who is your Sibylla, Grandpaw?

EZRA

Pythoness, Seer. Did you quit that job at the waffle shop?
(*He seats himself again on the bed.* SHERI *perches beside him.*)

SHERI

Yes, but now I don't know how—

EZRA

You must devote yourself to your painting. Don't worry about your rent—we'll take care of that.

DOROTHY

He used to say to me, "Stop wasting your energies on needlepoint, save everything for your watercolors."

SHERI

I'm really just an amateur . . .

DOROTHY

The true artist is always an amateur.

SHERI

Well then, this amateur is going to start on your portrait today,
Dorothy.
(*She takes out sketch pad, begins to work.*)
You're the color of a peach blossom.

DOROTHY

Now, now—
(*She tidies herself, begins to pose, obviously pleased.*)

EZRA

"Thus Undine came to the rock."
(SHERI *looks at him.*)
Water spirit. Unstable as the element itself. You are currents, tor-
rents, dangers. But once you are on your rock—ah, then the waters
are stilled.
"And if I see her not,
no sight is worth the beauty of my thought."
Will you draw me, too?

SHERI

I made you a drawing last night.
(*She takes a drawing out of her bag.* EZRA *examines it eagerly.*)
Look, Dorothy.

(*She shows it to* DOROTHY.)

I'm the sibyl, just like his poem, with a python in my hand.

DOROTHY

I'll take that—for my yellow wall.

(*She takes out checkbook, writes a check, hands it to* SHERI,
and takes the drawing, so that EZRA *cannot have it.*)

I expect this will be sufficient.

SHERI

(*Pocketing check*)

Thanks! I signed the lease for my apartment yesterday. It's only two blocks from here—your neighborhood, Dorothy.

DOROTHY

(*Folding up needlepoint, with irony*)

How lovely. Well, I must get started.

(*She kisses* EZRA.)

EZRA

You'll be back in the morning?

DOROTHY

First thing. Goodbye, Sheri.

(*They kiss.*)

Oh, by the way—would you care to accompany me to the garden party at the British Embassy on Saturday?

SHERI

I'd love to!

DOROTHY

It means, of course, a dress. Your hair will be quite the sensation.

(DOROTHY *exits.*)

SHERI

(*Kissing* EZRA)

I went to the cathedral yesterday afternoon, kneeled down, lit a candle, vowed never to leave you till you're free.

EZRA

No trial, 'cause I'm nuts. If I'm not nuts, a trial. Looks like I'll be here a while longer.

SHERI

(*Caressing him*)

And you don't really mind it here.

EZRA

Three squares a day, no expenses—and you and the other *jeunes* keep me supplied with delicacies.

SHERI (*Hurt*)

Me and the other jeunes?

EZRA

Well, what do you call them?

SHERI

They're just your disciples. I'm your muse.

EZRA

Whatever they are, they bring me treats. What have you got for
me today?

SHERI

(*Opening another bag*)

Oysters—in a can, I'm sorry. The fresh ones wouldn't keep.
Caviar—just this little pot, enough for the two of us. You'll have
to hide it when the disciples come. Some of that special blackberry jam you like on your toast in the morning.

(EZRA *is greedily examining each item.*)

I wanted to cook you an artichoke, but I couldn't find a single one—

EZRA

Try harder. Artichokes are Greece—the Greece of Helen, of H.D.
Of course, she had to insist Helen was in Egypt, not Troy—H.D.
always went her own way.

SHERI (*Hopefully*)

Was Undine Greek?

EZRA

From another tradition.

(*He begins to shuffle through papers, finds it, reads.*)

"Thus Undine came to the rock,

by Circeo

and the stone eyes again looking seaward . . ."

I'd restore that statue of Aphrodite in Circeo, if I had the means.
Dorothy controls all that—my "Committee." I can't even sign
a check.

SHERI (*Meaningfully*)

I know.

EZRA

Dorothy means well. She told Overholser to leave you in charge when she goes away next week.

SHERI

I'll take you out on the lawn, we'll sit under the trees . . . she never minds, does she?

EZRA

She believes in "The Objective," you see—always takes comfort in that.

SHERI

What do you mean, "The Objective"?

EZRA

An old theory of mine comes in handy . . . reality is a dream—that kind of thing. Only souls count, and only souls connect. Dorothy's a beautiful painting that never came to life. No light from Eleusis there, no divine rites—

SHERI

(*Trying to be fair*)

But you had a son—

EZRA

That was simply propagation.

SHERI (*Boldly*)

What about Olga, then? She had your daughter. Was that simply propagation, too?

EZRA

Mary was Olga's idea. She wanted it. I told her, "If you have it, it will be yours—yours, entirely."

"*Pensar di lieis m'es ripaus.*"

SHERI

I hate it when you talk those old languages.

EZRA

"Thinking of her is my repose." Olga understands the medieval sanity I found in Provence. From Arnaut. Dorothy, Olga, and me— we all lived together in Rapallo:

"If love be not in the house, there is nothing."

SHERI (*Hurt*)

You didn't tell me.

EZRA (*Placating*)

Everything was rationed, we had to pool our resources.

SHERI

I thought Olga was always up the hill, in Sant' . . .

EZRA

. . . Ambrogio. Olga and I share a passion for music; she was an up-and-coming young violinist when I met her in Paris. Together we rediscovered Vivaldi. True poetry is much closer to the best of music than to any other form of literature.

SHERI

I don't know anything about music, Grandpaw.

EZRA

That would ordinarily be a difficulty, but in your case—well, there are . . . compensations. You are my Painter of Paradise.

SHERI

And you are my Holy Man—I've searched for you all my life . . .
(*Caresses him*)

EZRA

Your work is finer than anything since the sixteenth century.

SHERI

We were going to talk about my adoption today.

EZRA

Let me be specific: finer than anything since 1527.

SHERI

If you adopt me, Dr. Overholser will let me take you into town.

EZRA

(*Rustling through tins*)

Have a cookie.

SHERI

(*Accepting cookie, laying it aside*)
You called me your daughter yesterday.

EZRA

You are my daughter, in spirit. Making it legal is meaningless.

SHERI

Not to me. One of your jeunes said to me on my way out, "I guess now you're Ezra's pound cake."

EZRA

(*Clearly pleased*)
One must make allowances for the vulgar mind.
(*Sly*)
I got your little note.

SHERI

Did you like it?

EZRA

(*Digging note with photo out from its hiding place; this is purposeful; he knows just where it is.*)
Very flattering, your bikini . . . but I can't translate your message.

SHERI

Oh, Grandpaw—you can translate anything!
(*She points out the letters on the note.*)
"F U Will Be My Valentine I Will Be Yr Kon Que Byne."

EZRA (*Flattered*)

I thought you wanted to be my daughter.

(*Kissing her*)

As Odysseus said to Circe, "Your bikini is worth my raft."

(*Enter* OLGA. *She stands staring at* SHERI. OLGA *is wearing a summer dress and carrying a matching parasol.* EZRA *looks up at her with a sheepish smile.* OLGA *snaps her parasol closed and lifts it over* SHERI*'s head.*)

EZRA

Hello, Olga.

SHERI

(*Confused by the new arrival*)

Grandpaw ?

OLGA

(OLGA *and* EZRA *kiss.*)

You've lost weight. And your hair's all white.

EZRA

So, you finally up and traipsed yourself across the ocean.

OLGA

(*Referring to* SHERI)

Why didn't Dorothy warn me?

SHERI

(*Gathering her things*)

I'm leaving.

EZRA

(*To* OLGA)

Let me get you something to eat, Lynx.

(*He bustles around, assembling scraps of food in various tins.
Offers* OLGA *the caviar.*)

SHERI

(*At the door*)

Not the caviar!

(*No response.* EZRA *serves* OLGA *caviar on a piece of bread.*)

Goodbye, Grandpaw. I'll see you tomorrow.

(*She exits, loud noises from the hall.*)

OLGA (*Furious*)

WHO IS SHE?

EZRA

A friend. A . . . disciple. A painter—

OLGA

Dorothy promised me there would be no one here!

EZRA

Waall . . . she took herself off . . . didn't say you was coming . . .
not today anyway . . .

OLGA

Falsehoods and subterfuges! It's been so long, *mi amore*, you don't
even answer my letters, and then to find—

EZRA

Please, Olga. No "argymints"!

OLGA

Confusion, mess, lies! The usual.

EZRA

When a man's down a well, you don't jump in on top of him!

OLGA

Seven years since we've seen each other!
(*Pause*)

Do you ever miss me?

EZRA

Yes, Ma'am. I want you back . . .
(*He tries to embrace her. She pushes him away.*)

OLGA

WHO IS THAT GIRL?

EZRA

Why, just Sheri—Sheri Martinelli.

OLGA

That girl I've been reading about in the newspapers . . .

EZRA

She's one of my students, brings me treats. She's very talented—

OLGA

Enough! Not another word!

EZRA

Spare me, Olga!

OLGA

No self-pity—we've never traded in that. You used to tell me, when I was wretched, to look inside for the cause—

EZRA

In here for twelve years—

OLGA

Do you think I was living high on the hog, in Sant'Ambrogio?

EZRA

You were free!

OLGA

Free—to struggle! Free—to worry!

EZRA

You're looking . . . fine, Lynx.

(*He pats her.*)

OLGA (*Softening*)

You're leonine, still!

(*She kisses him.*)

Do you remember, at the beginning, in Paris—I started keeping a journal—

(*She brings it out of her bag.*)

EZRA

Didn't you bring your violin?

OLGA

I'm not a traveling circus!

EZRA

Antheil said, after you played his concert: "I'll never find another fiddler like Olga, but she's getting careless."

OLGA

When do I have time to myself, to practice?

(*Looking at journal*)

Today is my fifty-seventh birthday . . .

EZRA

(*Presenting her with an olive from his collection of food.*)

'Gratulations, Miss, I'm sure . . .

(*As she kisses him*)

OLGA

I was hoping, somehow, to add more...?

EZRA

Not much privacy here.

OLGA

(*Turning pages of journal*)

I recorded each time we . . . your birthdays, our first Vivaldi concert, the evening we finished playing all the Mozart violin sonatas, the night after you first sung me your Villon opera—see, I've marked an *x* for each . . . sometimes two . . .

EZRA

Copulation and poetry flow from the same source. Not much of either left now.

(OLGA *intensifies the embrace,* EZRA *pulls away.*)

What have you been doing in Washington? Did you see your aunt?

OLGA

Still asking me why I never married! I told her I am married—in the eyes of God!

EZRA

How's Rapallo—much changed?

OLGA

The Café Yolanda is going in for ices, and Dante—our waiter—has a new white coat. Of course I don't have time to go lollygagging there. I've been working night and day to get you out. Gli Amici di Ezra Pound—we have almost three hundred signatures.

EZRA

Dorothy's agin it. Afraid they'll still have a trial if I get out—finally do it this time—

(*Garroting gesture*)

OLGA

(*Ignoring this*)

Your old friends haven't forgotten you. But you're not making it easier with the disreputable characters you let visit you here.

EZRA

Please—they amuse me.

OLGA

(*Pulling out newspaper*)

Even this John Kasper? You've seen the article in the *Herald Tribune*?

EZRA

You know how the Jew press pillories—

OLGA

(*Showing him the headline*)

"SEGREGATIONIST KASPER IS EZRA POUND DISCIPLE."

How can you, Caro?

EZRA

Well, at least he's a man of action, and don't sit around looking at his navel.

(*He leans back in his chair, closes his eyes. After a moment of watching him,* OLGA *seems to relent.*)

OLGA

All these years, waiting for a word from you, and almost nothing came.

(EZRA *gestures.*)

Oh yes, a letter every now and then, and once you sent me gladioli—when I saw the boy carrying them along the Zattere, I thought, "They can't be for me."

(*Furiously*)

WHAT IS SHE WAITING ALL HER LIFE FOR—NOW REACHING THE LAST DROP . . .

EZRA

(*Indicating Olga*)

The victim is always culpable.

OLGA

Knowing Dorothy was here with you, legally in charge, seeing you night and day!

EZRA

I did hope you'd bring your violin. No musick in the nuthouse, just the TV ravin' in the hall.

OLGA (*Ominously*)

You've forgotten the first evening the three of us spent together . . .

EZRA

(*His baby voice*)

She to have mercy, now.

OLGA (*Relentless*)

The afternoon you and Dorothy moved up to my apartment at Sant'Ambrogio—dragging God knows how much stuff! I was trying to be tactful. I went to my room early to leave you two alone, picked up my violin, played the Mozart Concerto in A Minor as well as I've ever done. Dorothy said NOTHING to me about it, good, bad, or indifferent, spoke to me later as she might have to a housekeeper. I never played—or was asked to play—again.

EZRA

Last time I heard music at Sant'Ambrogio.

OLGA

After that you two sat in the dark every evening, listening to the news on the BBC, while I tried to put together something to eat.

EZRA (*Faintly*)

"Some cook, some do not. . . ."

OLGA

All the cooking, the shopping, the cleaning, and she never thanked me, just told everybody, "We're spending a while up at Olga's house." Oh, we were civilized!

EZRA

(*Pottering around*)

Little Jimmy Laughlin, my American publisher, just sent me a fresh pineapple.

(*He cuts her a slice.*)

He wants to see my new Cantos, publish them in New Directions. More like No Directions.

OLGA

(*Refusing pineapple*)

You can work here, you can get on with it. But when do you think I have a moment, between your daughter's unsuitable alliance with her make-believe prince, and my twenty-four hours a day running the Siena Accademia? It's been hand to mouth since the start of the war—hand to mouth! I've guarded your things in Sant'Ambrogio—but I intend to let that place go, now! I've scraped together enough to buy a little place in Venice—start over! I'm fifty-seven . . . it's not too late. Great musicians go on and on . . .

(*She runs down.*)

EZRA

You fritter away your time.

OLGA

The war stopped me. Dorothy made use of me to the fullest, commandeered my house while I worked like a slave—just so you wouldn't suffer! I cannot understand to this day her terrible meanness—always in terror lest I have some advantage over her—her, with all the income, her child taken care of, I with no rights of any kind, high and dry in a country I never would have chosen except to be near you—

EZRA

You'd have preferred to spend your life in Youngstown, Ohio?

(*Pause*)

OLGA

No.

EZRA

Any funds coming in from your parking lot?

OLGA

I can't get at them since the war.

EZRA

Too bad you always have to pinch so hard.

OLGA (*Flaring*)

I never took money from you, except once, for Mary's schooling, and now Dorothy's been showering me with thousand-lire notes . . .

EZRA

I told her to pay your rent, long as you was in Sant'Ambrogio.
(*A pause. Again,* OLGA *relents.*)

OLGA

(*Opening purse, taking out papers*)

I'm moving to Venice as soon as I get back to Italy—you'll always be welcome there. And I've been putting together a group of your broadcasts, for publication—edited, of course.
(*Shows him the manuscript*)
I'm calling it "If This Be Treason . . ."

EZRA

Tom Eliot's against it, and my lawyer. Says it'll stir up trouble.

OLGA

I thought if people read what you actually said—

EZRA

Best forget it, for now.

(OLGA *starts to protest* . . .)

I was PAID, Olga. That's the only thing they care about. PAID—by a gov'ment the blamed-dad US of A was a-fighting. . . . Don't give a fig-nut I had to put food on the table for three people.

OLGA

Twelve years! People forget.

EZRA

MacLeish, Eliot—they're raking the prizes in.

OLGA

When all this business is over and forgotten, your Cantos will be remembered. Not Eliot. Not Frost.

EZRA

You believe that?

OLGA

You'll be the one studied at Harvard!

EZRA

"Said Mr. Adams, of education
Teach? At Harvard?
Teach? It cannot be done."

OLGA

I've staked my life on it!

EZRA

Mebbe you wuz a fool.

(*As she is absorbing this*)

How long you plan on staying?

OLGA

Three visits, two hours each—that's all your Dr. Overholser granted me! Because I'm not "kin."

EZRA

Waall . . . you ain't.

OLGA (*Deadly*)

That girl is not kin.

EZRA

Overholser makes an exception for my students. I call it the Ez-uversity .

OLGA

(*Gathering up her things*)

If Dorothy had not told me a direct LIE in answer to a simple question, I would have been prepared for what I've found here! I won't be needing the other two visits. Goodbye, Ezra.

(*Turns to go*)

EZRA

Wait!

OLGA

I've waited too long.

EZRA

Please—Lynx—after all these years—

OLGA

Yes, Ezra. After all these years.

EZRA

I've missed you. I've missed Mary . . .

(*She turns to leave.*)

Send me your photo—please. A new one.

OLGA

Your memory will have to suffice.

EZRA

(*Reaching for her*)

Let those I love try to forgive what I have made.

OLGA

Bats in the belfry—as always.

EZRA

If love be not in the house, there is nothing.

OLGA

Yes. Nothing.

(OLGA *exits.* EZRA *sits down dejectedly.*)

EZRA

"Oh Lynx, my love, my lovely lynx . . ."

    (SHERI *enters, having overheard this. She goes to him. She*
rubs his neck and shoulders.)

SHERI

She doesn't carry her life on her fingernails.

    (*Shows him her paint-stained fingers*)

Each one a different color, because I'm a working painter!

    (EZRA *groans, turns away.*)

A fighter, like you, in the Ethical Arena where you know what's
really wrong because you did it all yourself!

EZRA

Yes, all of it—

SHERI

(*Embracing him*)

Artist! Maestro!

EZRA

So much for him who puts his trust in a woman.

    (SHERI *begins, slowly, to undress.* EZRA *slowly looks up*
at her.)

CURTAIN

Act II

SCENE 1

Setting: The same, EZRA's room, St. Elizabeths Hospital.
A few days later, 1958

DR. OVERHOLSER

(*Testimony, as though in court, over a miocrophone.*)
Ezra Pound is not a dangerous person and his release would not
endanger the safety of other persons, property, or other interests
of the United States.

(*Recording of* ELDER SOLOMON LIGHTFOOT MICHAUX
*in all his glory, in his Radio Church of God. We hear him
deliver the end of a sermon and go into one of his famous gospel numbers. Note on* EZRA*'s costume at St. Elizabeths: Tan
shorts too big for him, tennis shoes and a loose plaid shirt, or
a loose sweatshirt, an old GI overcoat, baggy trousers, heavy
white socks, bedroom slippers, long underwear showing in
his lower legs.*)

ELDER LIGHTFOOT MICHAUX
(*Shouting into the microphone*)
Pilgrims! There's going to be a meeting in the air, Pilgrims. With Saints from Everywhere! W! J! S! V! W for Willingly! J for Jesus! S for Suffered! V for Victory! Willingly Jesus Suffered for Victory! W! J! S! V! H - A - P - P - Y - A - M - I. Is everybody happy? The whole world is happy!
(*Begins singing*)
HAPPY AM I . . .

(*The room in St. Elizabeths is if possible more disordered: trampled books, torn newspapers, dead flowers, boxes of left-over food, discarded clothes.* EZRA *is doing yoga. His movements have become less energetic; he is showing his age. On the radio,* ELDER LIGHTFOOT MICHAUX *continues to sing.*

JOHN KASPER *enters, carrying books, papers, a dough-nut box, etc. He stands watching* EZRA, *who does not for a moment see him.*)

KASPER
Unpretzel yourself, Pops.

EZRA
Kasp!
(*He jumps up. A bear hug.*)

KASPER
What's this crap—?
(*He snaps off radio.*)

EZRA

Most famous colored man in America—him can TALK! And him
can SING!

KASPER

(KASPER *grimaces.*)

And him a nigger.

EZRA

What did you bring me?

KASPER

(*Opening box*)

Crullers—best in Greenwich Village.

EZRA (*Disappointed*)

Only two?

KASPER

I had my breakfast on the train.

EZRA

I wait hours for the gosh-darned bell to ring, meaning breakfast—
    (*As* EZRA *begins to devour the crullers,* KASPER *spreads out
    papers and books on the bed.*)

KASPER

I've found the best corner in the Village for the bookstore.

(EZRA *nods.*)

Put together the circular for the first of your Square Dollar books.

(*He begins to read from circular.*)

"Square Dollar is starting with American writers who can hold their own either as stylists or historians against any foreign competition whatsoever: "*The Chinese Written Character, A History of Monetary Crimes, Bank of the United States, Roman and Muslim Moneys*"—

EZRA (*Eating*)

Basic education at a price every student can afford: one square dollar. You hear from Marshall McLuhan?

KASPER

He's agreed to serve on the advisory committee for the bookstore, also Norman Holmes Pearson, from Yale—

EZRA

I don't hear none of the lingo I give you for that thar circular.

KASPER

Wait!

(*Reading from circular*)

"JAIL NAACP, alien, unclean, unchristian;

BLAST irreverent ungodly leaders."

EZRA

Good old Kasp! You sign the lease for the bookstore?

KASPER

Yes, five years—landlord insisted.

EZRA

(*Mouth full of crumbs*)

Yid?

KASPER

Name of Mordecai. You guess.

(*They laugh.* KASPER *brushes crumbs off* EZRA*'s chest.*)
You're one hell of a mess, Pops.

EZRA

What you aiming to call your place of business?

KASPER

(*Showing design for the bookstore sign*)

MAKE IT NEW.

(EZRA *crows.*)

You approve?

EZRA

My gospel! The critics—they thought I meant words—just words. I
was talking about THE WORLD! MAKE IT NEW! Had a chance,
too—before the First War killed . . .

(*He scrabbles through papers, brings out manifesto.* KASPER
waits tolerantly. EZRA *reads.*)

"MAKE IT NEW:

1. TO PAINT THE THING AS I SEE IT.

2. BEAUTY

3. FREEDOM FROM DIDACTICISM . . ."

SALLIE BINGHAM

KASPER

How about you write me something for the bookstore opening, a few words re how you feel right now, the political situation et al. . . . OK? I'll have it printed up big, hang it in the window—right there in the heart of Greenwich Village where the so-called intellectuals and stuck-up academics will have to read it . . . Ez's voice from the grave! From the nuthouse, anyway.

(*Hands* EZRA *paper*)

EZRA

(*Accepting paper, hesitating*)

Brain's wore out these days.

KASPER

Just write the way you talk, Pops! Put your heart in it! Don't hold back! Those fools in New York City need to hear the truth— YOUR truth!

(*Gives* EZRA *pen*)

Come on, Pops! MAKE IT NEW!

EZRA

Use my manifesto—

(*Hands* KASPER *an old, yellowed paper*)

KASPER

That won't do it, Pops! That was, when?

EZRA (*Stopping*)

1908. I wrote it for H.D., Hilda Doolittle of Pennsylvania as was—booming her first poems—I got her published, she never would have amounted to anything if I hadn't . . .

KASPER (*Interrupting*)

This ain't about poetry, Pops, this is about the Mission! Cleansing the Anglo-Saxon race of befouling elements—Nigs, Yids and the rest of the gutter trash. Write that, Pops! That'll light them up, all those Greenwich Village left-wing pinkos.

(*As* EZRA *still hesitates*)

You got some of your Rome broadcasts somewhere?

EZRA

Believe I do.

(*He begins to scrabble through papers,* KASPER *assisting.*)

What about this—

(*Reading*)

"FEAR GOD AND THE STUPIDITY OF THE POPULACE."

KASPER

Not exactly what I—

EZRA

It'll have to do, Kasper.

(*Signs paper with a flourish, hands it over.*)

What you aiming to serve at your vernissage?

KASPER

(*Taking the paper, clearly disappointed*)

Cheese and crackers.

EZRA

Waall . . . at Natalie Barney's salon in Paris it was foie gras and
champagne.

(*Looking through* KASPER*'s bags*)

You brung me anything else?

KASPER (*Brightening*)

Apples.

(*He brings out two.*)

EZRA

(*Taking one*)

Good to get the bowels a-moving, I guess.

(*They sit on the bed.* KASPER *takes out a pocketknife, begins
to peel an apple for* EZRA.)

KASPER

Great rally in Louisville last week—you saw the papers?

EZRA

I don't read the Jew press.

KASPER

Police claimed only five hundred in the crowd, my people counted
over a thousand. Right on the courthouse steps; police everywhere
but they couldn't stop them.

(*Hands* EZRA *apple slice*)

Tennessee's next—I'm starting a newspaper there: "The Clinton-Knox County Stars and Bars. A Nationalist-Attack Newspaper Serving East Tennessee."

EZRA (*Eating*)

You giving 'em hell?

KASPER

You know it! Told those folks in Louisville I had it on good authority some Nigs have tails.

EZRA
(*Laughing, mouth full of apple*)

They get it?

KASPER

You bet they got it! You're spraying me, Pops.

(*Wipes himself off*)

Supreme Court's trying to force them to bus the kids, integrate their schools. They don't want it, busted all the windows of that goddamned pinko rag they call a newspaper! Some of 'em went to jail. Speaking of jail . . .

(*Hands* EZRA *another apple slice*)

I hear they brought that girl of yours to trial.

EZRA

I don't want to talk about it.

KASPER

Well, the story is all over town—"Pound's student, drug charges"—
didn't you see it?

EZRA

I told you I don't read Hymie lies. Undercover cops PLANTED
that junk on her—trying to get at me!

KASPER

Don't fool yourself. She's got herself a habit, Pops. I know it. You
know it.

EZRA

(*Starts singing to drown out* KASPER)
"Gentle Jheezus sleek and wild
Found disciples tall an' hairy
Flirting with his red hot Mary
Now hot momma Magdalene
is doing front page fer the screen
Mit der yittischer Charleston Pband
Mit
deryiddischescharles
tonband."
(*Ignoring this*)
Got to write Possum. He sent word he didn't want me 'sociating
with your kind . . .
(*He is looking for letter paper.*)

KASPER

I've got to be going, catch the five o'clock back to the city. Got an important engagement.

(*He begins to pack up his things.*)

EZRA

You coming Sunday? Dorothy's planning on serving cucumber sandwiches. Very British.

KASPER

If I can get away. "HONOR—PRIDE—FIGHT: SAVE THE WHITE!"

EZRA

Bravo, Kasp!

(*Gives the fascist salute, which* KASPER *returns.* KASPER *exits. A pause.* EZRA *writes his letter, muttering to himself. Enter Marcella Spann, carrying briefcase. She hesitates near the door.*)

MARCELLA

Professor Pound?

EZRA

(*Looking up*)

Who's lookin' for him?

MARCELLA

(*Holding out her hand*)

Marcella Spann. I wrote for permission . . .

EZRA

What you want from the old man?

(*He approaches, shakes her hand, scrutinizes her.*)

MARCELLA

(*Taking papers out of her briefcase*)

I teach high school English. We're going to study Eliot's *The
Wasteland* next week. I was hoping perhaps you could—if it's not
too great an inconvenience—

EZRA

I midwifed that thing, performed a caesarean.

(*He looks at cover of book she is holding.*)

Old Possum's gotten downright distinguished-looking. Three-
piece suit! Scraggly and none too sweet-smelling, when I knew
him. Sit down.

(*He offers her the chair.*)

Are you planning to teach the *enfants* the whole thing? How old—?

MARCELLA

Eleventh graders. Most of them are sixteen. It's a small private day
school—they're quite amazingly literate. I was planning to start
with a few of Eliot's shorter works—

EZRA

Don't coddle them, jump right in with the big stuff.

(*Finding a page in the book, reading*)

"For Ezra Pound: *il miglior fabbro*."

You know the meaning of that?

MARCELLA (*Translating*)

"The better craftsman."

EZRA

Exacto! Possum brought me this gosh-darned mess of papers—
never seen anything like it—no shape to it, I told him, "This thing
is going to be stillborn."

MARCELLA

Stillborn? Whatever do you mean . . .

EZRA

Deformed in the womb! Went at it night and day, took out an
arm and a leg. Then I had to get the thing delivered—find him a
publisher, raise enough money for him to quit the bank—and he
turned the money down, hurt pride, some such nonsense. But I
got the poem published.

(*He begins to read from "The Burial of the Dead" from* The
Wasteland.)

EZRA

"Son of man,

You cannot say, or guess, for you know only

A heap of broken images, where the sun beats,

And the dead tree gives no shelter, the cricket no relief,

And the dry stone no sound of water. Only

There is a shadow under this red rock,
(Come in under the shadow of this red rock),
And I will show you something different from either
Your shadow at morning striding behind you
Or your shadow at evening rising to meet you;
I will show you fear in a handful of dust."

(*Pause*)

Too long getting to the end, I shoulda taken my hacksaw to them middle lines . . .

(*He begins to scratch out lines in the book.*)

MARCELLA

Oh, please—

(*She takes the book.*)

I have to teach from this. Now, if you would be willing to explain . . .

EZRA

Always at the service of a pretty gurl.

MARCELLA

(*Ignoring this*)

For example . . .

(*Consulting the book*)

What do you take to be the meaning of "the red rock"?

EZRA

Wrong way to go about it. When you start out to read a poem, you got to go about it like a biologist: slice to the heart of the writer's method, examine it under a microscope! Now, Possum uses two types of metaphor: his wholly unrealizable, always apt, half-ironic suggestion, and his precise realizable picture. Which of these two types of metaphor is "the red rock"?

MARCELLA

The precise realizable—

EZRA (*Excited*)

Perfecto! And that's only the start! Those three words convey a whole situation! It's his constant aliveness, his mingling of a very subtle observation with the unexpectedness of a backhanded cliché—the red rock; what's special about a red rock? Nothing. But you see, he's taking it, turning it, linking its shadow to another shadow—

MARCELLA

"Your shadow at evening rising to meet you."

EZRA

Yes, yes!

MARCELLA

But then he disconnects, jumps to this marvelous image:
"I will show you fear in a handful of dust."
(*Pause*)

EZRA

It's always dangerous to single out devices. A poet has to create his own metaphors, draw them from another source. Possum uses contemporary detail the way Velázquez—you know his work?

MARCELLA

Mr. Pound, I'd heard that you give quite a lecture, but I didn't realize you gave it to all your—callers. Is it possible, do you think, for us to have a conversation?

EZRA

Later, later—don't want to lose my train of thought, happens too easily these days! You remember the cold gray-green tones in Velázquez's painting *Las Meninas*?

MARCELLA

Gray-green, yes—I remember those tones—but cold? Isn't that in the eye of the beholder?

EZRA

Yes, yes of course—you're starting to get it now! Show the kids that painting! A reproduction, anyway. Make them SEE the connection.

MARCELLA

And when they complain about this "old stuff"—

EZRA

Tell 'em the one big truth! The supreme test of a book—any book—is this: we should feel some unusual intelligence working behind the words. Ask 'em if their comic books, their junk—whatever they're reading—ask if they find an unusual intelligence behind it.

MARCELLA

They're all about emotion, at that age.

EZRA

There's no intelligence without emotion. Next you're going to have
to educate them about vers libre—Eliot claims there's no vers libre
for a man who wants to do a good job. Close to the mark, but not
on the button!

(DOROTHY *enters, looks at* MARCELLA. MARCELLA *sees
her, stands up.* EZRA *is oblivious.*)

In fact Old Possum is one of the very few who have given a personal rhythm, an identifiable quality of sound to free verse. Music,
you know—that's the essential link. I HUM what I write . . .

(*He is looking through books.*)

Billy Yeats, now—he WROTE in that heavy Irish lilt, I'd hear him
at night—we shared a cottage in Sussex, years ago, Dorothy was
supposed to cook . . .

(*Reading from a book, exaggerated Irish accent*)
"Swear by what the sages spoke
Round the Mareotic Lake . . ."

Nothing to Jimmy Joyce, though—Yeats give me one of his first
poems, I got it here somewhere.

(*Finding book, reading, again, in an exaggerated Irish accent*)
"I hear an army charging . . ."

What we lost—who we lost—you ever think of it? In these wars . . .
for an old bitch gone in the teeth—a botched civilization.

MARCELLA

(*Going to* DOROTHY, *shaking hands*)
You must be Mrs. Pound.

DOROTHY

Who are you?

EZRA

Morning, Mao. This here young lady's a schoolteacher, trying to knock some sense about poetry into a bunch of blockheads.

MARCELLA

(*To* DOROTHY)

I've taken up enough of Professor Pound's time . . .

(*She begins to gather up her things.*)

EZRA

No, no—we're just beginning!

MARCELLA

I don't mean to intrude.

EZRA

No intrusion! This is the Ez-uversity. Dorothy always offers the students tea. Did you bring us anything special today, Mao—those chocolate cookies like you brought last week?

DOROTHY

(*Beginning to lay out tea things. This is an elaborate ritual:
porcelain cups, teapot, spirit lamp, strainer, etc.*)
Lemon wafers, this time.

MARCELLA

Mrs. Pound, really—

DOROTHY

Go on with the lesson.

(*As* MARCELLA *still hesitates*)

I'm used to it, my dear! In fact—if I may say so—you are a good deal more—appropriate—than some of Ezra's . . . students.

MARCELLA

Thank you.

(*She sits down.*)

EZRA

Now, as I was saying about Jimmy Joyce—

MARCELLA

I don't teach Joyce, Professor Pound. I'm afraid his work would cause a reaction. Among the parents, that is.

EZRA

Set the cat among the pigeons—the whole purpose of serious literature!

MARCELLA

Probably! But for me—there are certain constraints. . . . Now, if you would be kind enough to elucidate . . .

(*She looks through* The Wasteland.)

What exactly is the source of the German quotation?

EZRA

(*Snatching the book*)

It's from *Tristan and Isolde*—Possum always a great one for forun tongues—don't believe he can speak a one of them, though. . . .

Then we get to the heart of it:

    "'You gave me hyacinths first a year ago;
    They called me the hyacinth girl.'"
      (*He and* DOROTHY *exchange glances.*)

MARCELLA

And the hyacinth girl was . . . ? I don't want to be literal, but the girls are sure to ask.

EZRA

"She" was a "he"—Brit infantryman, killed in the First War. I made Old Possum cut out all the other smarmy stuff about him.

DOROTHY

Very wise, too.

EZRA

Keep close guard over the personal, it blurs things.

DOROTHY

A cup of tea, Miss—

MARCELLA

Spann. Marcella Spann. Thank you.
      (*Accepting cup*)

DOROTHY

A lemon wafer?

MARCELLA
(*Taking one*)
You're very kind.

(*To* EZRA)
But surely—the personal reference can shed some light.

EZRA
Wrong sort of light. A searchlight—not the fire flickering from Eleusis. Give it up, Marcella.

DOROTHY
Here's yours, Mao. Two lumps of sugar, two tablespoons of heavy cream.
(*Hands him teacup*)

EZRA
No chocolate cookies, though.
(*He sips tea. Noise of patients in the hall grows louder.*)

MARCELLA
It must be very difficult for you to concentrate on your work here . . .

DOROTHY
(*Before* EZRA *can respond*)
Dr. Overholser finally agrees there's no reason for you to continue to be confined here. There'll have to be a hearing, of course.

MARCELLA

After twelve years . . . what wonderful news.

DOROTHY

More than twelve years. The horror of it. My husband is one of
the great men of his time.

EZRA

Now Mao, don' you go mekking me blush.

DOROTHY

(*To* MARCELLA)

You seem an intelligent young woman. Perhaps you can understand. A situation such as this one, for the foremost poet in the
English language—

EZRA

(*Clearly pleased*)

Turn off the trumpets, Dorothy!

MARCELLA

I have felt from the beginning, Mrs. Pound, that this was a gross
miscarriage of justice. And your fortitude, standing by him all
these years . . .

DOROTHY

I'm Ezra's "Committee"—in charge of everything. The court
plans to make his release depend upon my role continuing—in
perpetuity.

(EZRA *groans.*)

Don't groan, Mao, it's for your own good; you always had your theories but when it came to the actual handling of money . . .

EZRA (*Determined*)

Mao . . .

(*Pause*)

MARCELLA

You must be delighted.

(DOROTHY *assents.*)

Will you return to Italy?

DOROTHY

I believe so. Yes. But there are certain hurdles to overcome, first—

EZRA

Prime one bein' I DON' WANNA GO!

(*To* MARCELLA)

Nowhere to lay my head, outside this place.

DOROTHY

Mary has always said she'll take you in at Brunnenburg . . . you'll see your grandchildren.

EZRA

(*To* DOROTHY)

You'd go to Brunnenburg, too?

DOROTHY

For a while, to get you settled.

(*Privately*)

But it won't be as it was in Rapallo.

EZRA

I ain't heard from Olga in—

DOROTHY

(*Quickly, to* MARCELLA)

Robert Frost went to see the president twice, asking for a pardon.

EZRA

No way to pardon a man ain't been tried and convicted.

DOROTHY

A release, rather—into my custody. Robert's worked hard for it.

EZRA

Took him long enough. Some of them first verses he wrote at the start warn't too arwful. But then he had to go to pontificating.

(*To* MARCELLA)

For your genuine, homegrown product, never or hardly ever left Amer'cun soil, I propose to you good old Dr. William Carlos Williams. Though I don't hear much from him anymore. He's one-seventeenth Yid, you know.

DOROTHY

Miss Spann, would you mind terribly . . . my husband and I have some private matters to discuss.

MARCELLA

(*Hastily gathering her things, then to* DOROTHY)

Thank you for the tea. Professor . . .

(*She shakes* EZRA*'s hand, avoids his kiss;* DOROTHY *is watching closely.*)

Goodbye, Mrs. Pound. I'll call again before you leave.

(MARCELLA *exits.*)

EZRA

Good head on her shoulders.

DOROTHY

So it appears. I've asked Dr. Overholser to pay you a visit, Mao.

EZRA

Good old Overholser! He saved my neck, twelve years ago when they wuz fixing to hang me—what's he got to say to me now?

DR. OVERHOLSER

(*Appears at the door, taps*)

I'm not interrupting?

DOROTHY

Not at all.

DR. OVERHOLSER

(*Going to* EZRA)

Good morning Ezra. How's that bladder infection?

DOROTHY

The new medication seems to be working.

EZRA

Old pisser just about dried up—no more piddling!
(*Cagey*)
I only see you on Sundays, Dr. O. This is Wednesday.

DR. OVERHOLSER

I wanted to give you the news myself. The court has decided to quash the indictment because you'll never be well enough to stand trial.

EZRA

I guess that means I'm still nuts!

DOROTHY

Only Olga believes that.

DR. OVERHOLSER

And as a result of this, the court is releasing you into your wife's custody.

EZRA

(*Turning sharply away*)
I can't leave here, Overholser. My work is here—my students.

DR. OVERHOLSER

I can give you two weeks to get your things together, say your goodbyes. If that will help.

DOROTHY

That's most kind of you.

DR. OVERHOLSER

I've started reading your Cantos, Mr. Pound—or it might be more accurate to say trying to read them. Perhaps one afternoon you could . . .

EZRA
(*Sitting on bed, head in hands*)

Old man he tired.

DOROTHY

You'll have a good rest at Brunnenburg. Mary has started to bring your papers and books from Rapallo. Even your mother's portrait! You'll have your own apartment, in the castle.

DR. OVERHOLSER
(*Privately, to* DOROTHY)

You've booked passage?

DOROTHY

Two weeks from now—the *Cristoforo Columbo*. First class.

DR. OVERHOLSER

Good.
(*He shakes hands with her.*)
Goodbye, Mrs. Pound. Of course, we'll confer before you leave.
(*He approaches* EZRA *to shake hands;* EZRA *hides his hands.*)

You have many good years ahead of you, Ezra—no need to spend them here.

(DR. OVERHOLSER *exits.*)

EZRA (*Childish*)

Don't pull me out of here, Mao.

DOROTHY

Now, Ezra—there's no use in a scene.

EZRA

First real home I've had.

DOROTHY

Not our little apartment in Church Walk? The white house in Paris with the pretty garden? The waterfront apartment in Rapallo—

EZRA

I always had to take charge, those places—feuds and misunderstandings!

DOROTHY

You won't have to take charge anymore, Mao, I promise you.
(*Taking out steamship tickets, showing them to him*)
Steamship tickets, first class . . .

EZRA

There'll be no one to help me, in Brunnenburg—Mary so busy with

290

the enfants. I'll need typing, for the new work—get the Cantos together, tidy everything up.

DOROTHY

What are you proposing?

EZRA

A secretary. To go with us. Not going to find anybody in Italia.

DOROTHY (*Firmly*)

Not Sheri.

EZRA

No, no. That girl who was just here. Smart enough, and probably looking for a way out of teaching.

DOROTHY

Miss Spann.

EZRA

Yes. Decent sort. Teachable.

DOROTHY

I'll think about it.

EZRA

Dr. Overholser's a good friend of mine, if I tell him I don't want to go—

DOROTHY

Remember, in '48 when I quashed your habeas corpus appeal? It wasn't the right time to go, then. Now, it is the right time. The furor has died down. And I want to go home.

(*A standoff. They stare at each other.*)

EZRA

Dorothy—that summer, in Sirmio—

DOROTHY

I haven't forgotten.

EZRA

"If, at Sirmio,
my soul I meet thee, when this life's outrun . . ."

DOROTHY

"One hour <u>was</u> sunlit."

That was forty years ago, Ezra.

(*She begins to gather up the tea things.* EZRA *watches her.*)

Goodbye, Mao.

(*Ritualistic kiss*)

I'll see you tomorrow.

(*She exits. For a moment,* EZRA *stands as though stunned, staring vacantly. Then he turns to his papers, begins rapidly sorting through them, making corrections, muttering to himself.* SHERI *enters.*)

SHERI

I passed Dorothy in the hall, she wouldn't speak to me.

EZRA

Things on her mind.

SHERI

They acquitted me, Grandpaw.

EZRA

So that's why you're here.

(*He is still looking through papers.*)

SHERI

And I brought you an artichoke.

(*Takes out of bag*)

Steamed! And hollandaise sauce—that was one bitch to make!

EZRA

Always vinaigrette, in France.

SHERI

You told me you prefer hollandaise.

(*Spreading out food*)

The jury took one look at me—I was dressed right, my nice gray suit, hat, gloves—knew right off the bat there wasn't a grain of truth in the police story.

EZRA

(*Finally turning to her*)

Let's see your arms, honey.

SHERI

Grandpaw, what in the world—

(*She tries to resist him.*)

EZRA

(*Taking hold of her firmly, rolling up her sleeves*)

Old Kasp was just here, made me face some facts I needed to face.
But I still need to see for myself.

(*Sees the needle tracks;* SHERI *tries to cover them.* EZRA, *disgusted, turns away.*)

SHERI

It takes me ages to heal! Delicate skin bruises easily . . . Grandpaw!

EZRA

You can leave the artichoke.

SHERI

But I'm only half finished with Dorothy's portrait!

EZRA

She don't want it. Dorothy's an English lady, she don't hold with
carryings-on.

(*Pause*)

Goodbye, Sheri. I'll be leaving here soon, in any event.

SHERI

But Grandpaw, I made a vow—I told you about it! "Never to leave
you until . . ."

EZRA

Big mistake to make vows. They always get broken.

(*He is pushing her toward the door.*)

Goodbye, take care of yourself.

SHERI

A man can't just dispose of his spirit love!

EZRA

This one just has.

(*He pushes her through the door, closes it, listens for a moment to* SHERI, *pleading outside. The pleading stops.*)

The female is a chaos.

(EZRA *begins to eat the artichoke. Lights fade on* EZRA. *We see* DR. OVERHOLSER *reading the* New York Times *of April 19, 1958.*)

DR. OVERHOLSER

"Treason charges against Ezra Pound were dismissed today, opening the way for the 72-year-old poet's return to Italy. The case was never tried because the poet was found insane, and that he would in all likelihood never be mentally competent to stand trial and that the alleged radio broadcasts he made from Italy during World War II might have been the result of insanity. Medical advice to this effect had come from Dr. Winfred Overholser, superintendent of St. Elizabeths Hospital."

(DR. OVERHOLSER *puts the paper down.*)

Arrivederci, Mr. Pound.

CURTAIN

SCENE 2

Setting: The *sala* of a rundown, partly refurbished castle
in the Tyrol.

A month later, June 1958

(A *few sticks of old furniture, candelabra, big desk, the Gaudier-Brzeska* Hieratic Head of Ezra Pound, *ancestor portraits. Fresh flowers are everywhere.* MARY, *dressed for a festivity, stands looking out of a large window, watching for* EZRA's *arrival.*)

MARY
(*Seeing him—waving*)
Babbo! My Babbo!
(*She runs to the door to greet him.*)

EZRA
Leoncina!

MARY
Let me look at you—
(*With a sense of wonder*)
Babbo! Your hair's gone all white!
(*They embrace.*)

EZRA
From missing you . . .

MARY
Everything's here—your books, your papers, the manuscripts you sent. We'll work together again, Babbo!

EZRA

My homecoming—and Auld Robbie Burns's birthday.

MARY

Haggis and Johnnie Walker Black Label? Just as you requested.

EZRA

(*Looking at portrait*)

My mother, the proud Isabella! I had them send white roses, for her funeral.

MARY

She looked very majestic and serene in her coffin, in her precious cashmere shawl.

EZRA

I never appreciated what she did for me until after she was dead. Too late.

(*He continues to prowl around the room.*)

MARY

And Boris rang the castle bells—

(*Bells continue to ring.*)

EZRA

Your Prince! As bad as the bells at St. Mary's in Kensington—I petitioned the vicar to stop them, but "these bells have been rung, Mr. Pound, for seven hundred years." Will Boris go on ringing these for seven hundred years?

MARY

They're celebrating your return home. The villagers are coming up later, with torches and a band, for a feast—

EZRA

For me?

MARY

It's for my birthday, too, we have a tradition—
(*The bells stop.*)

EZRA

Thank God!
(*Collapsing in chair*)
Fatigue deep as the grave.

MARY

(*Kneeling beside him*)
Here you can rest. And for one beautiful day there will be peace . . .

EZRA

"I surrender neither the empire nor the temples
Nor the constitution nor yet the city of Dioce . . ."
(MARY *gets up, goes to the desk.*)

MARY

I've put the new Cantos here—the pages you sent me from St. Elizabeths; they're arranged chronologically, we can begin our work exactly where you left off . . . I thought you could read the new poems to me—your handwriting is still impossible to decipher,

Babbo!—and I can type them up as you read. Then you can go over what I've typed, make changes, and then I'll do a final draft. . . . There's a new ribbon in the typewriter, plenty of foolscap—

(MARY *indicates all the arrangements.*)

What do you think?

EZRA

The futility of "might have been."

MARY

Don't say that, Babbo! This is a new beginning!

(*No response*)

There're all these boxes—your papers from Rapallo to sort through—work that needs finishing.

(MARCELLA *enters with briefcase, papers, books, typewriter.*
EZRA *sits in the chair, eyes closed.*)

Babbo?

(MARCELLA *approaches* MARY. MARCELLA *holds out her hand.*)

MARCELLA

I'm Marcella Spann.

MARY

(*Shaking hands*)

How do you do.

MARCELLA

Surely someone told you.

MARY

In fact, no.

EZRA

(*Seeing the Gaudier sculpture*)

You have the Gaudier!

(*Caresses the statue*)

Henri got it right! Said, when he was carving this, "It will not look like you. It will be the expression of certain emotions I get from your character." Dead in the trenches, in the "Great" War. The war to end all wars, they said.

MARCELLA

Mr. and Mrs. Pound asked me to accompany them, to put his papers in order, type up the new Cantos, continue work on the anthology.

EZRA

The SPANNthology. "From Confucius to Cummings."

MARY

I haven't heard anything about the . . . Spannthology.

(*To* EZRA)

I thought we were going to work on the new Cantos—

EZRA

(*Springing to life*)

Look here, Marcella—everything's arranged, ready to go first thing in the *mattina*.

(*Shows* MARCELLA *desk and so forth*)

Here's my new pages from St. Liz—you'll need to type them up as I read them, handwriting's horrible—then I'll edit, you'll type the final drafts. There's a new ribbon in the typewriter, plenty of foolscap—

MARY

I don't understand, Babbo. I was counting on helping you—

EZRA

Marcella's a trained secre'try, takes shorthand—

MARCELLA

Now you know that's not true—I'm just here to help—

EZRA

And to see Italy.

MARCELLA

Yes—Dorothy wants that.

MARY

I'll have to find a room. The castle's not completely furnished, we're short on suitable beds.

MARCELLA

I'm very sorry to trouble you.

MARY

No trouble at all, when it's for Babbo.

(MARY *exits.*)

MARCELLA

You didn't tell her.

EZRA

Well, Mary's adaptable. . . . Open those boxes—I want to see what Olga sent from Rapallo, what I've got here—almost fourteen years in storage!

(MARCELLA *begins to open the boxes.* EZRA *goes through the papers with growing excitement.*)

My notes from the Languedoc—1912, the summer of Margaret Cravens's suicide . . .

(*He begins to go through the notes excitedly.*)

Marcella, look here. The notes I made for the book on the troubadours.

(*She comes to look, shares his excitement.*)

I want you to begin transcribing these.

(*As* MARCELLA *gets her typewriter and sets it up.*)

There's enough here for a book! Sit down . . .

(MARCELLA *drags a chair to the typewriter, puts in paper, gets ready to type.*)

MARCELLA

(*Looking at notes*)

Very difficult to read—

EZRA

Written under a tree! Here—I'll read to you . . .

(*Reads*)

"Roquefixade: the castle on the rock. I climbed up there this morning, took my life in my hands. The courtyard where the first Troubadours sang their verses—to the lady who could never be won . . ."

MARCELLA
(*As she types*)

Was Dorothy with you?

EZRA

Back in London, shopping for a bed.
(DOROTHY *enters, hears this. She is carrying more papers and books.*)

DOROTHY

I wrote you, "Let's not get soft-headed, the way other married couples do." The letter's there somewhere.

MARCELLA
(*Going to her*)

Let me help you with those.

DOROTHY

I can manage.
(*She begins to unpack* EZRA*'s own published works, arranging them on a shelf.*)

EZRA

Early stuff. Half-baked.

DOROTHY

(*Reading from a book*)

"I am torn, torn with thy beauty

O rose of the sharpest thorn!"

EZRA

I cut that out of my collected works.

DOROTHY (*Continues*)

"So have the thoughts of my heart

gone out slowly in the twilight,

toward my beloved,

toward the crimson rose, the fairest . . ."

EZRA

Oh Lord, those roses.

(MARCELLA *laughs.*)

EZRA

(*Leaping up, snatching the book from* DOROTHY, *cramming it onto the shelf.*)

After that I transformed the English language!

(*Seizing another book*)

And made all those gawdashed roses into THIS:

(*He searches for, and finds, another poem.*)

"In orchard under the hawthorne

she has her lover till morn.

Till the traist man cry out to warn

Them. God how swift the night,

And the day comes."

DOROTHY *(Tranquilly)*

I believe I prefer the earlier version.

EZRA

I was hammering word into word, bursting my way into Parnassus.

DOROTHY

Still, the earlier poems . . .

MARCELLA

(Still putting away papers)

. . . surely can't compare to the Cantos—their scope, their power.

(Pause. DOROTHY *stares at* MARCELLA, *who, realizing she
is being watched, looks up.* EZRA *flings himself into a chair,
closes his eyes.)*

DOROTHY

Did you like the Baths of Caracalla?

MARCELLA *(Startled)*

Very fine, of course . . . it was wonderful to have a whole day to
see Rome, but . . .

DOROTHY

But?

MARCELLA

There was something so oppressively massive about the Baths—
and intimidating, like Mussolini's railroad station across the street.
All those columns . . .

DOROTHY

The Duce knew what was worth copying. If you're settled, Mao,
I'll go down to help Mary—the villagers are coming up later, with
torches . . . and a band.

(*She kisses* EZRA *on his forehead. He does not open his eyes.*)
You're home, at last, Mao.

(DOROTHY *exits.* EZRA *is stretched in a chair, eyes closed.*)

MARCELLA

Shall I come back later, Ezra?

EZRA

(*Leaping up*)

No, no—must get started. No time to lose. Where are we in the
troubadours?

MARCELLA

(*Consulting notes*)

Roquefixada.

(*She reads.*)

"I have lain in Roquefixada,
level with sunset . . ."

Beautiful—

(*She types these lines, as* EZRA *continues to study the paper.*)
Read me the rest.

EZRA

"Oh God of silence
Purifiez nos coeurs . . ."

MARCELLA

(*Translates as she types*)

Oh God of silence, purify our hearts . . .

EZRA

(*Throwing the paper down*)

Give it up, Marcella. Scraps and rags.

MARCELLA

(*Beginning to go through papers*)

But there's a great deal more here—surely enough for a book.

(*She begins to read.*)

"'Tis not a game that plays at mates and mating,

Provence knew . . .'"

EZRA

(*Snatching it from her*)

I said give it up! The summer was ruined—I had to rush back to Paris to deal with Margaret Cravens's Indiana aunt, asking questions about Margaret's suicide. I gave her a poem, to explain it all—

(*He rummages.*)

Here it is.

(*He reads.*)

"POST MORTEM

A brown, fat babe sitting in a lotus,

And you were glad and laughing

With a laughter not of this world.

It is good to splash in the water

And laughter is the end of all things."

Her Indiana aunt wasn't satisfied.

MARCELLA

But—this is beautiful.

(*She takes it, begins to type it.*)

EZRA

(*Another poem*)

"The eyes of the dead lady speak to me."

(*Anguished*)

Give it up, Marcella.

MARCELLA

(*Dropping the papers*)

I'm very sorry, Ezra, I must have misunderstood. Shall we work on the Spannthology?

(EZRA *turns away.*)

EZRA

Margaret was transformed. Do you believe that, Marcella?

(*Before she can answer*)

The transformations I've made—tried to make—mistaken, all of them, some fatal. Dorothy—I wrote of her:

"How have I not laboured

To bring her soul to birth . . ."

MARCELLA

I'm quite sure she never understood that.

EZRA

She understood. She hated it.

(*Moving on quickly*)
Where are we in the Spannthology?

MARCELLA

(*Consulting stack of papers*)
Only up to Chaucer.

EZRA

(*Begins to go through papers.* MARCELLA *prepares to type.*)
Here are the lines I want—from the Prologue to the *Canterbury Tales*:

(*Reading*)
"Whan that Aprille with his shoures soote
The droghte of Marche hath perced to the roote
And bathed every veyne in swich licour
(EZRA *leans over* MARCELLA *as she types, hand on her shoulder.*)
Of which vertue is engendered."
Should have learned Old English but Provençal was my dish . . .
(*He leans closer, kisses her hair,* MARCELLA *continues to type.*)
We'll add this next:
"Western wind, when will thou blow,
The small rain down can rain?
Christ, if my love were in my arms,
And I in my bed again!"
(*They kiss.*)
We'll revive the old customs, the way we did in Rapallo. Mary has ordered in haggis and Johnnie Walker Black Label—we'll celebrate auld Robbie Burns's birthday.

(*He finds a small book of poems, begins to read.* MARY *and*
DOROTHY *enter, with the Johnnie Walker and glasses on
a tray. They stand listening. With an expansive gesture,*
EZRA *draws* DOROTHY *and* MARY *closer.* MARCELLA *gets
up from the typewriter and joins them.* MARY *begins to pour
the whiskey;* DOROTHY *passes it.*)

> "Or were I in the wildest waste,
>
> sae black and bare, sae black and bare,
>
> the desert were a paradise,
>
> if thou wert there, if thou wert there."

(*Music of the Tyrolean band approaching interrupts.*)

MARY

Oh, Babbo! It's the band from the village.

DOROTHY

Come see, Mao . . .

(DOROTHY *and* MARY *go to the window as we hear the
band approaching.* MARCELLA *starts to follow, but* EZRA
stops her.)

EZRA

(*Continuing the poem to* MARCELLA)

> "or were I monarch o' the globe,
>
> wi' thee to reign, wi' thee to reign;
>
> the brightest jewel in all my crown
>
> wad be my queen, wad be my queen."

(EZRA *grabs* MARCELLA *and begins dancing her around the*

*room to the louder and louder music of the band. They laugh
as they swirl.* DOROTHY *turns and watches them.)*

CURTAIN

SCENE 3

Setting: The sala of the castle in the Tyrol.

Several months later, winter, 1958–1959

(EZRA *sits in the sala, huddled in a chair, wrapped in blankets. A
broken chair, with tools, lies nearby.* MARCELLA *is combing his hair.*
EZRA *hums or groans while she is doing this.)*

MARCELLA

(*Giving* EZRA *a hand mirror*)

Look, Ezra—so much better.

EZRA

(*Pushing mirror away*)

A brown husk that is finished . . . maybe they should have shot me.

MARCELLA

You have no right to say that.

EZRA

Old man he tired . . .

MARCELLA

I've heard that a lot of that, lately. You might appreciate what we're doing for you; I've got the Spannthology up to Whitman at last, Mary is planting a magnolia tree by your Gaudier head, Dorothy's loaning you more money—

EZRA

Loaning! First the Jew bankers, now my wife!

MARCELLA

Reality, Ezra.

EZRA

Never my strong suit . . . I'm freezing! Damn castle don't have no heat.

MARCELLA

Here.

(*Marcella covers him with another lap rug.*)

EZRA

Damn castle cold as the tomb. Can't get away from here. Can't get no peace! Fuss and botheration! Worse than Rapallo.

MARCELLA

Mary's taking very good care of you.

EZRA

Learned that from her mother.

MARCELLA

Have you heard from Olga?

EZRA

She's mad at me. Wanted me to go to her when I got out of St. Liz. Couldn't face the climb, getting up to her place at Sant'Ambrogio. . . . But now, the altitude here—I'm gasping like a fish. Or is it the attitude.

MARCELLA

Mary adores you.

EZRA

My wrecks and errors lie about me.
          "This is the house of Bedlam.

          This is the man
          that lies in the house of Bedlam.

          This is the time
          of the tragic man
          that lies in the house of Bedlam."

MARCELLA

You didn't write that one, Ezra. That was Elizabeth Bishop, after she visited you at St. Elizabeths .

EZRA

It was quiet there after lights out. Here darkness brings the furies.

MARCELLA

Shall we deal with the mail?

EZRA (*Brightening*)

Lots today?

MARCELLA

Seven letters.
(*Opening one*)
T. S. Eliot.

EZRA
(*Grabbing it*)
Quick answer to mine!

MARCELLA

I didn't want to type that letter to him or send it. You questioned the value of everything you've written.

EZRA
(*Ignoring this, reading letter*)
"You are one of the immortals, and part at least of your work is sure to survive."
(*Suddenly revived, he cavorts and chortles.*)
Good Old Possum—never could admit Old Ez the greater poet!
(*Grabbing another letter*)
This here is about the crazy British tax. . . . Threatens to wipe out my Brit royalties if I don't maintain US residence.

MARCELLA

Why didn't you switch?

EZRA

Switch?

MARCELLA

Get an Italian passport during the war? Then there would have been no question of treason.

EZRA

Because I'm proud to be a 'Mercun. Crazy country, but mine. Did the maple tree seedlings arrive yet?

MARCELLA

Mary brought them up this morning.

EZRA

Good Vermont maples. We'll start a syrup industry—the Italians will have a new delicacy.

MARCELLA

They don't eat pancakes.

EZRA

Lots of other uses for syrup. Cooking, gelati! Must get somebody to water my grapevines—five hundred of them. Mary'll be able to sell white wine along with her red.

MARCELLA

If she'll do it.

EZRA

Hey, hey.

MARCELLA

You know how stubborn she is about suggestions.

EZRA

She calls you my bodyguard.

MARCELLA

I've heard her.

EZRA

(*Looking at letter.*)

Here's a missive from my lawyer. I asked him to help relieve me of my patient and long-suffering "Committee ."

(*Reading*)

"Dear Mr. Pound, Unfortunately, it is not possible formally to petition for Mrs. Pound's removal."

(*Looking up*)

Pride, jealousy, and possessiveness—the three torments of hell.

MARCELLA

I am not proud. I am not jealous. I am not possessive. But the situation here—

EZRA

We'll take a little road trip.

MARCELLA

Oh yes—and breathe fresh air.

EZRA

I want you to see more of Italy.

MARCELLA

(*After a pause for the penny to drop*)
With Dorothy?

EZRA

'Fraid so. She's legally responsible for me, I can't move a foot without her . . . can't even pay for a hotel room.

MARCELLA

Ezra . . .

EZRA

Come here.
(*She gets up and goes to him. He sits her on his knee, kisses her forehead.*)
"And to the garden, Marcella. . . . The long flank, the firm breast. . . . Sunlight and serenitas."
(MARCELLA *pulls herself off his lap.*)
I'll get a divorce.

MARCELLA

You've never understood . . .

(*She starts to go quickly.*)

EZRA

Marcella . . .

MARCELLA

You're behaving . . . foolishly.

(MARCELLA *exits quickly.*)

EZRA

After all these years I'm beginning to realize I'm not a maniac.
I'm a moron.

(*He turns to an old chair, which he is repairing, and begins
to hammer.* MARY *enters.*)

MARY

Babbo, those grapevines.

EZRA

(*He goes on hammering.*)

What is it now?

MARY

They're full of poison ivy.

EZRA

Impossible.

MARY

We've never had poison ivy in Italy.

EZRA

I introduced them to Vivaldi—so why not to poison ivy?

MARY

I'm afraid the vines will have to destroyed.

EZRA

But you told me yourself, there's a market for white, and these are
the best, from Californy . . .

MARY

All right, I'll see what I can do, when I have time. Dorothy has
taken to her bed, I have to carry her meals up on a tray. Can you
speak to her?

EZRA

No.

MARY

I can't do it all, Babbo. She won't eat at the same table as Marcella.

EZRA

We'll take a little road trip, relieve the tension. Dorothy, Marcella,
and I.

MARY

Oh, Babbo, do you think that's wise?

EZRA

You think I can escape my lawfully wedded wife? Can't even sign a check.

MARY

The conditions of your release. I'm afraid you have to live with them.

EZRA

You've turned hard on me.

MARY

I admire you more than anyone I've ever known, but you seem blind to the fact that other people have lives to get on with as well. I have so much work here with the children, the repairs to the castle, the vineyards. And Boris is no help. He's gone off again, says I have no time for him—

EZRA

Old man he tired. Just enough strength left for a road trip—to Sirmione.

(*Brightening*)

I want Marcella to see the lake, the little temple of Catullus.

MARY (*Wearily*)

What car do you plan to take?

EZRA

Yours. Marcella will drive. Sirmione—Ovid's bit of paradise.

MARY

I can't do without the car for more than two days, Babbo. I have to
get to the market, and if one of the children falls sick—

EZRA

Fine, fine—two days. "How sharper than a serpent's tooth . . ."

MARY

Hush, Babbo.

EZRA

Call Marcella—and Dorothy. They'll have to pack light. Walking
clothes, for the promenade around the lake.

"From under the rubble heap

m'elevasti—"

MARY

Babbo—are you sure?

EZRA

Dorothy understands! She always has. Call them!

(MARY *goes to the door, calls several times. Meanwhile . . .*)

EZRA

(*Chanting, ecstatic*)

"Dark eyed,

O woman of my dreams,

Ivory sandaled,

There is none like thee among the dancers,

None with swift feet."

MARCELLA

(*Enters, carrying a tray*)

Dorothy won't answer. She's locked the door of her room—left this outside.

MARY

Here—I'll take it.

MARCELLA

Let me—

(MARY *takes the tray from her, forcefully.*)

MARY

In my house I do the work.

EZRA (*Softly*)

The victim is always—

MARY

Don't say it, Babbo.

(*To* MARCELLA)

Of course Dorothy won't come down. She's an old woman, exhausted.

EZRA (*Firmly*)

She'll come.

(*He goes to the door, calls.*)

Mao! Please!

(*Pause.* MARY *begins to pick up coffee cups and glasses to add to the tray. She exits.* MARCELLA *busies herself with the manuscript.*)

DOROTHY
(*As she enters*)

You called me, Mao?

EZRA

Come here.

(DOROTHY *approaches. He sits her on his knee, runs his hands through her hair.* MARCELLA *quietly exits.*)

I remember when this was the color of the eyes of a wood nymph on Mount Olympus.

DOROTHY

A long time ago, Mao.

EZRA

When I came back from the Languedoc in 1912, after Margaret Cravens died. You were at the train station with roses, white roses, dozens of them.

DOROTHY

I spent more than I should, my mother was furious for days. "He's ruined you for any other man, with his attentions."

EZRA

Ruined—so she finally allowed us to marry—on your two hundred pounds a year.

DOROTHY

After four years' wait. I knew, at Sirmione, when I first touched your hair. Only the Objective—reality—could come between us!

EZRA

(*Taking letter out of his pocket*)

"One day you and I met—met in a blue, open place—we saw each other's hair and knew that we both loved the Sun. Later we loved each other as well."

DOROTHY

Yes!

EZRA

(*Continuing to read*)

"And you have forgotten me, left me behind."

(DOROTHY *buries her face in his shoulder.*)

"But because we are not real, it does not matter. We think we are in love—but that does not matter either. We have touched, and twisted ourselves together, floating . . ."

DOROTHY

Oh Mao—bright-haired one . . .

EZRA

(*As he strokes her*)

Dearest, whatever happens, we have touched, come together and slipped one round the other.

(*As she lifts her head*)

Come to Sirmione—where it all began.

DOROTHY

Where I first saw color . . .

EZRA

And let there be peace between us.

DOROTHY

The Gods be praised I've inspired you to write poems.

EZRA

Avanti, Madame Pound. Get your sketchbook. We return to Sirmione!

(DOROTHY *exits quickly.* EZRA *waits to be sure that she is gone, then calls.*)

Marcella!

(*After a moment,* MARCELLA *enters.*)

MARCELLA

Where's Dorothy?

EZRA

Get your things. We're going to Sirmione!

MARCELLA

With Dorothy?

EZRA

Of course! You and I will take the first walk around the lake together—to the little temple of Catullus that I told you about. We'll sit inside on the stone bench, look out over the water.

MARCELLA

But what will Dorothy think?

EZRA

(He begins to get to his knees.)
Give me your hand, Marcella.
(Uneasily, she gives him her hand, He kisses it.)
"'How many wonders are less sweet
Than love I bear to thee
When I am old.'"

MARCELLA

Ezra!

EZRA

Marry me, Marcella. Give an old man his last chance.

MARCELLA

I . . .

EZRA

I'll arrange everything—

MARCELLA

You can't do this!

EZRA

Dorothy's reasonable, she understands the Objective—always
has—she'll go back to London, live with Omar . . .

TREASON

(DOROTHY *enters during this speech, carrying her sketch-book, overhears.*)

MARCELLA

But surely, after all these years—

EZRA

Years piled up, crushing me!
(*He reaches for her hand, kisses it again; he is still on his knees.*)
There's some good in me yet, Marcella—take the good—

DOROTHY
(*Rushing forward*)

Ezra, how could you . . . !

MARCELLA

Mrs. Pound, I want you to know—

DOROTHY (*Furious*)

Please!

MARCELLA

I never intended—

DOROTHY

Marcella, please leave us now.
(MARCELLA *exits.*)

EZRA

I want to remember Sirmione as it was, before we were married—
before the war, before everything started to fall to pieces.

DOROTHY

Stop that!

EZRA

I gave you my name, I gave you an occupation. I gave you a son.
That was all you really wanted.

DOROTHY

Lies!

EZRA

Well, what else do you want, now?

DOROTHY

A little time alone with you!

EZRA

But you don't love me.

DOROTHY

Stop!

EZRA

Marcella might.

(MARY *enters.*)

MARY

Babbo, I . . .

(*Looks from* EZRA *to* DOROTHY, *sensing something wrong*)
Dorothy, has something happened?

DOROTHY

He asked her to marry him!

MARY

Marcella?

DOROTHY

Who else?

MARY

Oh, Babbo.

EZRA

I thought she might love me.

DOROTHY

I won't stand for this. After all these years. No divorce. No!

MARY

(*To* EZRA)

What did Marcella say?

EZRA

She sees . . . the difficulties.

DOROTHY

Difficulties!

MARY

Babbo. You can't do this.

EZRA

(*To* DOROTHY)

You wanted peace—no sorrow, no anguish, no horror—nothing but gentleness—floating above the world.

DOROTHY

I was young, I knew nothing.

EZRA

Oh, please . . . Dorothy.

DOROTHY

She must go.

EZRA

She have mercy on him now.

DOROTHY

When did you ever show me mercy? From the beginning, you trained me to accept your work, your genius as an excuse for every-thing—an excuse for every cruel and unfeeling act!

(EZRA *begins to sob.*)

Oh yes, now the tears! When it's too late, when nothing can wash away the dryness of my heart—all these years loving in the desert.

EZRA

Why don't you discard me here? Then I won't be any trouble
to anyone.

MARY

Oh Babbo . . .

(*She takes out a handkerchief, wipes his face.*)

DOROTHY

(*To* MARY)

I put up with the others—all of them—I knew he had to have them,
for his poetry. Even Sheri. I understood, I built my life on understanding! But at least I was always his wife, I presided. Perhaps
you mock that—

MARY

No.

DOROTHY

But it mattered to me, greatly! On the lawn at St. Elizabeths—I
poured the tea, I passed the little sandwiches. I will never surrender my place.

EZRA

"How have I laboured to bring her soul into separation;
  To give her a name and her being!"

DOROTHY

I remember that poem, Ezra—I remember it very well! Surely you
have not forgotten the way you ended it . . .

"I beseech you enter your life.

I beseech you to learn to say 'I,'

When I question you;

For you are no part but a whole,

No portion, but a being."

It has taken me almost a lifetime—but finally I have learned to say "I." "I" will call Marcella.

EZRA

No!

DOROTHY

(*She goes to the exit, calls.*)

Marcella!

EZRA

No, no, please—

MARY

Babbo, it won't work.

DOROTHY

Marcella! May I see you for a moment, please!

(MARCELLA *enters with her suitcase.*)

MARCELLA

Please believe me, Mrs. Pound, I . . .

DOROTHY (*Briskly*)

I believe you've seen enough of Italy.

MARCELLA

(*Notices* EZRA *is crying, goes to him.*)

Ezra?

DOROTHY

He has something to tell you.

EZRA (*Sobbing*)

I can't . . . can't . . .

MARCELLA

(*Standing up*)

This was never what I wanted.

DOROTHY

You encouraged him!

MARCELLA

I only tried to comfort him.

DOROTHY

You should have realized the consequences of allowing him to hope.

MARY

I'm so sorry, Marcella—

MARCELLA

(*To* MARY)

You want me to leave, as well.

MARY

I can't see any other solution.

EZRA
(*To* MARY)

Just a few days longer—

DOROTHY

Like a little boy cheated out of a sweet.
(*She has won; she pulls herself together.*)

MARCELLA
(*To* MARY)

How soon—?

DOROTHY

At once.

MARY

I'll drive you down to the station—the fast train to Rome comes through at seven. Can you be ready?

MARCELLA

Yes.

DOROTHY
(*In control now*)

I'll make you a sandwich for the train. Would you like that?

MARCELLA

I would "like" five minutes alone with Ezra.

DOROTHY

No.

(*Consternation. Finally,* MARY *takes control.*)

MARY

Dorothy—it's only right. They'll never see each other again.

DOROTHY

Very well. Five minutes.

(MARY *and* DOROTHY *exit.* MARCELLA *kneels by his chair. A long silence.*)

EZRA

(*Taking her hands*)

Stay with me. You're all I have—out of the wreckage.

MARCELLA

I won't do that to Dorothy. No.

EZRA

Dorothy will come to understand, in time.

MARCELLA

She'll come to understand—like she did with all the others.

EZRA

Yes!

MARCELLA

But I'm not like "all the others." You've never understood that.

EZRA

I understood you might love me . . .

MARCELLA

Yes, and for that I want to thank you.

EZRA

Thank—!

MARCELLA

I came to Washington a year ago looking for what I'd never found—in my family, in my teaching, in my wanderings—

EZRA

My errors and wrecks lie all about me.
(*Faintly*)

The Wasteland.

MARCELLA

You were my teacher—but more than that: a man I could admire, a man I could, without compromising, love. In the end that's what matters: that you exist—and you do exist—without me.

EZRA

Not without you.

MARCELLA (*Rising*)

You've given me what I came to find: the measure of a man.

EZRA

There's so much more to do—the anthology to finish—

MARCELLA

It's finished, Ezra, all but your introduction.

EZRA

And there's so much more of Italy to show you . . .

MARCELLA

Actually, I didn't come here to see Italy. That was Dorothy's idea.

EZRA

(*With difficulty*)

I have so much more . . . to give . . .

MARCELLA

You have given me . . . everything. Goodbye, Ezra.

(*She kisses him.* EZRA *turns violently away, as though to dismiss her.*)

No—that won't do. A proper goodbye.

(*They kiss.* EZRA *holds onto her. She detaches his hands, turns away as* DOROTHY *and* MARY *enter.* MARCELLA *leaves, without looking back.*)

MARY

Babbo—I'm so sorry.

(*She embraces him. He sobs.*)

DOROTHY

Please—don't encourage him. It will take me weeks to get him over this.

MARY

We can be gentle with him.

DOROTHY

When was he gentle with me?

EZRA

Mary, you could have helped me!

MARY

Not this time, Babbo.

EZRA

I thought you were my rock.

MARY

I've tried to be—I told myself, Babbo has a right to do whatever he likes—anything that makes him happy. Whomever he brings into my home is welcome. He makes his own laws, and I accept them.

DOROTHY

You might have anticipated there would be difficulties.

MARY

I did. From the first day, I realized I was up against something beyond Babbo's control. He expected me to help him . . . he was in great need of shelter and tenderness, so he could write Paradise.

EZRA

For one beautiful day, there was peace—but you couldn't keep it up.

MARY

More than one—but no, I couldn't keep it up. This house no longer contains a family. We shouldn't even be breaking bread together.

EZRA

You want me to be a demigod.

MARY

The vision has withered. I'm so weary of it all—I feel as though my skin is a bag of bones.

EZRA

"If love be not in the house, there is nothing!"
(MARY *exits. To* DOROTHY)
I want to go back to Sant'Ambrogio.

DOROTHY

No, Ezra—I can't manage you there, alone—

EZRA

You managed before, you can manage now.

DOROTHY

There are tenants in my apartment.

EZRA

Get rid of them . . .

DOROTHY

Where do you expect me to find the strength . . . ?

EZRA

Throw them out!

DOROTHY

No—they pay me.

EZRA

Get a hotel room!

DOROTHY

Very well. I'll start packing tomorrow.

EZRA

Now—now!

DOROTHY

Tomorrow.
 (*Suddenly sinking into a chair*)
He never know how tired . . .

LIGHTS FADE

SCENE 4

Setting: A hotel room in Rapallo.

Several days later

(EZRA *stands alone in the middle of the floor. He is dressed as in the first scene: cloak, sombrero.*)

EZRA

(*He begins to undress, slowly and laboriously.*)

To abuse words, to be abused by words: they sink under the weight. Like swallows up in the air—flying at the beginning, carrying all thought and meaning on their wings. But "'Tis the white stag, fame, we're a-hunting, bid the world's hounds come to horn!" Those hounds have dragged my words to the ground.

"The ant's a centaur in his dragon world.

Pull down thy vanity, it is not man

Made courage, or made order, or made grace,

Pull down they vanity, I say, pull down."

(*Now naked, he climbs onto bed, lies flat, staring at the ceiling. Enter* MARY *and* DOROTHY *with suitcases.*)

DOROTHY

(*At the bed, covering him hastily*)

He's resting—exhausted. I thought we'd have to call an ambulance.

MARY

Old, and sick, and very tired.

DOROTHY

We're all very tired.

(*Pause*)

He's asking for Olga.

MARY

And you don't object?

DOROTHY

There are times when one must simply be practical. I'm seventy years old. Ezra has been my delight and my burden for almost fifty years. Olga is sixty-three—tell her to take him to her house, with my blessing. I've done all that I can.

MARY

I'll call her right away.

DOROTHY

I telephoned her already. She said she'd hurry over from Sant'Ambrogio.

MARY

My poor mother—after all these years. I'll go downstairs and look out for her.

(*Exit.*)

EZRA (*Confused*)

Olga?

DOROTHY

No—Dorothy. Olga's coming.

EZRA

You—?

DOROTHY

I'll go to London.

EZRA

(*Reaching for her*)

Dorothy . . . "If, when this life's over . . ."

DOROTHY

Goodbye, Mao.

(*As she turns toward the exit,* OLGA *enters, wearing a red Chinese jacket embroidered with gold. They face each other in silence.*)

OLGA

Rest, peace.

DOROTHY

Yes.

OLGA

"What thou lovest well remains . . ."

DOROTHY

The Cantos. He'll never finish them, now. Lately I've begun to realize—to admit to myself—to KNOW that his poetry—

OLGA

I can't agree with you, I can't acknowledge—

DOROTHY

His poetry, which I bore for him, suckled as I never did our son—

OLGA

Don't say it!

DOROTHY

Died. Departed. Gone—

(*A beat.*)

OLGA

(*In spite of herself*)

When—?

DOROTHY

Perhaps years ago, when we left London—fled, really, he'd made so many enemies.

OLGA

Not his fault. Greatness is always misunderstood.

DOROTHY

Or when we realized Paris wasn't going to work, either, and went into exile, in Rapallo.

OLGA

Hardly exile.

DOROTHY

Or when we were all three living together, and quarreling, and he was so horribly disappointed—"If love be not in the house"—

OLGA

How he could have believed it would work—

DOROTHY

He loved us both.

(OLGA *is speechless.* DOROTHY *continues calmly.*)

But really, I believe his ruin came with the children.

OLGA

But we made sure the children never interfered.

DOROTHY

Just that. We prevented them from changing his life. What might he have understood—what might he have written—if they had come, as living beings, into his imagination. Instead—restrictions, protection—overprotection—

OLGA

He needs peace and quiet.

DOROTHY

Yes, yes. You and I were united, in giving him that. But did you ever feel . . . saddened? I believe there was a loss . . . a great loss . . . for all of us. There are hours—days—when I regret . . .

OLGA

When our children were born, Dorothy, he was already becoming forgotten.

DOROTHY

He set out to become the greatest poet of the twentieth century. I loved him for that. I suppose I encouraged him.

OLGA

He could have done it—before these wars.

DOROTHY

You encouraged him, as well.

OLGA

I believed in him. I believe in him.

DOROTHY

Very well. Then, care for him. Love him.
                    (*They embrace, tentatively.*)
Goodbye.

OLGA

Remember: "This cannot be wrest from thee"—all those years . . .
            (OLGA *moves to the bed and* DOROTHY *exits.*)
Dolcezza mia, how happy she is to see him . . .
                    (*Caressing him*)
The most beautiful head, the most expressive hands.

EZRA

(*He sits bolt upright suddenly.*)

Let those I love try to forgive what I have made.

OLGA

There's nothing to forgive. I chose my life.

LIGHTS SLOWLY FADE TO BLACK

SALLIE BINGHAM is the author of fifteen books, including
most recently *Treason: a Sallie Bingham Reader*; *Silver Swan: In
Search of Doris Duke*; *The Blue Box: Three Lives in Letters*; and
Mending: New & Selected Short Stories. The latter collection won a
Gold Medal in Fiction from *Foreword Magazine* in 2012 and she's
been included in both *Best American Short Stories* and *The PEN/O.
Henry Prize Stories*. Her nine plays have all been produced, includ-
ing the one in this book, *Treason*, directed by Martin Platt at the
Perry Street Theater in New York City. Bingham is founder of the
Kentucky Foundation for Women, The Sallie Bingham Center for
Women's History at Duke University, publisher of *The American
Voice*, from 1989 to 1998 and Book Editor at *The Courier Journal*
from 1983 to 1989. She has received fellowships from Yaddo,
MacDowell, and the Virginia Center for the Creative Arts, along
with many other honors. She lives in Santa Fe with her dog Pip.

SARABANDE BOOKS is a nonprofit literary press located in Louisville, Kentucky. Founded in 1994 to champion poetry, short fiction, and essay, we are committed to creating lasting editions that honor exceptional writing. For more information, please visit sarabandebooks.org.